Nothing had prepared *for Mac....*

He was all wrong for her. He didn't wear expensive cologne. His clothes were casual, and he just plain didn't give a damn about anything.

But he did know how to kiss a woman.

Her blood heated to a boil as his mouth shaped itself against hers. She melted against him, reaching up to slip her arms around his neck.

"You're trouble," he said huskily, dragging his mouth from hers.

She pulled away, tried to regain her breathing. *Mac* was trouble. He was everything she'd never dealt with before.

He stepped close again. "I won't apologize," he whispered.

"I wouldn't expect you to," she whispered back. "Not when I wanted it as much as you did."

Dear Reader,

The year is ending, and as a special holiday gift to you, we're starting off with a 3-in-1 volume that will have you on the edge of your seat. *Special Report,* by Merline Lovelace, Maggie Price and Debra Cowan, features three connected stories about a plane hijacking and the three couples who find love in such decidedly unusual circumstances. Read it—you won't be sorry.

A YEAR OF LOVING DANGEROUSLY continues with Carla Cassidy's *Strangers When We Married,* a reunion romance with an irresistible baby and a couple who, I know you'll agree, truly do belong together. Then spend 36 HOURS with Doreen Roberts and *A Very...Pregnant New Year's.* This is one family feud that's about to end...at the altar!

Virginia Kantra's back with *Mad Dog and Annie,* a book that's every bit as fascinating as its title—which just happens to be one of my all-time favorite titles. I guarantee you'll enjoy reading about this perfect (though they don't know it yet) pair. Linda Randall Wisdom is back with *Mirror, Mirror,* a good twin/bad twin story with some truly unexpected twists—and a fabulous hero. Finally, read about a woman who has *Everything But a Husband* in Karen Templeton's newest—and keep the tissue box nearby, because your emotions will really be engaged.

And, of course, be sure to come back next month for six more of the most exciting romances around—right here in Silhouette Intimate Moments.

Enjoy!

Leslie J. Wainger
Executive Senior Editor

Please address questions and book requests to:
Silhouette Reader Service
U.S.: 3010 Walden Ave., P.O. Box 1325, Buffalo, NY 14269
Canadian: P.O. Box 609, Fort Erie, Ont. L2A 5X3

Mirror, Mirror
LINDA RANDALL WISDOM

Silhouette®

INTIMATE MOMENTS™
Published by Silhouette Books
America's Publisher of Contemporary Romance

For me, December is more than Christmas
and my wedding anniversary. Twenty-one years ago this
month—on my wedding anniversary, no less—I sold my first
two books to Silhouette Books. Twenty years ago this month,
my first book, *Dancer in the Shadows,* was published.

If it weren't for my readers, I wouldn't still be here.
A heartfelt thank you for buying my books.

 SILHOUETTE BOOKS

ISBN 0-373-27119-0

MIRROR, MIRROR

Copyright © 2000 by Words by Wisdom

This edition published by arrangement with Harlequin Books S.A.

® and TM are trademarks of Harlequin Books S.A., used under license.
Trademarks indicated with ® are registered in the United States Patent
and Trademark Office, the Canadian Trade Marks Office and in other
countries.

Visit Silhouette at www.eHarlequin.com

Printed in U.S.A.

Books by Linda Randall Wisdom

LINDA RANDALL WISDOM

is a California author who loves movies, books and animals of all kinds. She also has a great sense of humor, which is reflected in her books.

IT'S OUR 20th ANNIVERSARY!
December 2000 marks the end of our anniversary year.
We hope you've enjoyed the many special titles already
offered, and we invite you to sample those wonderful titles
on sale this month! 2001 promises to be every bit as
exciting, so keep coming back to Silhouette Books,
where love comes alive....

Desire

#1333 Irresistible You
Barbara Boswell

#1334 Slow Fever
Cait London

#1335 A Season for Love
BJ James

#1336 Groom of Fortune
Peggy Moreland

#1337 Monahan's Gamble
Elizabeth Bevarly

**#1338 Expecting the
Boss's Baby**
Leanne Banks

Special Edition

#1363 The Delacourt Scandal
Sherryl Woods

#1364 The McCaffertys: Thorne
Lisa Jackson

**#1365 The Cowboy's
Gift-Wrapped Bride**
Victoria Pade

#1366 Lara's Lover
Penny Richards

#1367 Mother in a Moment
Allison Leigh

#1368 Expectant Bride-To-Be
Nikki Benjamin

Romance

**#1486 Sky's Pride and
Joy**
Sandra Steffen

#1487 Hunter's Vow
Susan Meier

**#1488 Montana's Feisty
Cowgirl**
Carolyn Zane

#1489 Rachel and the M.D.
Donna Clayton

**#1490 Mixing Business...with
Baby**
Diana Whitney

#1491 His Special Delivery
Belinda Barnes

Intimate Moments

#1045 Special Report
Merline Lovelace/Maggie Price/
Debra Cowan

**#1046 Strangers When We
Married**
Carla Cassidy

**#1047 A Very...Pregnant
New Year's**
Doreen Roberts

#1048 Mad Dog and Annie
Virginia Kantra

#1049 Mirror, Mirror
Linda Randall Wisdom

#1050 Everything But a Husband
Karen Templeton

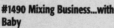

Chapter 1

Women like her never walked into his office. Women like her never requested his services. Hell, women like her never existed in the world he inhabited.

He thought only the fictional Travis McGee and Philip Marlowe met gorgeous women.

The women who came to him for help were sad, sometimes downtrodden. They were there looking for answers they hoped he could give them, even if the answers weren't the ones they wanted to hear. Their clothing came from thrift stores instead of designer boutiques and their cologne was whatever was on sale. They wouldn't have dreamed of smelling like something that probably cost a couple hundred dollars an ounce or sporting expensive French manicures. In essence, this lady looked as if she could easily afford his fees.

Things were looking up, and he hadn't even had to take out an ad.

He figured he'd just sit there and enjoy the ride. And the view.

"You came highly recommended as someone who works discreetly and gets the job done," she explained in her cool, calm voice as she sat in the lone visitor's chair. Her glance around the room told him she couldn't imagine why he came so highly recommended when his office looked as if it had been furnished by picking up whatever he found left on the sidewalk.

Mac nodded. "I do my best." He wanted to sound humble and self-assured. Let the client believe you can do anything, was his rule of thumb. So far, it had worked pretty good.

He leaned back in his chair with his hands folded over his flat stomach. While she was giving him the once-over, he was doing the same to her.

He doubted her hair, the rich color of honey, came from a stylist's bag of tricks: styled no-nonsense short, parted on the right side and curved behind her ears. Her cobalt silk sheath dress fit her businesslike demeanor, just as her body language stated loud and clear she wasn't to be toyed with. Eyes that matched her dress faced him squarely. The scent of expensive perfume floated in the air between them. Definitely better than any brand of air freshener he'd ever used to chase away the lingering scent of cheap cigars left by a previous client.

Her immaculate appearance was a far cry from his more casual dress consisting of jeans and a rumpled white cotton shirt with the sleeves rolled up to his elbows. His dusty brown hair shot with silver was combed by his fingers and long overdue for a haircut. There'd been more important things to do than finding a barber. He'd been up all night on a surveillance. Right now, he wanted nothing more than a few hours of sleep and a hot meal that didn't arrive via a drive-thru window. Trouble was, interviewing a prospective client, who could actually pay, was more important than catching some much-needed shut-eye. Which resulted in his gray-green eyes looking bloodshot. He probably looked like he'd just gotten off a weeklong drunk.

Dana Madison slowly turned her head as she surveyed the small office. A hint of distaste crossed her face. He had a pretty good idea what she saw. *Office* was a relative term, since Mac always thought the space had once housed brooms and mops. Luckily, his kind of business didn't require a lot of space. Just room for his desk, a file cabinet and a couple of chairs.

"For a man reputed to be successful in his line of work, you don't like to show it outwardly, do you?" Dana Madison commented.

Mac shrugged. "Success isn't always measured by a person's bank account. It's results that count, not what surrounds you to make you look successful. If you want the outer trappings, I can give you the names of a couple of good agencies that have offices in one of those fancy highrises. They'll trot out all their spy goodies, tell you exactly what you want to hear and gladly take your money. That doesn't mean they can give you what I can." His catlike eyes met hers squarely.

She didn't even flinch.

"Tell me why you're here, Ms. Madison," he said, when he finally figured she wasn't going to get all huffy over his blatant attempt to unnerve her. *Nope.* She hadn't gotten up and walked out the door.

Good thing. Rent was due tomorrow, and he was a little cash poor. Okay, a lot cash poor.

"I'd like you to follow me," she replied. "I don't feel I require twenty-four-hour surveillance. Just from, say, six p.m. to eight a.m."

"All right, you want me to follow you," he repeated, just to make sure he got it right. And here he thought he'd heard it all.

She nodded.

"Any reason why you feel the need to be followed?" Mac asked. "Protection from an old boyfriend who doesn't understand why you broke off the relationship?"

"The reason why is no concern of yours." She coolly put him off. "Naturally, I would like a daily written report as to my activities between those hours."

"Everything to do with a case I take on is my concern, Ms. Madison. When someone comes in here and asks me to put a tail on a person, they usually are talking about me following someone *else*."

"Then there's always a first time, isn't there." She opened her bag that doubled as a briefcase and pulled out a checkbook. "What are your fees?"

Mac shook his head. "I think we need to get something clear here, Ms. Madison. I don't operate on a need-to-know basis. In my line of work that kind of thinking can get a fella hurt, and I've got to be honest—I'm not into pain."

In his estimation, her tension level upped a good fifty points. Whatever she was hiding must be a doozy.

"This isn't easy for me," she admitted in a tight voice.

"You're not the first person who's been in a little trouble." He softened a little. He figured the lady wasn't used to not being in charge. She probably preferred to handle things her way. Now she was forced to come to someone else for help. Something must have happened to spook her big-time. The usual scenario was an ex-husband or ex-lover stalking the lady. Either way, a guy could get hurt if he didn't know what could be waiting for him around the corner.

"I'm not in trouble," she hastily denied.

Dana's tongue appeared, dampening her lower lip. Judging from the death grip she had on her bag, she was not only nervous, she was scared to death of something. The question was what.

"For the past two months I have experienced some

strange things," she said slowly, apparently reluctant to disclose any of this. "Unexplained things that involve me, yet I have no recollection of them happening." She paused and waited for his nod for her to continue. "People I have never met come up to me and claim they know me. Clothing I have never seen before has shown up in my closet. Some mornings I discover that my car's gas tank is almost empty, yet I know I had filled the tank the night before— and I hadn't gone anywhere but home after that."

Mac nodded. "Is there any history of sleepwalking in your family?" he asked. "I knew of one woman who carried on a complete second life while sleepwalking. Any mental disorders you're aware of?"

She shook her head. "No, nothing. And I do not have a split personality, if you're going to ask about that next. There has to be a logical explanation for what is happening to me. I need to know what that is."

Mac silently agreed. But then, his years with the police force told him even the looniest of people could look as normal as...well as normal as him.

"Logic is nice, but that doesn't mean what's going on is logical." He pulled the yellow legal pad toward him and picked up his pen. He glanced up. "First off, how many people have keys to your house?"

She thought for a moment. "Myself, my housekeeper, my mother. I keep a spare in my office, but that's in a locked drawer. I believe that's it."

"Were you the original owner?"

She shook her head.

"When you moved in, did you change the locks?"

She nodded.

"Any brothers or sisters who might be playing some sick joke on you?"

She shook her head. "I'm an only child."

He wrote on the pad. "Do you have an alarm system?"

Dana nodded. "I had it installed before I moved in. Our community also has a private security patrol that is very vigilant. Our neighborhood has an almost nonexistent crime rate."

"Maybe that's what they tell you, so they look good. If you think someone's breaking into your house, there's a big need for an alarm. If nothing else, the noise will alert your rent-a-cops," Mac said flatly. "I'd like to look your place over first before making my recommendation for one. Also, I might be able to get an idea how someone's breaking in without setting off the alarm. If it is someone else."

She leaned forward, her face an icy carving. "That *is* what is happening!" She opened her purse and pulled out a small paper bag. The name of a well-known jewelry store was written in tasteful script, teal ink on gray paper. She pushed it toward him. "I found these yesterday, and I can assure you they are not mine."

Mac immediately withdrew a pair of latex gloves and slipped them on. He doubted there would be any usable prints after who knows who handling them, but he wasn't going to take any chances.

Once he'd looked at the contents, he couldn't imagine they conformed with the woman seated across from him.

It wasn't anything he hadn't seen before. Two foil-wrapped condoms, a matchbook from a bar across town—one he knew had a fairly wild reputation—a small bottle of perfume and a hotel key card. He laid them out in a row. He picked up the perfume bottle, opened it and sniffed. The scent was heavy, musky—something a woman would wear if she was in heat. He couldn't imagine the woman seated across from him wearing this fragrance.

"None of these ring a bell with you?"

"No." Her tone could have turned a heat wave into a blizzard.

He picked up the hotel key card. The name was stamped

on one end. "Yeah, this place isn't exactly known for its ambience. More for its hourly rates. I've heard they don't offer room service, either. Unless you're talking about the kind that doesn't exactly come on a linen tablecloth."

He should turn her down. The lady might be easy on the eyes, but she was also loony tunes. Not something he needed after dealing with Raymond Cutter for the past month. The guy had wanted Mac to follow his wife. There was only one problem. He had never been married. But that didn't stop him from being convinced he was married to the woman in the next apartment. Luckily for the woman, Cutter was harmless, but Mac still didn't waste any time having a talk about the situation with an old buddy at the police department. He also contacted the woman and helped her obtain a restraining order. Last he heard, Raymond Cutter moved out of the state.

Yeah, even with the rent due, Mac didn't need a case like this. Of course, he could recommend someone who would come to the same conclusion he had. Except, they'd gladly take her money and probably not even do a proper job.

Fact is, Mac believed that when a woman asked for help, a man did whatever was necessary to keep her safe. Dana Madison had come to him. That meant it was up to him to find out what was going on.

He rattled off his fees and what he required for a retainer. "All right, Ms. Madison. You have yourself a watchdog. I'll send you reports at the end of each week," he explained. "There are some things I'll need right now. I want you to give me your housekeeper's schedule and a list of anyone else who's on your property on a regular basis. I also suggest you keep a log of your mileage. Write it down every time you park the car in your garage and even when you leave it at your office. Keep the mileage log in your purse."

She looked relieved. Obviously, she hadn't expected him to accept.

"Anything you need," she replied.

He nodded. "As I said, I'll want to go through your house. And your office."

"You have to understand that I must have complete secrecy in this matter. No one can know about this," she insisted. "Since the death of my father, my business has taken some nasty hits. He'd been the heart and soul of it, and some of the long-term clients are having trouble shifting their loyalties to me. I'm having to prove to them I can do just as good a job as he did. If word of this got out, I'd be finished."

"Maybe I don't have the fancy office, but I do have my honor. Nothing said between us leaves this room." He squinted at the squiggles he'd made on the notepad. Damn, pretty soon he'd need reading glasses. Not a good image for a tough private investigator. "If someone's trying to gaslight you, I'll find out who it is."

"And why," she said. "Right now, I'm not sure which is more important. Who or why. But I need to know." She quickly wrote in her checkbook, tore the slip of paper out and handed it to him. She wasted no time in writing out the information he requested. She passed it over, along with her business card on the back of which she'd jotted numbers. "This should cover a month. Here are my cell and pager numbers."

"Yes, it will." Mac was proud of himself for not whooping with joy at the amount written on the check. His retainer and one month's worth of his daily rate. He was positive this check would clear first time around. Not like other checks he'd banked. "Don't worry about your office staff. They won't know anything you don't want them to know."

Dana looked at him squarely. "When can you start?"

What was another night without sleep?

"Tonight," he said promptly. "But don't bother looking for me. Surveillance doesn't work if the subject is busy looking around for the watcher. From now on, you're to let me know immediately when you find anything else of a questionable nature. Don't touch it or pick it up with your bare hands. Use a handkerchief to pick it up and slide it into a clean envelope. If we're lucky, we'll get some workable fingerprints."

"Of course." She rose to her feet in one fluid motion. She held out her hand. Fingers sleek with a French manicure, the skin silky to the touch. A fire opal ring on one finger flashed orange, blue and green at him. Funny. A woman with a no-nonsense image should be wearing pearls. What was the ring trying to say about her? He'd be curious to find out. Not that he'd try to think of her in any way other than as a client. Getting emotionally involved with a client, no matter how beautiful she was, would be breaking the Eleventh Commandment he'd instituted the day he opened the office.

Thou shalt not mess with gorgeous clients.

"I'll be in touch in a couple days," he told her. "From now on, you don't need to worry about any of this. Go about your business the way you always do. Above all, don't change your routine. You have to act as if nothing has changed."

She nodded. The uncertainty that flitted across her features before she composed herself was proof she wasn't as in control of herself as she'd like.

She stood up and offered her hand, which he took.

"Thank you," she said softly.

The scent of her perfume still lingered in the air hours after she'd left the small office. Yep, better than those cigars.

*   *   *

"Dammit!" Dana pounded her steering wheel with the heel of her hand. Anger was something she rarely displayed.

The last thing she'd wanted to do was hire a private investigator. She didn't want anyone prying into every corner of her life. She knew this man would do just that, citing it was his job. She knew he wouldn't find anything scandalous in her background. It was just that she preferred keeping her life private.

Why did this have to happen to her?

There was no answer to that question. But she could clearly remember the day it started. The telephone call from Harold Curtis that distressed her. She hadn't detected even a hint of the warmth she usually associated with the man. During that call, he'd kept a cool distance as he abruptly informed her he would not be renewing his contract with her firm. It took her some time to find out exactly why he was severing a business relationship that had begun with her father more than twenty years ago when her father managed Harold's first building. Now Curtis was going elsewhere because he claimed to have seen her acting very improperly at a downtown hotel. Harold was an upright conservative citizen who refused to tell her exactly what he'd seen because, as he explained, he didn't want to *think* about what he'd seen. No matter how much she protested that it couldn't have been her, he hadn't budged an inch. In the end, she'd sadly closed his file.

She realized there was nothing she could say to convince him that it hadn't been her. Further, how could she convince someone else he was sadly mistaken when she feared he could be right?

There had been too many mornings when she'd left for work and discovered her car's gas tank was registering almost empty, when she was positive it had been more than half-full the night before. And there was the morning she found a nightgown casually thrown on the floor of the closet—a nightgown she knew wasn't hers. But it was finding the matchbook in her wastebasket that upset her the most. Especially after she drove past the bar in question. There was no way she would have entered such an establishment.

That was when she knew it was time to do something about it. She knew most women would have discussed their troubles with their friends. Confessed their worries in hopes one of them would have a solution. Except, Dana realized, the friends she had, she'd virtually ignored since her father's death and then her mother's stroke. She'd buried herself in her work and pushed them away. All she had were acquaintances and business colleagues in whom she wouldn't dream of confiding.

She was completely on her own as she started making discreet inquiries about private investigators. With each inquiry, John McKenna's name was brought up with the recommendation that if anyone could solve the problem, he could.

She hadn't discovered a lot about the man, other than that he was a former police detective. That he'd received many commendations—even if he was known as a cop who didn't mind flaunting authority if it meant getting the job done the right way. All his arrests were done by the book, and woe to any prosecutor who screwed up one of John McKenna's cases.

"You wouldn't know it to look at him just how successful he is in his work. He's too committed to helping people who can't afford his fees and he doesn't seem to care if his rent gets paid or not," one person told her. *"But I can't think of anyone else I would want on my side."*

No one really knew the complete story as to why he finally left the police force and opened his private investigation office. But everyone who recommended him said they would trust him with their life. She knew that that was the highest praise any man would receive.

She hadn't expected a private investigator who was so highly regarded to have an office that looked like something straight out of a Raymond Chandler novel. She wouldn't have been surprised if he had a bottle of whiskey in the bottom drawer of his desk. Even the neighborhood was highly suspect. After leaving, she didn't breathe a sigh of relief until she found herself in the parking garage of her office building. Security personnel patrolled on a regular basis, magnetized key cards were required for the entrance gate, excellent lighting and cameras were also placed at strategic spots. The knowledge that no one who wasn't authorized could get in here was a relief to the building's occupants, who gladly paid the high fees to feel secure.

Dana didn't consider herself someone who was easily spooked. She prided herself on allowing nothing to unsettle her.

Then her life had started to turn itself upside down. Someone was out to get her, and she had no idea who, or why.

She pulled into her parking space and stopped but didn't shut off the engine.

She didn't want to leave the safety of her car. The walls of the garage seemed to crowd around her, constricting her breathing. That was when she knew she had to get out of there.

She pulled her cell phone out of her purse and hit the speed dial. The ringing on the other end sounded unusually loud in her ear. Even the sound of her administrative assistant's voice didn't calm the shivering deep in her bones.

She made a decision. "Marti, I need you to cancel my three o'clock appointment with Terence Little." She spoke crisply. "No, there's no problem. I just won't be in for the rest of the day."

She wasted no time in backing out of her parking space, and almost raced out of the parking garage. She couldn't face returning to the office just yet. Right now, she needed fresh air so she could banish the uneasiness clouding her mind.

She hadn't expected her meeting with John McKenna to leave her feeling so unsettled. His strong personality seemed to shear through her defenses like a hot knife through butter. She didn't like that.

She was used to men who dressed in Saville Row suits, not jeans. They were always clean shaven, not sporting a face that had missed a blade for the past few days. Their hair was expensively styled, not hanging in thick strands that looked ready to be shorn like that of a sheep. But one thing John McKenna didn't lack was self-assurance. The man had enough for an army.

There was something about him that sent strange feelings through her. He gave her a quivery sensation she'd never encountered before, and she wasn't sure she liked it. His eyes, a misty gray-green color, seemed to look deep within her and ferret out all her secrets. And find her lacking.

She shouldn't care what he thought of her. She'd hired him because he had the skills she needed, not because he liked her as a person.

So why did his opinion of her matter?

She needed to put such thoughts aside. Ordinarily, she would have driven to her old family home. There, she would have sought the comfort of her mother's arms. She always knew what to do and say to make her feel better. Except that Alice Madison had been felled by a stroke, and right now, any kind of stress was detrimental to her recovery. Dana couldn't go there to find her father working or reading in his study. She had always enjoyed the spacious comfortable room where she could curl up in one of the large leather chairs and discuss her problems with him. She

reminded herself that she shouldn't feel the need to tell him
her worries. Past experience told her what his advice would
have been had he still been alive. He would have told her
that she was an adult and she could handle this herself. It
hurt that the only way she could talk to her father was to
visit his grave.

The way Dana looked at it, she had no one to turn to.
She was used to handling personal and professional problems on her own. It stung that this time she couldn't.

She hoped John McKenna would find out who wanted
to make her life so miserable.

It was dark by the time Dana finally made her way home.
She pulled into the garage and looked around as the garage
door slid down behind her. She had always considered her
home a quiet refuge. A place she could retreat to and renew
her energy when her work proved to be too much. Now,
even that had been violated. She hesitated as her hand covered the doorknob. She couldn't find the strength to turn it.
Not when she didn't know what she would find on the other
side. The thoughts raced through her mind like dark clouds
obscuring the sun.

Would she find her things moved around?

At first glance, her kitchen looked the same as it always
did. She stopped long enough to leave her packages on the
counter and put her groceries away. Even that simple task
couldn't erase the sense that an unauthorized visitor had
probably looked through the cabinets.

"Stop it," she ordered herself. She picked up the mail
Connie, her housekeeper, had left on the counter, and sorted
through the envelopes. There was no way she could tell if
anyone other than Connie had looked at these.

Dana turned on all the lights as she walked down the
hallway to her bedroom. Before, she wouldn't have bothered because she'd never felt afraid to be alone in her

home. Now, she didn't feel safe unless lights were blazing in just about every room—just as she couldn't stop silently asking herself if someone had come in here between the time Connie had left and Dana had arrived.

Dana pretended her life was absurdly normal as she hung up her dry cleaning and changed into a robe. She had no appetite, but since she hadn't eaten much for lunch she warmed up the casserole Connie had left for her.

While the food was excellent as always, she ate little. Keeping up her self-imposed charade of spending a quiet evening at home, she curled up on the couch and watched the news. Watching people whose lives were in worse shape than hers helped her get things in perspective: her life wasn't all that bad, after all. She knew it didn't make for an exciting evening, but she didn't care. The last thing she needed was anything to upset the balance she'd worked so hard to achieve.

She kept up her pretense as she called her family home to speak to her mother's nurse. The woman's report that Alice Madison had had a restless afternoon left Dana wishing she could do other than provide excellent medical care for her mother. She'd hoped she would feel assured she was doing everything she could. She informed the nurse she would be out to see Alice the next day.

Dana usually prided herself on not imagining sounds that weren't there or fearing there was someone lurking just outside her property line. She'd always considered herself a brave woman who met life head-on. Her father had brought her up that way. But now she prayed John Mc-Kenna would do what she couldn't.

Dana took a pre-bedtime glass of wine into her bedroom and settled in bed with her drink and a book. The thought that her new watchdog wasn't far away eased her mind in a way she hadn't felt in some time. After reading a few pages, she set her book on the nightstand before she fell into a deep sleep.

If anyone entered her house, she was sleeping too heavily to notice.

Mac had the seat back as far as it would go so he could stretch out his legs. Stakeouts used to be his least favorite activity, since department-issued cars didn't provide enough room for a tall man. The first thing he did when he set up on his own was make sure he had a vehicle, an Explorer, that wouldn't give him that problem.

Since he'd promised Dana Madison prompt service, he hadn't wasted any time before driving over to her office building. What he hadn't expected was to see her car shoot out of the parking garage like a bat out of hell. He told himself it was a good thing he hadn't waited until evening to keep tabs on her. He kept his distance as he followed her, while she performed fairly normal errands before driving to her house. He noticed that while she smiled at whomever she dealt with, there was still a hint of tension tightening her features. Something bothered the lady, all right.

He studied his surroundings—at least what he could see beyond the streetlights. Dana Madison lived in an upscale neighborhood where he guessed the residents paid a hefty price for woodsy areas that might have looked as if they'd been there for years, but were only a part of the developer's designs. Each home was set back from the road with a lush lawn rolling before it. Discreetly placed signs in the woods indicated paths set aside for walkers and joggers. He guessed it gave the homeowners the feeling they lived in an rural area. As a security expert, all he could see was that the surroundings were heaven sent for burglars who could sneak in from those well kept woods and then get out before anyone knew what was going on.

He'd bet the streets were busy during the day with gardening crews who kept the lawns and shrubbery a rich green. He wouldn't be surprised if a few nosy neighbors checked out any unknown cars loitering in the area. He'd learned long ago that people who kept themselves abreast of what went on with their neighbors made his job a little easier. He didn't worry about his position that night since this side street didn't have any houses nearby, just the woods. From here, he could easily watch Dana's house and not worry about being seen by neighbors.

His musings were interrupted by a low growl coming from the back seat.

"Again?" he muttered, looking over his shoulder. "It's only been ten minutes since the last time. It's a good thing those rent-a-cops don't drive past as often as our client thought they did. Of course, what's so dangerous about a guy walking his dog, right?"

A massive black-and-white head lifted upward and propped itself on the seat's headrest. A broad muzzle bumped the back of Mac's head in a canine demand for attention.

"Okay, okay." Mac dug a beefy dog biscuit out of a small plastic bucket he kept on the floor of the passenger side and tossed it over his shoulder.

The dog's jaws snapped open long enough to catch the treat. It was devoured in one bite.

"You may work cheap, Duffy, but you sure don't make it easy," Mac told the St. Bernard, who was happily drooling all over the blanket draped over the seat to keep it relatively fur free.

Mac had just shifted his position when he noticed Dana's garage door gliding upward. He checked his watch. It was just a little after midnight. Two minutes later, her spiffy Jaguar convertible backed down the driveway and out onto the street.

''My guess would be you're not going out for milk,'' he muttered, starting up the engine.

Five hours later, Mac was back on the side street near Dana's house. He watched as she drove her car into the garage. Within moments, lights winked out and all was quiet.

He muttered a few choice curses. When she'd said she wanted him to follow her he'd had no idea just where her request would take him. Now he had the task of figuring out how to word his report in a way that wouldn't sound downright insulting to the lady.

How do you tell your client that when it turns dark, she turns into a major party girl? And not just any party girl, either. This one hit some pretty heavy-duty clubs and didn't seem to mind whom she spent her time with. She even cruised a few of the sleazier motels he didn't think he'd even heard of when he worked vice many years ago.

He spent the night feeling as if he'd entered one of those weird films that tried to disguise itself as art.

Except this wasn't a movie, and there was no way he could call what had gone on any kind of art. He wasn't looking forward to giving this particular report.

He reminded himself that what he'd seen wasn't anything new. Just because Dana Madison looked the part of a nicely dressed, corporate type, didn't mean there wasn't a wild side that came out after dark. He'd seen proof of that wild side tonight. Few things surprised him anymore. His years with the police department carved that out of him in no time. But after his meeting with Dana Madison the previous day, he hadn't expected the reckless behavior he'd witnessed the past five hours.

''What's wrong with this picture, Duff?'' he said out loud. ''Do you think she's doing all this for kicks? Do you think she decided to go one step further and find a PI to follow her and watch what she does? Maybe she likes to be watched. Do you think she's sleepwalking? Has a split personality? Any of those sound good to you?''

A contented doggie snore was his answer.

Mac sighed and hunched down in the seat. Even though he doubted his client would be going anywhere until it was time for her to leave for her office, he didn't dare catch a nap. He'd do that later. He'd have plenty of time to sleep after his newest client received his report—and, in all probability, fired him. He swallowed a yawn. At least his retainer paid up the rent and office utilities.

Please God, no. She just couldn't handle a migraine first thing in the morning.

Dana fumbled with the prescription pill bottle and finally managed to get it open. She tossed two tablets in her mouth, followed by a healthy swallow of water.

Here she thought she'd slept so well, yet she woke up feeling fuzzy-headed and out of sorts. After she'd gotten up, she'd started to feel the stabbing pain in her head and had feared the worst. If the old-fashioned work ethic hadn't been drummed into her from a young age, she would have called in sick and pulled the covers over her head.

Her sense of feeling out-of-it intensified when she went downstairs. She knew immediately that something was wrong. There was the faint hint of cigarette smoke in her kitchen that she knew hadn't been there the night before. She told herself it had to be her imagination, since she didn't smoke and her housekeeper was allergic to cigarette smoke.

But she couldn't blame her imagination again when she opened her closet and found a bright pink lacy bra wadded up on the floor. It wasn't hers.

She picked up Mac's business card and left a message insisting he call her as soon as possible.

If he was doing his job the way he'd said he would, she'd have some answers today.

Chapter 2

"Call your office and tell them you'll be late."

"Excuse me?" Dana groped for her coffee cup. She figured she didn't have enough caffeine in her system to grapple with John McKenna first thing in the morning.

"I'll be over there in about ten minutes to look over your house." He hung up.

"Goodbye to you, too," she muttered.

She watched the minute hand sweep ten times before Mac rang her doorbell. He nodded a silent greeting and walked past her toward the kitchen. He opened the back door and inspected the lock.

"A five-year-old could get in here with little effort," Mac muttered.

"Last I heard, five-year-olds weren't listed on America's Most Wanted." She sipped her coffee. The caffeine wasn't proving to be enough to keep her alert.

Mac looked up. "You need a dead bolt on this door and your front door." As he crossed the kitchen, he glanced at the immaculate counters. "You must use paper plates." He thought of the dishes from a week ago that still resided in his own sink.

He took stock of his surroundings. Fancy counters that looked as if they were made out of gray granite, cooking island, bleached cabinets with etched-glass doors. Nothing out of place here. He resisted the urge to wash his hands before continuing. Instead he slipped on a pair of latex gloves. Under Dana's watchful, and wary, eye, he went to work.

Drawers divulged little other than that he couldn't find anything remotely resembling a junk drawer. Her personal phone book noted numbers for the usual medical needs, various repairmen, her housekeeper, and a few names and addresses he gathered belonged to friends.

He noted there were a few times when she looked as if she wanted to snatch something out of his hands, but she managed to restrain herself. She remained seated as he left the kitchen.

He bypassed the family room and living room, and headed straight for her home office.

It was just as he expected. Desk drawers were all neatly arranged, all the files in order. Even her correspondence was arranged in chronological order. *No wonder she looked shell-shocked when she saw my office,* he thought, glancing at the tiny boxes holding stamps, paper clips and rubber bands. He doubted she ever had to tear her desk apart to find a lousy stamp.

Dana was standing in the hallway as he headed for her bedroom.

"Do you have to go through every room?" she demanded tautly.

"Only if I want to find out who's harassing you," he replied. "Don't worry. I won't make a mess or mishandle any of your delicate lingerie."

"That's not what I'm worried about."

The minute he stepped into her bedroom, he detected the same scent he remembered from his office.

If he expected to find it decorated with ruffles and lace, he was sorely disappointed. But not too much. What he found was even better.

The carpet underfoot was plush and a muted shade of spearmint green. He couldn't imagine a dog in this room. Especially his dog. Big mistake even thinking like that. The silk bedspread was a rich cream color with an abstract swirl design of green, pale pink, peach and soft blue. Solid color throw pillows decorated the head of the king-size bed. He hated to think what Duffy would do to a bed like that. Actually, he shouldn't even think of himself anywhere close to that bed.

He inched open the closet door and studied the variety of clothing that hung there. The contents were all well made and expensive. Work clothing and casual clothing divided. Dresser drawers disclosed lingerie that momentarily had him visualizing the silk and lace on her. He tucked that thought out of the way the minute it appeared. Not a good idea thinking of your client wearing a black lace bra, panties and garter belt. Tended to take away the professionalism. He was headed for the bathroom, when a bright color caught his eye.

"Well, well, well," he murmured, reaching into the wastebasket and pulling out a hot-pink lace bra that screamed sex. It wasn't remotely like the ones he'd found in her dresser drawers. The ones that were demure yet seductive. Victoria's Secret versus Frederick's of Hollywood. He pulled a plastic bag out of his pocket and secured it inside. He tucked it inside his jacket pocket.

The bra didn't go with the clothing he found in the closet. He did a quick search of every closet in the house.

He couldn't find anything else that went with the underwear.

He returned to the bedroom and went on through to the bathroom. Here the colors weren't soothing soft pastels, but colors of the ocean. Brilliant turquoise, bright lime and a smattering of deep lavender for accent.

Mac doubted a professional decorator had stepped one foot in this house. No, Dana would have done all this herself. That way she could keep her house under her control just as she kept control over her workplace.

Since she'd hired him, she obviously felt her life wasn't behaving the way she'd planned.

There. It was so subtle, it could easily have been overlooked. Especially by a man. Even by Mac. But he'd been looking for another clue to go with the underwear and had hoped he'd find it here. He got lucky.

A former girlfriend had once set him straight about a woman's cosmetics. There were those who were strict about what brands and colors they used. Dana was one of these. All the lipstick cases he found were black. But one silver case stood out among the others. He carefully picked it up and studied the label, then twisted the tube so the lipstick would swivel upward.

"Passion," he murmured, checking out the color. "Interesting name." He held the tube upward, the shimmery red shade almost blinding his eyes.

Not one of Dana Madison's, that's for sure.

He dropped it in a second plastic bag and stuffed it in his pocket.

A cursory search of the living and family room didn't tell him anything other than that Dana Madison seemed to live a pretty quiet life.

Maybe the lady needed a shrink instead of a private investigator. Still, his curiosity was growing by the moment.

He returned to the kitchen, where Dana was again sitting

at the table. Her delicate features were still taut and her lips were pressed together tightly. He guessed it was so they wouldn't tremble. He wondered if she ever dared show any emotion. Maybe she did have an alter ego that could only come out at night. It might be something he'd have to discuss with her.

"Well?" She faced him with a challenging stare.

"First off, buy some timers for your lamps. Set them up in each room and program them for different hours. Make sure at least one lamp comes on just before it gets dark," he instructed.

She nodded. "What else?"

"I'll call you when I have my report ready," he said, before striding out the door.

As Mac walked to his truck, he thought about what he'd seen in the house. Except for the bra and lipstick, nothing there indicated a woman who liked the nightlife.

One thing was sure. The past twenty-four hours was more than enough to tell him Ms. Dana Madison was turning out to be one hell of an interesting case.

"You've been very popular this morning."

Dana paused at her assistant's desk long enough to pick up her phone messages. She swiftly checked the name on each one but didn't see anything that required immediate attention.

"Anything else I need to know about?" she asked.

"Scott wants to see you about the contracts for the Brand Corporation," the silver-haired woman replied. "I told him you'd be free at three, and he could have fifteen minutes."

Dana smiled. Marti Cameron had kept her father's office running smoothly for more than thirty years. After his death, Dana had asked Marti to remain with her, since her own assistant had resigned when her husband accepted an out-of-state transfer. It was a decision Dana had never re-gretted.

"What will I tell him during those fifteen minutes you've allotted him?" she asked.

Marti arched an eyebrow. "You won't need to tell him anything. All you'll have to do is sit there and let him tell you why he feels the amendments to the contract are in our favor. Then you'll explain to him they aren't in our favor. When he asks you why you feel that, you can tell him he needs to do some more homework."

Dana perched herself on the corner of her assistant's desk. The smile she flashed was natural and warm. It was a smile few were allowed to see.

"Are you sure you wouldn't rather keep this meeting for me?"

The older woman looked horrified. "As if I would pre-sume to do such a thing." She picked up her reading glasses with the multicolor frames and slipped them on. "Now go on and return those telephone calls. I have cor-respondence to finish so you can sign them before the end of the day."

"Yes, ma'am." Dana saluted her and slipped off the desk.

Dana couldn't enter the office that had been her father's without feeling as if she were entering a sacred area. At first, she feared she wouldn't be able to run the large man-agement leasing company as well as he had, but with Marti's help and many hours of work, she felt more con-fident with each passing day.

It helped that one of her father's last instructions was to redecorate his office the day she took it over. He'd told her to make the space her own. And she had.

The heavy mahogany furniture and hunter-green drapes were replaced with a lighter-shade wood furniture, more modern in design, and sage-green drapes. A green-and-rose tweed sofa was placed against one wall with a coffee table in front of it and a chair on either side. Her father had refused to use a computer, claiming he didn't trust them, but now a laptop sat on Dana's desk. Though she'd put her stamp on the space, she felt her father's spirit still existed in the large office. That feeling helped her gain the confidence she needed to lead the company.

That confidence, so hard won, had begun to ebb when strange things started happening.

Dana sat at her desk and laid the pink message slips out like a deck of cards. She ignored them as she picked up her phone and punched out a number.

"McKenna Investigations. Leave a message."

"As always, cryptic to the point of rude," she murmured, waiting for the tone. "Mr. McKenna, this is Dana Madison. I'd appreciate hearing from you."

A *click* sounded in her ear. "What would you appreciate hearing?"

"What happened last night." She could be just as blunt.

"Like I told you, you'll get a weekly report. I'd like more than twenty-four hours before giving you my observations. See you at the end of the week, Ms. Madison. Come by around five, and we'll talk." He hung up before she could say a word.

Dana looked at the phone receiver as if it had somehow betrayed her.

"If this is how he treats paying clients, I hate to think how he treats the world in general," she murmured, using her fingertip to push one of the message slips away from the others.

She thought of the bra she'd found that morning. She had been instructed to contact him if she found anything. Instead, she'd thrown it away because she couldn't stand to look at anything so disgusting. Should she call him back and tell him about it? Or just pretend it never existed?

Lately, she preferred acting as if nothing happened to her between dusk and dawn. Safer to keep it that way.

As the afternoon lengthened, the curt tones of John McKenna's voice reverberated through her head. She didn't know how or why, but she was positive his first night working for her had given him clues about what was going on. Clues she was not going to like hearing.

She plunged into her work. Long ago, she'd discovered it was the best way to keep her fearful thoughts at bay. Keeping her current clients confident that she could manage their buildings as well as her father had was proving to be more than a full-time job. One she was now grateful for.

By the time she felt she could take a break, her eyes were burning from staring at the computer monitor and her back ached from staying in one position too long. It was dark out, and only the lamp on her desk was lit. Deceptive shadows hung from every corner of the room.

She imagined her father lounging on the couch.

"You chose something much too soft, daughter," he'd tell her, shifting around to find a comfortable position. *"This kind of couch is only handy if you want an afternoon nap. Don't think about making your clients too comfortable. They might think you're as soft as your couch."*

"You're wrong, Dad. I use it to soften them up for the kill," she murmured, saving her work before she closed the files and shut down her computer. She stretched her arms over her head to relieve some of the ache that had settled in the small of her back, and stood up.

She walked through the dark empty offices and relocked the main door on her way out. As she descended in the elevator, she felt the silence of the entire building surround her. She felt the stark solitude as she crossed the parking garage to reach her car. The yellow lights cast a harsh glow over the area, as if she had been thrust inside something dark and evil.

Dana tried to cast off the apprehension that flowed through her mind as she grew closer to her car. But it increased as a chill skittered along her spine.

She felt a pair of eyes focused on her. She turned around in a tight circle to view everything around her. She tried to peer into every corner, but the shadows mocked her with their stillness.

"Is anyone there?" She hated it that her voice trembled. "Ed, are you out there?" She called out the name of one of the security guards who routinely patrolled the parking garage.

The answering silence was equally mocking.

Dana disarmed her car alarm and got in. She started up the car and hastily backed out of the parking stall, her tires squealing as she raced around the corner toward the exit.

She was so intent on escaping that she didn't see a figure detach itself from behind a post and stand there watching the car's taillights disappear.

"Run little mouse, run." The figure laughed throatily. "But no matter how fast you run, you still won't be able to escape me. Before you know it, the day will come when you'll be the one in a cage, and I'll be the one with all the cheese."

Dana might not be able to see John McKenna, but she knew he was nearby no matter where she went.

As she left her office each evening, he was out there somewhere. He was nearby when she stopped at the dry cleaners, when she walked through the drugstore, picking up a prescription and necessary sundries, or when she made a quick stop at the gas station. It wasn't easy to resist looking around to see if she could find him.

The feeling of John McKenna watching her was different from what she felt when someone else watched her. She didn't sense any unease or nasty prickling of fear. She wasn't sure what to label the feeling; it was something she hadn't experienced before.

But no matter how comfortable she felt during those hours, she still suffered during the few minutes just before she fell asleep. She was overwhelmed by a terrifying sensation that her life was spiraling out of control. A cold feeling that warned her her slumber would steal the control she'd always held onto so tightly. And worries she'd never had before.

Of course, she'd never before had to worry about someone trying to destroy her life.

Now, Dana drove down the winding driveway. She'd always thought of the trees lining the drive as comforting. Tonight, they felt as if they were closing in on her. She breathed a sigh of relief when she reached the house. After she shut off the engine, she pulled down the visor and stared at her reflection in the lighted mirror. Lines of stress were lightly carved along her mouth and eyes. She smoothed her fingertip across them and reapplied her lipstick, deciding the color gave her a much-needed boost.

She got out of the car, and carriage lights along the steps showed her the way to a front door she knew well. She unlocked the door and stepped inside. A woman in her sixties appeared from a side room. Her silver hair was cut short and feathered around her face. Her plump body was clothed in a floral print blouse and dark blue slacks.

"Dana." She held out her arms for a hug. "Have you eaten, dear?"

"Even if I say yes, you'll tell me I don't eat enough and insist on stuffing me with food." She welcomed the embrace that brought memories of afternoons spent in the kitchen learning to bake cookies and cakes. Over the years, the woman had gone from a trusted employee to a valued family member. Dana couldn't imagine what it would be like if she lost her, too. "How are you, Harriet?"

"Pretending my arthritis doesn't bother me in the mornings," the housekeeper joked.

"Which is why I insisted someone come in to clean," Dana told her. "You know very well you're not expected to do all that work. You should be taking it easier now instead of trying to work harder."

"Lord, child, I don't have enough to do now," she protested, laughing. "Even those nurses don't cause that much work. Most of them seem to think a small salad is a huge meal."

"They're doing all right?" She knew she could get the truth from Harriet.

Harriet nodded. "They're just fine. They seem to prefer keeping to themselves, but they always take excellent care of...your mother." Her smile disappeared.

Dana could feel the area around her heart tighten. "She's worse?"

"Not worse, not better," the older woman said gently, keeping her arms around Dana. "Honey, the doctor told you there was a good chance your mother wouldn't fully recover."

Dana shook her head, refusing to listen. "Mom's always come back before. She will this time. She's had excellent care."

Harriet's eyes softened with the love she felt for the young woman she'd cared for since childhood. "Sweetheart, please don't take this the wrong way, but the last time your mother was very ill, your father was here."

She wouldn't take it the wrong way. She knew just how strong the bond between her parents had been. She envied them their love, but knew she never lacked for love of her own. Now her mother lay in a hospital bed, her mind trapped in a frail body. How sad her body could never keep up with her mind. And now, her mind had trouble even keeping up with her body. Every time Dana sat with her, she silently willed her mother to come back to her. To be with her.

She looked upward. "Do you know if she's awake?"

"I'm sorry, dear. She had a difficult afternoon. She just dropped off to sleep about an hour ago." Harriet kept an arm around her. "Why don't you come with me and I'll fix you something to eat. We can go upstairs afterward to see if she's awake."

As the housekeeper guided her toward the kitchen, Dana purposely pushed her troubles out of her mind. For the next hour or so, she would let Harriet fuss over her and she would pretend nothing had changed.

Time enough to worry when she left the house.

Mac stared as the pages slid into the printer's paper tray.

Funny how words could change a person's life.

The report he was printing would tell a woman that her husband wasn't her husband, after all. She might have the marriage license and the wedding video, but her alleged husband had a secret she knew nothing about. He had a wife living in another city. A wife he'd married some years before.

She'd come to him because she feared her husband was having an affair and she needed to know the truth. Mac normally didn't like following errant husbands. It never seemed to do any good, only bringing pain to the one needing to know. Except, she was so young, so vulnerable that he felt as if he'd kick a puppy if he gave her a flat no. He also didn't want her looking for another private investigator and ending up with one with few scruples. So he followed the man who held an executive position in a medical supply corporation. Mac soon learned the man traveled extensively between two offices. That way he could stay part of the time with wife number one. Mac did some nosing around and learned that wife number one believed he had to travel a great deal. Wife number one gave him a boy and a girl. Wife number two was currently five months pregnant with their first child.

Mac ran two copies of his report, which included the two marriage certificates and information about the first wife, who was also the legal wife. He'd leave it up to wife number two how she wanted to handle this problem. He knew he wouldn't mind escorting the man straight to jail. This wasn't going to be pleasant either way. He sensed she had an inner core she was probably unaware of just now, but it would appear when needed. She'd need that and more in the coming months. He figured wife number one wouldn't waste any time in throwing the man in jail for bigamy. Jailhouse orange would replace his expensive suits, and a sheriff's van, his fancy Cadillac.

"Some guys think they can have it all," he muttered, putting the stacks of sheets in two separate manila envelopes.

"Don't all men think they can have it all?"

Mac looked up to find Dana standing in the doorway of his office.

"Ms. Madison." He nodded toward his extra chair. "Have a seat."

She stared at the envelopes on his desk. "A soon-to-be-satisfied client?"

"Probably not," he said cryptically. "What do you think of this?" He turned around and pulled an envelope off the top of the shelf behind him. He tossed it onto the desk next to the envelope. The contents spilled out. The bright pink lace lay there mocking her.

Dana eyed the bag as if it would reach out and bite her. She looked up with her jaw jutting forward and eyes the hard color of cobalt marbles.

"You didn't tell me you found anything."

"I didn't think I needed to. Maybe I'm wrong, but I had a hunch it didn't belong to you. Didn't look your style."

She pulled in a sharp breath that stabbed at her midsection. She sat still but her body vibrated with the fury she felt inside. No matter what she said, his excuse would be that he'd told her he wanted to inspect her house. She just hadn't realized it meant going through all her personal belongings, too.

"I would like to read the report now."

He cocked an eyebrow at her crisp order.

"How do you spend your nights, Ms. Madison?"

She laughed, a harsh humorless sound. "That's what I hired you to find out."

"Humor me." He leaned back in his chair, fingers laced, hands resting against his flat belly. "What did you do three nights ago after you left your office?"

Dana took a deep breath as she thought back. "I left my office early. I stopped at the Valley cleaners. Then I dropped by Flora's bakery for a loaf of my favorite bread. After that, I went straight home. My housekeeper had left a casserole in the oven for me. I ate my dinner while watching the evening news, set my dishes in the dishwasher and called my mother's house. She has great difficulty speaking since her stroke, so I spoke to her nurse. I finished a book I'd been reading the past few nights, had a glass of wine and went to bed." Her smile was faintly mocking. "My, my Mr. McKenna. I seem to be doing your work for you. Was that exciting enough for you or do you want to know what brand of toothpaste I use?"

His reply wiped the smile off her face.

"Three nights ago, your bedroom light went out at 12:03. At 12:26, you backed out of your garage and drove downtown. You were dressed in a skirt that was up to your navel, a strapless top that could have doubled as a Band-Aid and come-hither high heels. You headed for the Crystal

Tree Lounge, which is known for its 'interesting clientele.' There, you met up with a character named Big Al. Big Al's a long-haul truck driver from Little Rock. The two of you drank tequila shooters until two a.m., when the bartender announced last call. You somehow found a liquor store that was still open. You bought a bottle of tequila and headed over to the Mayfield Motel. Room six. Not exactly the Hyatt, but they don't ask any questions about lack of luggage.

"The two of you played the horizontal mambo until about five, when you left good ol' Big Al and drove back home. I gotta give you credit, Ms. Madison. I saw you that morning and you looked about as bright-eyed and bushy-tailed, pardon the pun, as any woman I've seen. You had one hell of a busy evening and didn't even suffer a hangover. I'd sure like to know what vitamins you take. Then you pretty much went through the same routine night before last. That time with a guy named Bud.

"I also gotta say your community's so-called private security patrol is a joke. They drove past your house twice and didn't seem to think it odd that a strange man was parked along a side street for most of the night. I want you to get a security system ASAP."

Dana stared at Mac as if she'd never seen him before. Her pinpoint pupils and labored breathing warned him she was going into shock.

"You're lying," she whispered between stiff lips. Her eyes lit upon the envelope. She picked it up and tore the papers out. After she scanned the pages, she shoved them back into the envelope. She dropped her hands back into her lap.

Mac remained quiet, preferring to study her reaction. He wasn't sure what he expected, but this quiet show of pain wasn't it. Maybe because he was used to his female clients picking up whatever was handy and throwing it at him while screaming that he was scum.

A lone tear made its way down her cheek. She did nothing to stop it.

He had to break the silence. Concentrating on business at hand seemed the best way. He felt if he offered any word of comfort, she would shatter.

"Did you keep a log of your mileage like I told you to?"

She nodded jerkily. She took a deep breath and reached into her bag. She pulled out a small book and laid it on the desktop.

Mac picked it up and leafed through the pages. The mornings that listed a different mileage than the night before coincided with the nights he'd followed her. He handed back the book, which she promptly returned to her bag. She stared at him as if knowing it wasn't over. But her gaze also accused him.

He hated to think how she'd react to his next piece of evidence. He pulled a photograph out of his drawer and tossed it on top.

Dana's eyes didn't leave the damning photo. She looked defeated and physically ill as she gripped the desk edge.

The woman in the photo was her. Yet not her.

Mac remembered when he'd taken the photo. She was exiting a motel room. Her clothing was minimal, the kind a woman would wear if she worked standing on a street corner. Her hair was mussed and the look on her face was that of a woman very satisfied with herself.

Dana refused to believe what she saw.

"No," she whispered, feeling the raw pain tear through her limbs. "No."

Mac pushed back his chair and stood up. He grabbed the battered brown leather jacket off the file cabinet and shrugged into it.

"Come on," he said abruptly.

She stared at him, baffled by his order.

"There's only one thing the body needs in matters like this." He walked over to her and grasped her arm, pulling her to her feet. He kept hold of her hand as he left the office and closed and locked the door behind him.

"Are you saying you think you need to feed me?" she demanded, straining to pull away, but she could have been fighting a tree for all the attention he gave her.

He flashed her a sideways look as he pushed the elevator call button.

"Hell, no, we're going to get a drink."

Chapter 3

"A bar. Of course. Is this a man's idea of a cure for all ills?" Dana looked around the darkened interior. She wrinkled her nose at the faint hint of smoke. She wouldn't be surprised if most of the occupants ignored the no smoking signs posted on the walls. "Go to a dark bar and let alcohol solve all his problems."

"Not all his problems. Just the important ones. Thanks, Taffy." Mac smiled at a voluptuous waitress wearing two circles of multicolored glitter and a G-string, as she deposited a bottle of beer in front of him and a filled wineglass in front of Dana.

"Anytime, hon." Her smoky voice fit the atmosphere. "You want to just run a tab?"

"Sure. Why don't you get us two of Barney's cheeseburgers and some onion rings." He looked Dana's way. "Want barbecue sauce or chili on your burger? Either is guaranteed to put hair on your..." His eyes fastened on her chest. "Then again, maybe you don't need it."

"I'll have the barbecue sauce, please," she told Taffy. "Do you have any salads?"

The waitress's friendly laughter was as smoky as her voice. "Nope, sorry, hon. Can you honestly see a salad bar in here?" She moved away.

Dana picked up her glass and drank down half her wine.

"You brought me here for a reason, didn't you? In fact, probably more than one. You thought I'd be embarrassed to be in a bar. Or that I'd refuse to eat a cheeseburger. Your test seems to have backfired."

He shrugged. "Maybe I was hoping the place would jog your memory."

Dana looked around again. Scarred wooden tables and chairs that could have been there since the Second World War. A bar along one wall, fluorescent advertisements for various beers and one light sculpture that was definitely X-rated. She was positive the woman in the picture would be at home in this place.

She wondered vaguely if the waitresses ever got cold in their scanty attire, but noticed the customers treated them with respect. She was positive it had more to do with the burly-looking man standing behind the bar than good manners. She'd learned quickly that the jukebox didn't play anything past 1972, and that anyone drinking too much was escorted outside to a cab paid for by the bar. The bartender tagged the car keys with the customer's name and placed them in a locked box.

This neighborhood bar knew its customers and did what was possible to keep them safe.

John McKenna was obviously a regular here, since many greeted him by name. She felt the looks of curiosity directed her way, but he didn't introduce her to anyone as he guided her toward a table in the rear.

"Mr. McKenna—" she began.

"Mac."

"Excuse me?"

"Mac." He tipped the bottle toward his lips. "Mr. Mc-Kenna's my old man and we've never exactly been on speaking terms."

She took a sip of wine, more to reorganize her thoughts than to quench a thirst. "What do you think it is? Sleep-walking? Split personality?" Neither possibility sounded plausible. But she wanted a reason, any reason, to explain the insanity she'd just read about.

"Either of those is up to a doctor, and you don't seem to want to check it out that way." He rolled the bottle between his palms. "All I know is what I saw. Sorry I couldn't have taken more pictures. Of course, most of them couldn't have been taken to your local photo shop."

She felt heat brush across her cheeks. She couldn't have done any of those horrible things, could she? If she had, why wouldn't she remember events such as he'd described to her?

She automatically murmured her thanks when Taffy set a red plastic basket in front of her. It was filled with the largest cheeseburger she'd ever seen. A separate plate loaded with onion rings the size of dessert plates was set down between them.

The aroma tempted her into carefully picking up the cheeseburger and taking an experimental bite. The almost narcotic rush of medium-rare hamburger and melted cheese along with the tangy bite of barbecue sauce jump-started her appetite. A second bite quickly followed, and she snatched an onion ring. She ate as if she hadn't consumed anything in days.

"You can't have seen me," she said, once half her cheeseburger was eaten. "Maybe you were looking at a neighbor's house and thought you were looking at mine. That picture was taken in the middle of the night. It could have been someone who looked like me."

Mac shook his head. He held up a hand as he chewed and swallowed. "Sorry, sweetheart, you can lie to yourself all you want, but the story won't change. There weren't any mistakes. The houses on your block are too far apart to mix up your house with a neighbor's. Plus, your closest neighbor is a sixty-year-old man with a bad-tempered bulldog who appears to be blind in one eye. The other neighbor is a scholarly type who cusses out the bulldog when he goes out to get the morning paper. No way either one of them could have gotten away with the outfit I saw."

She swallowed her food and hoped it wouldn't come back up.

"Was that the only time?" she whispered, pushing her food away.

"Nope. The next night was pretty much the same." He eyed her unfinished burger. "You going to finish that?"

She shook her head and gestured for him to feel free. He did.

"Do you think it will happen again?"

"You said things were going on before you hired me. Since they haven't stopped, I'd say it will."

Mac stared at her stricken features. He called out to Taffy and waited until she returned with a glass of club soda. He picked up Dana's wineglass and handed it to the waitress. He waited until Dana took several sips of the soda.

"My father dies, I suddenly have to placate clients who don't want to negotiate with the daughter, my mother has a stroke that has left her without speech and unable to take care of herself. Now I have this to deal with," she murmured, more to herself. "Maybe I should have seen a doctor instead of hiring you. I'm certain he would have suggested a vacation in a quiet, out-of-the-way place with a friendly staff." She took a deep breath. "But leaving town won't make this go away. I have to know."

Mac nodded. "Don't take this the wrong way, but seeing

a doctor might be a good idea. Have a checkup from top to bottom. Ease your mind, if nothing else. I've heard of people sleepwalking. Practically living another life without being aware of it.''

She shook her head. She wasn't disagreeing with his idea, just shaking her head as she thought about the events of the past hour.

"Why do you think all this is happening?" he asked. "For most women going through this kind of harassment, it usually has to do with an old boyfriend who wasn't happy about being dropped. They want to get even, and that way is to scare the hell out of the woman.''

She shook her head again.

"Then you won't mind if I check it out further?" Mac polished off the last onion ring. "It never hurts to cover all the bases.''

"No, I won't mind," she murmured.

"Anything else?" Taffy asked, gathering up the baskets and Mac's empty beer bottle.

Mac cocked an eyebrow, silently questioning Dana. She shook her head.

"Tell Barney all of it was great," he said. He picked up the bill against Dana's protests. "Don't worry, I'll just tack it on my expenses.''

"Hey, Mac, don't forget Duffy!" the bartender called out in a rusty voice.

"Like he'll let me." Mac stood up and walked around, pulling Dana's chair out for her. He guided her toward the front of the bar, then stopped and opened a door off to the side. A loud *woof* greeted him as a dog, as tall as the man, stood on his hind legs. He washed Mac's face with a tongue as broad as a beach towel. Dana stood back, afraid the monster would attack her next. "Don't worry, he's harmless," he assured her, pushing the dog down onto all fours. "Trouble is, he thinks he's a lap dog." He snapped a leash onto the dog's collar and headed for the door with the St. Bernard leading the way. He raised his hand in farewell to the remaining customers.

"I would have thought you'd have a rottweiler or a German shepherd." Dana kept a wary distance from the dog, who stopped to sniff the building's exterior before lifting his leg.

"Duffy was on death row at the shelter," he explained. "Seems his previous owner didn't like him chewing all his shoes."

"You didn't worry about him chewing yours?"

"Not after I sprinkled them with cayenne pepper. He's good company on a stakeout."

Dana halted when they reached her car. A chirping sound announced she'd disengaged the alarm. Mac cast her a wry smile.

"Any reason why you'd have an alarm for your car, but you'd never consider installing one in your house?" he asked in an all-too-casual voice.

"It's necessary. There're times I carry important papers," she explained. "I don't see it necessary to install one in my house. The community security patrol always seemed to offer adequate protection. Or so I thought."

Mac shook his head. He thrust his hands in his jacket pocket, while Duffy tugged on his leash and investigated the tires on a nearby car. Mac gently tugged the dog away when he realized what Duffy's intentions were. "We'll talk about that. Look, I know what you heard tonight was a shock."

"Shock is an understatement," Dana murmured, not even wanting to recall what Mac had told her. She refused to believe any of it. "What you saw was a mistake."

"Cameras don't lie."

She flinched. "That doesn't mean they always see the truth. I guess we'll just have to wait and see what happens next.'' She climbed into her car and closed the door. Without looking at Mac again, she started up the engine and drove away.

Mac dragged Duffy away from a nearby bush and headed for his vehicle. The large dog jumped into the back seat and settled down.

''What's up with her, Duff?'' he asked as he pulled out of the parking lot. ''She's got all the signs of a nutcase, but, I don't know. Something doesn't ring right. Think I'm losing my objectivity because of a pair of blue eyes?''

His partner's reply was a contented doggie snore.

''Some help you are.'' He spied Dana's car and sped up a little. He kept her in sight until she pulled into her garage and the door slid down behind her. He parked on his usual side road and watched a few lights turn on inside the house. A few hours later they were all extinguished.

Maybe Barney's bar didn't bother her because she's spent evenings in places a hell of a lot worse than Barney's, he thought.

This whole deal was something out of a movie made for television. Heroine frightened by unknown fears; macho hero brought in to protect her and save her from a faceless villain.

He wondered what happened if the heroine and the villain were the same. He hoped that wasn't the case. There was something about Dana that pulled at him. Something about the shape of her mouth that had him wondering what she would taste like. He knew when he went to the office in the morning he'd find her scent still lingering in the air.

How many men had had the chance to check out that delectable-looking mouth and inhale that intoxicating perfume? How many guys like that truck driver did she party with?

During his time in vice, Mac had been assigned to follow more than a few women like Dana. Women who might as well have been prostitutes, even if they didn't charge the men they were with.

Dana Madison. She was as changeable as day moving into night.

"Spending the night thinking about the lady isn't a good idea. She's a client, and that means no fooling around. Not to mention, all her eggs might not be in one basket," he said out loud. He knew some people would think he was crazy discussing his cases with his dog. He didn't care. As far as he was concerned, Duffy was the perfect partner: he didn't give his opinion when it wasn't wanted and he worked for Milk Bones. "Just because she looks so damn normal doesn't mean she is. Remember Myra Frasier? She looked normal, too. Just like the sweet old grandmother you read about in books and see on TV. No one would have guessed any different if the neighbor's dog hadn't dug a hole in her rose garden. Turned out there were six men buried there, and she was living off their life insurance. Just goes to show you can't trust anyone."

Duffy sat up, draped his massive head over the back of the passenger seat and exhaled a deep doggie sigh.

"Yeah, life's a bitch." Mac chuckled as the dog whined a reply. "Okay, okay, you wish."

He slid his seat back to allow room for his legs and settled in for a long night.

So, dear little Dana had gone out and got herself a watch-dog. How interesting. When had this happened? She didn't remember seeing him before. But then, she also hadn't been looking for one.

She liked the idea that she was watching the watcher. It gave her the delicious feeling of knowing something he didn't. It gave her something to do, since she had no plans to invade Dana's space tonight. Some nights she preferred standing outside where she felt free, just contemplating her surroundings. She enjoyed those hours of freedom. These were times when she could dream of what it would be like when everything was hers, and dear, darling Dana no longer existed.

Had Dana had any wine tonight? There was enough sedative in the liquid to ensure a good night's sleep. Dana hadn't woken up once any of the times her house had been occupied. She hoped Dana was grateful to her for those undisturbed nights of sleep.

She'd spent many an hour getting to know the house when Dana was asleep. She liked to explore every corner and study the contents of cabinets. It was so delicious to have the chance to ferret out Dana's boring little secrets.

She wondered if Dana liked the little presents she made sure she left behind. How satisfying it was to find just the right item. A little something she could drop in a convenient place for prissy Dana to discover. How horrified she must have been when she found the offerings. She only wished she could have seen Dana's reactions.

It didn't matter. She wasn't in any hurry. After all, there were plenty of other nights for games. It was better if she took her time. That way, Dana would feel more and more paranoid. It seemed only fair Dana suffer. Who knows, if she had any luck she might even find time to play with Dana's watchdog.

She craved a cigarette but tamped down the need. This wasn't the time. Not when she could look around and survey her future kingdom. Dana had chosen a lovely quiet neighborhood. She'd enjoy living here after Dana was gone.

She glanced toward the darkened vehicle again. She didn't worry about his seeing her. Didn't people always believe what they saw? And she knew exactly what people saw anytime she wanted to be noticed.

* * *

Dana stared at the three names and telephone numbers she'd written on the notepad set in front of her. It had taken her almost the entire morning to summon up the courage just to get this far. Now she had to dredge up the courage to make the call.

With the same meticulous care as before, she'd done her homework. The results were the three names. She prayed one of them would hold the answers she was looking for.

Her hands shook as she picked up the phone. She hated that her fear caused them to tremble.

She'd just tapped out two of the numbers, when her intercom buzzed.

"What is it, Marti?"

"Ms. Madison, there's a Mr. McKenna here. He doesn't have an appointment, but he feels you would be willing to see him," her assistant informed her. "I'm afraid he wouldn't say what he wanted."

Her first thought was to say she was busy and couldn't see him. Her second was that perhaps he had some news for her.

"Mr. McKenna doesn't believe in making appointments. That's all right. I'll see him."

She deliberately remained seated as Mac entered the office. He took his time walking around the perimeter of the room. He paused every so often to study a piece of furniture or look out the windows, before he finally turned to her.

"Nice digs," he complimented, sitting down on the chair across from her. "No wonder you looked as if you wanted a pair of rubber gloves and a bottle of disinfectant when you walked into mine." He smiled.

Dana could only stare. When the man smiled, his entire demeanor changed. The rough craggy features didn't soften, but something happened to his face that directed a punch to her stomach.

Whenever she thought of a private investigator, she visualized the debonair Remington Steele. Definitely not Mac McKenna, who looked as if the word *tuxedo* didn't belong in his vocabulary, with his faded jeans, tan cotton shirt and battered black leather jacket. She expected to see boots on his feet instead of top-of-the-line running shoes that looked as if they'd been through a few wars.

She couldn't detect any hint of cologne on him. Just some kind of spicy soap. But he fit the idea of the rough-and-ready man in every other way.

"For someone not having an appointment and who's unknown to your staff, it wasn't all that difficult to get back here to see you," he said, settling his ankle on his opposite knee.

"This is the type of business where the head needs to be accessible," she countered.

"Not if you're afraid someone is looking to get you."

Dana froze. "What else have you learned?"

"Not a thing," Mac admitted, pulling a small notebook out of his jacket pocket. "And that's what puzzles me. If someone is running around town impersonating you, they're now keeping a low profile. Your car hasn't left the garage for the past six nights. Since you haven't called, I gather you haven't found any more surprises in the house." He cocked an eyebrow as a silent reminder that she hadn't told him about the bra.

She shook her head.

"Perhaps whoever is doing this has gotten tired of the game and moved on," she said, uncomfortably aware of hope filling her voice.

"Do you really think so?" he asked.

Dana didn't want to think it might be the calm before the storm. She preferred to think it was over. She wanted her life to return to the way it was. She wanted her father alive again, her mother healthy and everything the way it should be.

She didn't want to answer his question. "Is that why you're here? To ask me if I think it's over?"

"Nope, just giving you my weekly report, as promised." He glanced at the papers on the desktop. His gaze settled on the sheet set squarely in the middle. "Antonelli, Robinson and French. All long established in their field, all multi-published in their field and all a bunch of pompous idiots. If you're going to see a shrink, at least get one who cares more about the patient than the hourly rate." He noticed her astonishment. "The art of reading upside down is a useful skill in my line of work."

"These are all well-respected professionals," she argued.

Mac leafed through his notebook until he found what he wanted. He reached over and grabbed the sheet of paper with the three names, then he crossed them out and wrote down a name and phone number. He pushed the sheet back across the desk.

She looked down at the name, which didn't look familiar to her. "What makes Abby Moore better than the three best psychiatrists in the city?"

He was unfazed by her challenge. "Easy. She's not in it for the money."

"A philanthropist like you."

"Her office is in a better neighborhood."

"That's reassuring."

"She won't look for a quick fix, and even when it hurts, you know she'll do what she can to make it better."

There might not have been a change in Mac's expression, but Dana still sensed there was more to his statement than he was letting on.

Had he seen the lady doctor on a professional basis—or perhaps a personal one?

"You tell me what alarm company to contact, what doctor to see. Are you in the habit of taking kickbacks?" she asked.

Her question would have made any other man respond in anger at having his honor questioned. She was surprised to see a hint of a grin lift Mac's lips. Again, she felt that mysterious punch to her stomach.

"You don't mince your words, do you? I didn't take kickbacks when I was a cop and don't believe in taking them now. I just figure if someone needs the skills of a professional, they should seek the best."

"The best...in your opinion."

"The one that counts." He looked around. "Since I'm here, why don't you give me the nickel tour. Show me what Madison Property Management is all about."

Dana pushed back her chair and stood up. "I hope you don't mind that I avoid mentioning you're a private detective I hired to follow me. That kind of news would give the office gossips some wonderful material to feed on."

Mac walked beside her to the door. "The best thing to do in a situation like this is to keep it simple. Just tell them I'm your boyfriend," he murmured in her ear.

Dana tipped her head back, eyeing him as if he were some strange animal let loose. Now that punch to her stomach had turned into a strange heat that seemed to make its way all through her body.

"I wouldn't suggest it," she advised.

Mac didn't remove his arm as Dana twisted the doorknob and opened the door. She tried to bump him to one side with her hip, but he smiled and easily sidestepped her gentle attack.

Marti looked up as the two stepped out of the inner office. If she was surprised by the familiarity the visitor displayed toward her boss, she was too well trained to show it.

"I thought I'd show Mac the offices," Dana explained. "Marti, this is John McKenna. A close friend of mine." She felt a faint blush steal across her cheeks as she said the words. She knew her reaction would make the story more believable. "I'm afraid he's correct. He doesn't need to have an appointment to see me."

"I promised her I wouldn't show up too often," he told the assistant, flashing her a warm smile guaranteed to charm any woman.

The administrative assistant nodded. "Of course." She smiled at Mac.

"I don't know what I would have done without Marti after my father's death," Dana explained. "She knows more about this office than I ever will."

"Only because I've been doing it longer," the older woman replied. "Don't let Dana fool you. She took to this like a duck takes to water. She has the know-how to take this company far."

"Now you see why she gets paid the big bucks," Dana joked, as Mac guided her away from the desk.

"Which I'm sure I'll see in my next paycheck," Marti called after her.

Mac remained at Dana's side as she explained the inner workings of the company. Now and then Dana could detect that faint scent of spicy soap, but she also sensed something more elemental and male.

"How long has Marti been with the company?" he asked in a low voice.

"Since the day my father left the firm he was working for and started this one. She was his secretary then, and she left to work for him because he promised full medical benefits from day one. Her husband needs constant care, and my father made sure she never had to worry about it," she replied. "He believed in doing whatever was necessary to keep his employees happy. We offer a full benefits package, competitive salaries and other perks our rivals don't provide. As a result, we have a very low turnover rate."

"What else do you have? A company picnic during the

summer and an annual Christmas party?'' He nodded his head and smiled at various office staff members as they gazed curiously at him. ''Sounds too good to be true, Dana.''

''Not your style, I'm sure, but our people are happy.'' She paused in front of a room that housed the usual kitchen appliances. ''I can guarantee the coffee is excellent.''

''Sounds good to me.'' Mac waited as she poured two cups and handed one to him. He shook his head when she offered cream and sugar. He leaned against the counter and sipped the hot brew. Just as she promised—excellent. ''I'll have to come here for my coffee. The place I go to claims it's coffee, but I think they get it out of the backyard.'' He took a healthy swallow.

Dana glanced out the door and turned back to face Mac.

''What do you expect to get out of this?'' she demanded. ''You come in here acting as if you're my...''

''Lover?'' He said the word she wasn't about to voice.

''Close friend,'' she amended.

Mac watched with fascination as a dark pink blush flashed across Dana's cheeks. He guessed a lot of men would call her prim. He'd call her the cool, calm, collected type. She liked being the one in charge.

Right now she was acting a bit cranky because *he* was the one in charge. He actually liked seeing her cranky. It made her seem more human.

''I checked out some of the more dubious hangouts,'' he said by way of conversation. Better to bring it back to business. Watching her in that slim-cut skirt showcasing a great pair of legs was pretty distracting. She didn't make it easy for him to remember he was a professional. Funny, he'd never had this problem before. He wasn't sure it was a good idea now.

''A lady going by your description has been prowling them for the past six months,'' he continued. ''She's well remembered for being one hot number, a good tipper, overly friendly, and, considering everything, didn't cause any trouble. Guys fall over their tongues to buy her a drink, and the ones who leave with her think they're in heaven. She's not known to be a tease. In other words, she's only too happy to put out.''

Dana looked away. Her fingers tapped nervously against the side of the cup.

"What name does she give?" she asked hoarsely.

"Alice."

Her head snapped up. "Alice?"

Mac moved swiftly, snatching the cup out of her hands just as her fingers loosened their grip. He set it to one side. When he grasped her hands he found them ice cold.

"My mother's name is Alice," she whispered, feeling the cold steal through her body.

"You have any other relatives named Alice who could pass for you if they wanted to?"

She shook her head. "My parents were both only children. My last grandparent died four years ago. There's no one."

"Wrong. There's someone out there who knows you." He rubbed her fingers until he felt the warmth return.

"Then you believe me?" she asked. "That this isn't me doing all this?"

"A good cop has to rely on his instincts. It can save his life more than once. It has mine. Something tells me there's someone out there doing this to you—but without proof…" He shrugged, silently telling her he needed something tangible to work with. "Your deciding to see a doctor might answer some of the questions."

Her hope deflated at his words. "Deep down, no matter what you say, you still think it's me, don't you."

"You hired me to follow you and find out what's going on," he replied. "The easy part was finding out what's going on. The trouble is, I couldn't find out why. I think you might have to do some more digging of your own to find that out. Now—" he set his cup on the counter "—it's time to finish that tour. We'll talk more later when there isn't a chance of being overheard."

Dana should have known Mac could be charming, even if he hadn't shown her that side the few times they met. He alternately charmed the women and bonded almost instantly with the men. Nothing was said, but she'd have to be blind not to see how her staff silently speculated about the relationship between their boss and the man with her.

As she looked around, she felt the tension rise in her body, until she felt so taut she feared she would snap. *Could one of them be behind everything I've suffered? Can't I trust anyone?*

Would Greg in Contracts do something like this? His love for practical jokes was legendary. Talk still hasn't stopped about his using the copier for pictures of his private parts at the last Christmas party. He'd supposedly joked that he wanted to loosen Dana up.

Or what about Fran Harris in Accounting? She was furious when she was denied her last promotion. It didn't matter that her work hadn't been up to par and she was told maybe next time. Fran still hadn't forgiven Dana. Marti once said Fran had a "diabolical side." Could she plan something like this? Would she sink so low as to find a way to turn her boss's life into a living hell?

How could Dana continue to walk through these offices without wondering if someone here was behind it all? How could she talk to them without wondering if they were secretly laughing at her? Secretly hating her.

For a woman who prided herself on her self-control, she sadly felt it was spiraling out of her hands.

The touch on her arm was fleeting, barely felt. But it

instantly calmed her. She turned her head and looked up into Mac's face.

"Nothing new with a person thinking the world is against them," he murmured. "You just have to be strong enough not to think it all the time. Paranoia can be dangerous if you allow it to take over your life."

She took a deep breath and nodded.

He led the way back to her office. "Grab your purse and let's get some dinner. Come on, Madison. They'd expect it," he added, when she opened her mouth to protest.

"I choose the restaurant this time," she told him. She told her assistant she'd be leaving and went into her office.

Marti smiled at Mac. "It's good to see her leaving here at a decent hour," she told him.

"I told her I'm starved and she has to feed me," he joked, as Dana walked up to him.

Dana couldn't help but notice the curiosity still directed her way as she and Mac left the offices. She'd left herself open to gossip. Something she didn't believe in doing. She wouldn't have accepted his dinner invitation, except that she desperately wanted to know why he'd come.

As they walked toward the elevator, Mac's glance shifted sideways when a shadow caught his attention. He was certain he'd seen the man before when he'd crossed the downstairs lobby to the elevator. Ordinarily, he wouldn't have thought anything of it, since this floor housed several businesses other than Dana's. Except, the man seemed to be watching her with a little more than passing interest. Mac made a mental note of the man's description. He wouldn't overlook him again.

"We'll take your car," he said when they exited the elevator into the parking garage. When they reached the Jaguar sports car, he held out his hand. "The keys?" he prompted.

"I don't allow anyone but my mechanic to drive my car," she argued.

"You've just added someone else to the list." He kept his hand out.

She grudgingly dropped the keys into his palm. He disarmed the alarm and opened the passenger door.

"I guess your boyfriends don't show up at the office," he said, skillfully guiding the car out into heavy traffic.

"I prefer to keep my personal life just that. Personal."

"So no one there knows very much about you." Mac darted a quick glance in her direction.

"The ones who've been there as long as Marti have known me for about twenty years, but as I said, I don't like to mix business with my personal life."

"Not anymore, Dana. You said a client allegedly saw you in improper circumstances. That means someone decided it was a good idea to mix your personal life with your business life."

Chapter 4

Dana kept Mac's casual attire in mind and chose a restaurant that wouldn't require the male diners to wear a tie. She didn't miss the hostess casting wary glances Mac's way. She thought of when she was little and was warned not to touch the burners on the stove because they were hot. The warning hadn't stopped her from trying. She was tempted to advise the hostess that Mac's form of charm could be lethal. But she doubted the hostess would listen to her any more than she had listened to warnings about the stove.

In no time he was served his beer and she, her glass of wine.

"Do you enjoy intimidating people?" she asked, picking up her glass and sipping the tart liquid.

Mac shrugged. "I can't help it if people see me as a bad ass."

"I think you enjoy it," she accused him.

He flashed her a wolfish grin. "Hell, yes."

"I'm surprised the criminals didn't just break down and confess the minute they saw you."

Mac looked off into the distance as if his past were depicted on the far wall. "They didn't believe in making anything easy for me. I was known for not giving the perps an inch. They did wrong, I dragged their asses off to jail. Unfortunately, some of them got out before I could finish filling out the paperwork and they worked on adding more to their list of offenses."

She heard a note in his voice that she could only describe as yearning. Not a word she would have thought of in connection with him and his former profession.

"You miss it, don't you," she said softly.

His jaw worked furiously as he kept his eyes averted. She had begun to think he wasn't going to reply, when he started to speak.

"Miss it? Not exactly. What I miss is my satisfaction when I got scum off the street. Trouble is, that satisfaction soured when I saw too many of them were getting back on the street."

"Is that why you left the force?" She was curious to find out about him as a man and not just as someone she'd hired. "Because you felt the system was failing you?"

"Maybe I just needed to do a better job," he replied, after taking a healthy swallow of his beer.

She studied him and saw a man whose eyes never stopped scanning the room, as if he was making sure trouble wouldn't catch him off guard. She doubted anything ever caught him off guard.

"Something tells me you did an excellent job. Which makes me wonder why you left."

"If you're smart, you get out when you realize you're past feeling anything," he murmured, apparently still lost in the past. "A cop who's lost his edge can lose his life."

More questions cropped up in Dana's mind. But she

didn't think Mac would answer anything she cared to ask just now. As she looked at him, she could see more than memories dimming in the gray-green depths of his eyes. She also read a lot of pain and loneliness.

She couldn't miss emotions she knew so well.

What secrets does she hide? What goes on in her mind?

Mac could imagine well-oiled gears moving at warp speed inside Dana's brain. He could see the questions she was fairly bursting to ask. How was she managing to remain quiet?

What the hell was he doing here with her? This was all wrong.

He'd made a major mistake taking her out to dinner. He was here with her as if she were his date, not a client. Not that he'd know what to do with a date. It'd been some time since he'd socialized with a woman.

Because he had brought her out, she started to see him in a different light. Not the way he wanted her to see him. So the inevitable happened. Like all women, she wanted to know everything about him. Hell, she didn't need to know anything more about him. She knew all that mattered.

She had to know he would do his job to the best of his ability. He would protect her from harm, and if there was someone out there with the intention of hurting her, he would stop them.

She didn't need to know he didn't like imported beer or that his beloved leather jacket was more than thirty years old. His needs were few. His office was a dump, but it was *his* dump, now that he'd gotten up to date on the rent. The only thing in his life that mattered was his dog. And the knowledge that women didn't fit into his life. If he couldn't keep a wife happy, he didn't expect he could keep any woman happy. Easier not to try. Besides, Duffy was enough company—and he could take him on stakeouts.

"Your father was a strong influence in the company, wasn't he?" he said, wanting to get her thoughts directed elsewhere before she decided to ask a question he'd have to rudely refuse to answer.

She seemed surprised by the change of subject. "It was more that Dad *was* the company. He'd started it from scratch more than twenty years ago. My dad had the kind of personality that drew people to him. He worked hard and expected no less from his staff."

"A parent with that kind of workload usually has a lousy home life," he commented.

Dana's reply was postponed as the waitress appeared to take their orders.

"Dad considered his home life as important as his work," she continued. "I don't know how he managed it, but I can't recall one piano recital or school play that he missed. My father once said that his daughter would be a little girl only once and he wanted to make sure he didn't miss any of it. I guess I was more lucky than others. My mother's health has always been frail and she couldn't be as involved with my activities as my father was."

"You mentioned she'd recently suffered a stroke, but she was home now," he commented, tackling his salad as if he hadn't eaten all day. "I gather she's been receiving home health care?"

Dana nodded. "She isn't able to care for herself at all, so she has round-the-clock nursing care." She looked up as their salads were set before them. "Harriet, our house-keeper, has been with my parents for many years. She lives in. She looks out for my mother and oversees the household. I guess I think of her as a second mother."

"If you couldn't talk to your mother about this, why didn't you talk to Harriet? Ask her if she has any idea who would do this." He shook his head when the waitress asked him if he'd care for a second beer.

Dana frowned at the idea. "I couldn't tell her. She has enough to worry about with my mother without fretting about me, too. Before now, if I had a problem I talked it over with my father."

"And he's no longer here." He stated the obvious. "So who do you talk to if you're afraid of causing everyone to worry about you? You don't have a dog or cat. And believe me, animals make good listeners, and you never have to worry about them ratting on you."

A brief smile touched her lips. "My mother was allergic to dog and cat fur, so I couldn't have pets."

"A guard dog is always a good idea," he pointed out.

"Except they shed, chew things they shouldn't, dig holes in the backyard and bark when they shouldn't."

"Sounds as if you've been talking to Duffy," he quipped. "They're also good company and don't let anyone uninvited in."

"I don't think I'll worry about finding a puppy just yet." She smiled her thanks when her lemon grilled chicken and rice pilaf was placed in front of her.

Mac looked down at his steak and loaded baked potato, then over to Dana's plate. "That kind of food wouldn't keep my energy up for more than an hour," he stated.

"Perhaps, but I can imagine my arteries are a lot less clogged," she retorted, cutting her meat into bite-size pieces.

"Goes along with those whole-grain cereals you eat." A corner of Mac's mouth lifted in a grin.

"I intend to be an extremely healthy old lady," she informed him. Her smile dimmed a bit.

Mac figured she was thinking of her mother. With the older woman in such bad health, he guessed he could understand why Dana would do whatever she could in hopes she wouldn't suffer the same fate. Since his old man imbibed a quart of whiskey a day and was still going strong, he didn't think he had anything to worry about.

He waited until the waitress served them coffee after their meal. "Just because it's been quiet lately doesn't mean it's going to keep on that way."

Dana stirred her spoon in tight circles in the hot liquid even though she hadn't added anything. She didn't need to ask him what he meant. She just didn't want to talk about it. She kept on stirring her coffee.

"You know, this was always one of my favorite restaurants," she said in an artificially bright voice. She looked everywhere but at him.

"Dana." One of his hands covered hers while the other gently took the spoon out of her hand and placed it on the saucer. "I don't want you to let down your guard just because you think it's safe now."

She stared down at the table. His fingers looked strong and capable of handling anything.

"Even a crazy client," she murmured.

"Is that what you think the doctor is going to tell you?"

She uttered a short laugh that was anything but humorous. "If I admit it now, I'd save myself a lot of money in medical fees."

"Admit what?"

Dana shook her head. "Admit I sleepwalked. Admit I have fifty other selves straining to break out. Admit I do crazy things because I feel the need to do them. To be honest, I wish I knew what I should admit," she whispered.

When she lifted her face, he saw the sorrow in her eyes.

"I'll call Doctor Moore first thing in the morning."

"I think that would be a good idea," he said softly.

As they left the restaurant later, Mac knew what was going on in every direction. For a moment, he almost pulled Dana to a stop. He could have sworn he again saw the man he'd noticed back at Dana's building. If he hadn't had her

with him, he would have checked it out. But he didn't want
to chance leaving her alone.

He wasn't going to worry. If the guy was following
Dana, Mac knew he'd see him again. And next time Mac
caught sight of him, he'd take the time to ask what the hell
he was doing. If the guy decided he wasn't willing to talk,
well, Mac would just have to persuade him it was in his
best interests to tell all.

"Thank you for seeing me so quickly, Dr. Moore," Dana
said, trying not to fidget as she sat in the comfortably up-
holstered chair.

"You were lucky. I had a last-minute cancellation."

Dana looked around the office in an attempt to get an
idea of the kind of woman she would be dealing with.

She was used to doctor's offices that were antiseptic
looking, but Dr. Abigail Moore's office resembled a comfortable sitting room more than it did a medical office. Her
desk was an old-fashioned writing desk and the chair she
now sat in was a cushioned rocking chair, while Dana's
chair was overstuffed and big enough for an afternoon nap.
She wouldn't mind having one in her own home.

Nothing was what Dana expected, beginning with the
male receptionist out front whose suntanned good looks
could make him a star on *Baywatch* and ending with the
petite dark-haired woman seated across from her.

Dark violet eyes that rivaled Elizabeth Taylor's in intensity, were warm as she gazed back. A yellow legal pad lay
in her lap.

"Why don't you start at the beginning?" she suggested
in a voice that held a hint of a Southern drawl. "What made
you think you needed to see a shrink?" A hint of a smile
touched her lips.

Dana immediately relaxed under Abby's gentle prodding. She told Abby what had happened, why she felt she

needed the services of a private detective and why, after learning what Mac had found out, she knew she needed to find out if her problem might be medical.

Abby didn't interrupt her as she penned notes. When Dana finished, Abby began asking questions.

"Did you notice any of these unusual happenings before your father's death?" Abby asked.

Dana shook her head. "The first time I felt something was odd was about six weeks after."

"And what was that?"

She cast her mind back. "I remember waking up feeling very strange. Heavy headed. And I was positive I could smell cigarette smoke in my room, but I don't smoke and neither does my housekeeper. There was also a tube of mascara among my makeup that I knew wasn't mine. It wasn't my brand or my color."

"Anything else?" she probed.

"I suffer from migraines," Dana explained.

"Since when?"

"Since a few weeks after my father's death. My doctor felt it was a reaction to my father's death."

Dr. Moore jotted notes on her pad. "Did he prescribe anything for the headaches?"

Dana named one of the popular drugs targeting migraines.

"Do you remember anything that might trigger the headaches?" the doctor asked.

"I never thought about it before."

"You might want to start keeping a log. Detail what you are doing before the headaches begin. Even what you might have eaten."

Dana nodded.

Abby was gently relentless in her questioning, delicately pulling out information that Dana thought she'd forgotten.

"I can understand why you came to me," Abby said

once they'd finished. "Considering everything, I don't think it would hurt to run a few tests. Nothing that smacks of Dr. Frankenstein," she assured with a low-voiced laugh. "Just so we have a starting place. But I'd also like to see you again in three days."

Dana agreed. "If you need to call my office, my assistant thinks I'm seeing a therapist to deal with my father's death."

Abby nodded. "Actually, that could be exactly what's happening to you."

"Insanity doesn't run in my family," Dana said.

"Let's do the tests before we even start thinking diagnosis. For now, I'd like to suggest you try to cut back on the extra hours at the office. You need to do whatever possible to lessen your stress level."

Dana reached inside her purse, pulled out a notepad and began writing.

"Dana." Abby leaned forward and placed her hand on top of Dana's. "What I'm saying is not written in stone. Don't feel you need to take notes. I'm only going to make a few suggestions that I hope will help you relax."

"I'm a type-A personality," Dana confessed.

Abby grinned. "I gathered that. Let's hope I can help you find a way to cut back."

She began outlining ideas for Dana, while Dana replayed them in her mind with the intention of heading for the nearest ladies' room...and writing them down.

By the time she left Abby's office, she was feeling a combination of relief and trepidation. She glanced at her watch and realized her office would be closed by now. Her first thought was that she could return and easily get some work done. "The doctor tells you to cut back and you can't even leave the building before you're doing the exact opposite," she muttered, climbing into her car. "You need to lighten up, Dana."

As she pulled out into the early evening traffic, she racked her brain for something, anything, to help herself do something out of the ordinary. When an idea came to mind, she didn't see it as a perfect one, but at least it would be a beginning.

What was going on here?

Mac stretched his legs in an effort to ease out a few kinks. He'd gone for a five-mile run that morning, something he hadn't done in a while, and he was paying for it tonight.

He knew Dana had gone to see Abby the day before. He would have liked to find out about that visit, but past experience told him that Abby, damn her, would only spout patient confidentiality. He'd have to wait and see if Dana would tell him anything when he met with her at the end of the week.

When he'd parked on his usual side street tonight, he hadn't expected later to see the light by Dana's front door come on, not long before a sleek Mercedes rolled into the driveway. Judging by the guy's demeanor when he climbed out, Mac guessed he wasn't there to sell insurance. His hunch was verified when Dana opened the door at the stranger's knock. If Mac wasn't mistaken, she looked like a lady dressed for a date.

He didn't waste any time picking up his binoculars to get a better look. With the front light on, he could easily see the scene before him.

She didn't look like the Dana he'd seen those nights when she'd gone out and partied like there was no tomorrow. Damn, she looked classy in a long-sleeved black dress that clung to all the right places. Her hair was brushed up in loose waves that curled around her face, and he'd just bet she smelled like heaven on earth.

Her smile was genuine as she greeted the man and appeared to invite him into the house. The door closed after the man stepped inside.

Mac swore under his breath as he tossed the binoculars back onto the passenger seat. What the hell was she trying to do? Damn her! She'd never told him she was going out on a date. Who was this guy? She should have told him so he could have run a background check. For all he knew, Mr. Suit-and-Tie could be behind Dana's troubles. Mac vowed to have a talk with her as soon as possible. If she was going to pay him to watch over her, she was going to have to work *with* him.

A faint flicker of light off to one side caught his attention. If he hadn't been concentrating so hard on Dana standing in the doorway, he might have missed it.

"Hello." He whistled tunelessly between his teeth as he snatched up his binoculars. He swung them in the direction of the light and peered through them. There was no mistaking the outline of someone crouched among the trees. "Guess what, scum. We're about to have a talk." He was ready to creep out of his truck and head in that direction, when he noticed Dana walking out the door with the other man. He swore softly under his breath and switched on the engine. He picked up the binoculars and checked the watcher again.

He was gone.

No matter. Mac knew he'd be seeing him again, and if he wasn't mistaken, one of those times would be later that night when Dana returned home.

Dana didn't believe in acting on impulse, and after tonight, she knew she would never do it again.

After her appointment with Dr. Moore the day before, and the woman's suggestion that she start trying to relax more, Dana thought of Alan Baxter, who had been asking her out for the past year. She finally decided it might not be a bad idea to begin building a social life, and Alan could be a good beginning.

A corporate attorney with his office in her building, she had known him for several years, even if their relationship had been confined to sharing the elevator at times or running into each other in the parking garage. Nice looking, always well dressed, he was the kind of man her father would have approved of. Except, when she looked at him, she didn't feel any connection. Not the way she felt when she looked at…Mac. After tonight, she vowed never to do anything impulsive again.

Not that Alan did anything wrong. He was the perfect gentleman from beginning to end. The restaurant he chose had an elegant ambience and food arrayed on the plate as if it were fine art.

Alan was an excellent conversationalist, but Dana found herself bored to tears.

Now all she wanted to do was go home.

"I'm glad we had a chance to do this," Alan said as he later parked his car in her driveway.

"Yes," she replied automatically. She resisted the urge to look around and see if she could find Mac's truck. She knew he'd been in the vicinity all evening. She could feel him as if he were right beside her.

Alan got out of the car and walked around to the passenger side. He kept his hand on Dana's elbow as they walked to her front door.

She unlocked the door and stepped inside. When she turned around she could see the look of expectation on his face.

"Alan, thank you for a lovely evening," she said politely, keeping a hint of warmth in her voice. "I'm sure you'll understand, it's been a long week."

He looked disappointed but said nothing. He kissed her on the cheek and left.

The moment his car left the driveway, Dana closed the door and threw the dead bolt. She pulled off her high heels and dug her toes into the carpet as she walked across the room.

She was on her way to her bedroom, when the doorbell rang.

Dana sighed. She hoped it wasn't Alan thinking he could change her mind. When it rang a second time, she started to head for the telephone so she could call Mac.

"Dana, it's me. Open up!" Mac's voice rang clear through the door.

She rushed to the door and released the dead bolt before opening it.

Mac's appearance was a far cry from Alan's impeccable presentation. His clothes were rumpled, his jaw was dark with stubble and his eyes were shadowed with fatigue.

"Tell me you looked through the spy hole before you opened the door," he growled, brushing past her.

"I didn't need to. You said it was you, and I recognized your voice." She was puzzled by his unexpected arrival and by his anger.

He grabbed her shoulders and held on tight. "Next time, you don't open the door unless I use a password only you and I know. If you don't hear that word, you tell me to go to hell and don't hesitate to call the cops. Do you understand?"

Her head bobbed up and down. "Password," she whispered.

Mac's face darkened with fury. "Dammit, Dana! A voice can be imitated. Someone could tape-record my voice and make me say anything you wanted to hear. You have to take the proper precautions."

"All right," she said, still stunned by his reaction.

Her quiet words brought him to his senses. He lifted his hands from her shoulders as if her skin had suddenly emitted an electric shock. He turned away, his hands propped on his hips as he worked at composing himself.

"Why didn't you tell me you were going out tonight?"

She immediately realized why he was upset with her. "I'm sorry. I should have told you."

Mac shook his head. Frustration was written across his face. "Yes, you should have. You hired me to watch over you from the time you leave your office at night until you leave your house in the morning. When I saw that guy showing up, I had no idea what was going on. It's not as if you have visitors every night of the week. This is something out of left field for me. In order for me to be effective at my job, I need to know what's going on."

"Dr. Moore suggested I try to relax more. To be impulsive sometimes," Dana explained. "Alan is a corporate attorney with an office in my building. He's asked me out several times, and I decided it was time to accept. He's absolutely harmless." *And dull.*

"Yeah, that's what they all say." He walked into her living room and started pacing the floor. His movements reminded her of a caged animal fighting to get out.

"I guess I didn't realize it would be important." She sat down on the couch, then immediately stood back up when she realized his standing gave him the advantage. Right now, she needed every little bit she could get.

Mac spun around and stalked toward her. "Look, Dana, if you want me to keep on working for you, you have to do things my way," he insisted.

She held up her hand to ward off any more of his lecture. "Maybe you should have handed me a list of your rules and regulations."

He thrust his fingers through his hair, doing nothing to tame the unruly strands. He shrugged off his jacket and dropped onto the couch. "You have any coffee made?" he asked.

"Coffee?"

"Yeah, I really need the caffeine."

Dana muttered under her breath as she stalked into the kitchen. "He couldn't have stopped at one of his favorite fast-food restaurants and picked up some coffee there?" She set up the coffeepot with none of her usual grace.

When she returned to the living room, she found Mac sprawled back against the couch cushions. He looked very tired. She handed him a cup and watched him down the hot drink as if it were water.

"Where's your partner?" she asked.

"Out in the truck. I didn't think you'd appreciate him coming in and shedding all over your carpet." Mac set the cup on the coaster she'd placed in front of him.

Dana couldn't stop looking at Mac's face, at the shift of expression that briefly revealed itself before disappearing.

She wasn't sure what had triggered an internal alarm. Just that as she looked at him, that alarm rang loud and long in her head. And it had nothing to do with his previous lecture.

"You found out something, didn't you."

Mac lifted his eyes and stared at her. "Do you know a Gary Carter?"

Dana was puzzled by his question, but she was getting used to his asking questions from out of the blue.

"The name doesn't seem familiar to me. I don't think he's one of our clients, but I don't know the names of every one. I'd have to check our files to see if anyone handles him."

"He's not a client," Mac stated.

She frowned at him, now wondering what was going on. "Fine, he's not a client. Why don't you tell me what this Gary Carter has to do with me."

"Gary Carter is the reason someone has been following you." He grimaced. "I should have noticed him sooner. At first, I'd only seen him in your building, so, naturally, I thought he worked there." He paused. "Then tonight I saw him hiding in the trees, watching you when your date came to pick you up. He also followed you to the restaurant where you had dinner."

Dana caught her cup just as it started to slip from her fingers. She set it down on the coffee table, the ceramic rattling against the polished surface. "How long has this person been following me?"

"Longer than I'd like," he ruefully admitted. "I should have noticed him the first time out. I'll give him credit for using a different car every time he followed you."

She was incredulous at his confession. "I hired you to protect me, and this man, who could be a homicidal maniac for all we know, could have slipped in here and murdered me in my sleep!"

Mac wasn't too pleased with her attack and let it show as he again shoved his fingers through his hair. "I admit it. I screwed up." Now he sounded just plain testy. "But I rectified my mistake."

Pure terror seeped into her bones. "How did you rectify it?" she whispered, as her mind started to imagine the worst.

He instantly read her thoughts and shook his head. "I'm not into hitting a guy unless he hits me first. Since he also followed you and Mr. Suit-and-Tie, there was no problem in introducing myself to your secret admirer."

"So there wasn't a fight?" she demanded, checking him out for any cuts and bruises.

"This guy wasn't into anything that could result in pain," he said wryly.

"And this Gary Carter told you why he was following me?"

"No, he told me that he's not Gary Carter. He's a private investigator who was hired to follow you," he explained.

Dana reeled from the shock waves rippling through her body. She gripped the edges of the chair seat with her fingertips.

"You're confusing me," she whispered. "Why would someone I don't even know hire a private investigator to follow me?"

"Probably because Gary Carter's wife, Melinda Carter, hired him when she was told he was having an affair with you," he explained. "According to the evidence he's gathered, you are having an affair with Gary Carter."

She could feel the nausea swirling in her stomach. "That's not funny."

"Melinda Carter didn't think it was, either."

"But you know better. You watch over me every night," she protested, fighting to keep the nausea down.

"It seems your trysts—" his lips twisted as he spoke the word "—were pretty much restricted to nooners at a hotel two blocks from your office. I saw the pictures, Dana. Whoever the woman in the picture is, she looks a hell of a lot like you."

Dana wasn't so dazed that she missed the fact Mac didn't believe she was the woman.

"Then someone is playing a sick joke and using fake pictures," she said.

He sprawled lazily on the couch, looking as if he might fall asleep at any moment. She knew that lazy exterior was a good cover for the alert man inside.

"This PI is legit, and what he has is pictures of some steamy raw sex that's usually seen in X-rated movies."

Her face burned a deep rose color. "But you told the man it wasn't me, right? And he'll tell this Mrs. Carter it's all a mistake," she implored. What if her clients found out about this fiasco? She'd be out of business in a matter of hours. "And if he doesn't do it, you'll beat him up, right?" she added in a rush.

Mac chuckled. "Watch it, Madison. You're turning blood-thirsty."

"Lies like that can ruin my business in no time. My father didn't spend all these years building it up to have me destroy it," she said.

Mac picked up his coffee cup and drained the contents. He got up. "Go to bed, Dana. Let me do the worrying, okay?"

As he opened the front door, he studied the dead bolt and shook his head. "I want the authorization to get an alarm installed here."

"Something tells me if I didn't say yes, you'd do it, anyway," she muttered.

"Damn right I would. I want to hear that dead bolt shoot into place." He closed the door after him.

Dana shot the dead bolt home, then heard Mac's footsteps fade away.

She collapsed against the door. Right now, she could only hope a hot bath would relax her tight muscles.

Except, even a long soak in the tub with the water laced with her best bath oil didn't calm her as she'd hoped it would. She cursed under her breath and climbed out of the tub. Thanks to Mac's news, she couldn't even enjoy her favorite form of relaxation. Since the night was chilly, she pulled on a light green print flannel nightgown that could be tucked under her feet when she lay in bed. Once under the covers, she opened the book she'd been reading lately, but the words didn't make sense. In a fit of frustration, she finally tossed it to one side.

Memories of Mac's visit were still strong in her mind, and the more she thought about it the more unsettled she felt.

She didn't want to turn the light off. Curling up under

the covers and going to sleep no longer offered her any form of security.

After all, things always happened when she was asleep.

She kept the light on as she slid down under the covers. She lay there, staring at the opposite wall.

When she was little, she'd been afraid that monsters lived under her bed. Now the monsters had returned.

But this time, she feared the monsters lived inside her.

Chapter 5

What had happened to her wonderful life? Would she ever go back to what she'd had?

Dana hated the questions that crowded her mind because she didn't have answers for any of them. And the questions multiplied every time she returned to her family home.

The house she'd grown up in had once represented safety and the love her parents lavished on her. Now she had trouble seeing the light and serenity she used to take for granted. She feared the house would always be dark and quiet with the pall of illness seeming to hang over it like a black cloud, even if Harriet did her best to keep the house filled with flowers and quiet music playing in the background.

Dana grieved each time she visited her mother.

She recalled the days when the master bedroom suite was filled with an antique four-poster bed where a little girl could lie on the mattress and among the many lace-trimmed pillows, imagining she was a princess. The bed where she could hide from the world merely by pulling the bed curtains shut. The sunlit corner surrounded by large windows had been the perfect spot for a tea party a daughter could hold for her mother.

The four-poster bed had been replaced by a sterile-looking hospital bed. The only homey touch was a pale blue afghan draped across the end of the bed. The antique furniture had been moved out, and medical monitoring equipment moved in.

The drapes had been drawn to keep out the afternoon light. Gone was the soft classical music that used to play; only soft beeps from the monitors broke the silence. Dana silently reminded herself to ask the nurse to play her mother's favorite CDs. She hoped the gentle music could bring her mother back to her, even if, for some reason, Dana couldn't.

The soft-spoken woman Dana knew as her mother lay still as a statue. Her normally pink coloring was paper-white and her lips bloodless. Any makeup applied to her skin either sank in or looked garish. The only thing familiar was the Swiss cotton nightgown she wore. Dana didn't feel her mother needed to wear a hospital gown, and the doctor agreed.

Dana sat by the bed, holding her mother's hand. The skin felt dry even though Dana had personally rubbed in a rich hand lotion only moments before. Instead of the rich fragrance of Chanel she always associated with her mother, she could only detect the sharp scents of rubbing alcohol and medicine.

The older woman's eyes were closed and her breathing slightly labored.

"I need you so much, Moms," Dana whispered, calling her the pet name she'd used as a child. "I want you to come back to me."

Alice Madison stirred and muttered in her sleep, but her eyes didn't open to indicate she heard her daughter's plea.

"Honey, she isn't going to wake up any time soon," Harriet murmured in Dana's ear. "For some reason she always sleeps best this time of day."

"I had to see her. Talk to her." She blinked rapidly but it didn't keep the tears from streaming down her cheeks. "I'm greedy, Harriet. I want my mother back."

"I know you do, sweetheart. I know you do." Harriet guided her to her feet and walked with her out of the room. "The doctor said she'll need lots of rest, and once she recovers there will be rehabilitation therapy. Don't you worry. Your mother and I know you can't be here all the time. But I'm here for her. It's not as if she's been left with strangers all the time. That's what counts."

Dana slipped an arm around the housekeeper's waist and hugged her tightly. "I know that and I'm so grateful you stayed here after Daddy's death. I just wish he were here. He'd know what to do."

Harriet stopped short. She grasped Dana's shoulders and turned her to face her.

"What's wrong, Dana?" she demanded. "And don't tell me there's nothing wrong."

Dana forced herself to smile. "Nothing is wrong," she assured Harriet, purposely lightening her voice. "I just feel lonely and sorry for myself."

Harriet didn't say a word as she peered into Dana's eyes. Then she uttered a word Dana had never heard come from the older woman's lips.

"Harriet!"

"Don't you 'Harriet' me, young lady. I've lived a lot more years than you and I can tell when you're lying to me," she said flatly. "Something's happened that's upset you. What's going on?"

Dana continued her pretense. "I told you, I feel lonely. I miss Moms."

She walked out of the room, her steps slow as she moved down the hallway. She stopped at one door and cupped the knob, turned it and pushed the door open.

She looked into the room that had been her bedroom until she left home to attend college. Nothing had been changed. Not the peach and cream decor or the stuffed animals that still lined the shelves high on the wall. It portrayed a former life.

She took great care in pulling the door shut.

"If you're feeling lonely, go out there and find a man. Once you find one, do what comes naturally when you're with a member of the opposite sex. That's what you really need," the older woman said bluntly.

Dana felt her face burn. She thought about Mac. She seemed to think way too much about him lately.

"I don't have time for a man," she muttered, keeping her face averted from the housekeeper's sharp eyes. "I have a business to run."

"Honey, there's always time for a man. I let mine know it, too," she proudly announced. "Frank might not look like much, but, honey, he has what it takes. If you know what I mean." A twinkle appeared in her eye.

Dana groaned and walked swiftly down the hallway. "I'm not sure I want to know any more."

As she descended the staircase, she looked around the large expanse. She thought of the times she had walked into the family house and found her mother busy arranging flowers with the same care an artist used in creating a masterpiece. She knew no one could have designed anything more beautiful than the floral centerpieces her mother did.

Dana didn't want to think of her mother lying so still in the bed upstairs. She wanted to walk into the house and see her mother turn and greet her with a smile the way she always had. She didn't want to think that the flowers were now provided by a florist.

Illness tended to frighten people into staying away. Phone calls from Alice's friends had dwindled.

Dana jealously hoarded the memories of what had once been, and more, for fear there would never be new ones.

Harriet led Dana toward the rear of the house and into the kitchen. The housekeeper poured an ice-filled glass with orange juice and warmed a cinnamon-apple muffin in the microwave oven. She placed both before Dana.

Dana tore off a small piece of the warm muffin and popped it into her mouth. She almost groaned with bliss as the flavors exploded in her mouth.

"Please tell me I can take some of these home with me." She gave the woman a look filled with theatrical pleading.

Harriet smiled and held up a bag filled with muffins. She laid them down. "The price for these muffins is you telling me what's going on."

Dana's smile disappeared. She plucked bits of her muffin with her fingertips and dropped them onto the plate. "There's nothing going on."

"Sweetheart—"

Dana refused to look up. Maybe if Harriet didn't look at her face, she wouldn't find out her secrets. "There's nothing wrong, Harriet."

Harriet didn't budge. "Honey, whatever is bothering you will only get worse unless you share it. Let me help you."

Tears started trickling down Dana's cheeks, dropping onto the muffin. She sniffed and swiped at her eyes with her hand. "Harriet, do you know if there's any mental illness in my family history?" she asked in a voice so soft the other woman almost couldn't hear her words.

"Mental illness?" Harriet sounded incredulous. "Why in the world are you thinking about that nonsense?"

Dana lifted her tear-streaked face, knowing it portrayed

a misery that seemed to rise up out of her soul. "Things
are happening to me," she admitted in a whisper. "Things
I can't explain."

Harriet sank down on the stool next to her. She covered
Dana's ice-cold hands with her own, then began rubbing
them between her palms.

"Tell me."

Dana took several deep shuddering breaths before the
words started to spill out. Once she began, she found herself unable to stop as she related everything that had happened to her. She even admitted her visit to the psychiatrist
and the fact that she feared she was losing her mind.

Harriet uttered a soft cry and enfolded Dana in her arms.
"Oh, my darling girl. To think you have been going
through this horror by yourself."

Dana's tears flowed faster. "You have enough to worry
about with Moms."

The older woman sighed heavily. "Yes, I worry about
Alice, but I worry about you, too. I sensed something had
been bothering you for some time, but I thought you were
having problems at the office. What about this private investigator? He must be good or you wouldn't have hired
him. Has he found anything so far?"

Dana made a face. "Mr. McKenna has discovered some
things that prompted me to seek psychiatric help." She
leaned against Harriet, absorbing her strength the way a
sponge absorbs water. "I'm so scared, Harriet," she whispered. "I go to sleep scared. I wake up scared. What if a
part of my brain has gone haywire and causes me to do
these things without my being aware of it?"

Harriet grabbed her by the arms and gently shook her.
"I swear, you can be the most stubborn child," she scolded
lovingly. "Dana Marie, you are the child I never had. When
you hurt, I hurt. I just wish you'd come to me sooner and
told me what was going on." She pulled a handkerchief

out of her pocket and dabbed at Dana's eyes. "You don't need to shoulder such problems all by yourself."

"Daddy always said a person needs to solve their own problems," Dana replied with a watery sniff. "I thought I could do it."

Harriet shook her head. "I'm sure your father didn't mean something like this. Then he'd expect all of us to get together and do whatever we can to help. There's times when a body needs help.

"First off, I cannot believe you are doing this to yourself. You were never a sleepwalker, you've never suffered any type of depression other than normal grief because of your father's death. In all the years I've known you, you've never exhibited any kind of mental instability. I'm sure that doctor you're seeing will soon tell you the same thing."

"But if it isn't mental or physical," Dana asked miserably, "what is doing this? Or who?"

"Thought you'd like to know I got Gary Carter's wife off your back before she did something really stupid," Mac announced when Dana entered his office.

"I thought you'd taken care of that the night you talked to that private investigator," she said.

"I thought so, too, but my new buddy Norman, who's Mrs. Carter's private investigator, gave me a call and said Mrs. Carter wanted blood. Namely, yours. When I went over to her house, she was talking about going to your office and making a big scene. I had a talk with her and explained her husband had concocted the whole deal to make her jealous," he explained. "Norman backed me up." He clasped his hands behind his head and rocked himself back and forth on the chair.

"And she believed your story?" she asked in a deceptively mild voice.

Clearly pleased with himself, he nodded. "She said she

should have known he'd try something stupid like that. She was calling her divorce lawyer when we left.''

"I'm not surprised," she said. "I wanted to know exactly who this man was, so I did some checking of my own. His wife won't be ending up with very much. Gary Carter was forced to file for bankruptcy because he's run his business into the ground and the creditors are hot on his heels," she said. "The reason his wife wants a piece of him is that the money he sunk into the business was hers. He'd assured her it was a sweet deal. Instead, he used the money to pay for prostitutes he listed under Entertainment. To top it off, three former employees have filed sexual harassment charges against him," she finished.

"All three were settled out of court," Mac added. His gaze softened. "He's not your nightmare, Dana. I'm sorry."

She smiled and shrugged as if the news wasn't disheartening. "I can always hope."

"How are your sessions with Abby going?"

"There're times I convince myself it's me and other times I know deep down it isn't," she replied. "I visited my mother yesterday and I asked our housekeeper if she knew of any mental illness in my family's background. She said there was none."

"That should have relieved your mind," he said, studying her. Damn, she looked good to his tired eyes. Her coral silk pants and matching short-sleeved shirt were accented by a braided belt in shades of turquoise, bright green and coral. Her hair was tousled by the windy afternoon, which had also added color to her cheeks.

"It should have, but it didn't," she admitted. "Maybe I'm the first crazy person in the past hundred years." Instead of sitting down in the chair he waved her to, she walked around the office until she reached the window. She wrinkled her nose at the grime covering the glass. She had started to turn away, when a flash across the street caught her eye. It only took her a second to realize the flash came from a pair of sunglasses worn by a woman.

As she looked down she suddenly felt pain explode inside her head. She closed her eyes and prayed it wasn't a migraine. The last thing she wanted was to suffer when she was away from her bed. Except, this pain wasn't like the warnings of a migraine. Instead of a stabbing behind her eyes, she felt it against her temple. She swallowed a moan and just concentrated on riding out the pain.

"What's wrong?" Mac asked, noticing her frozen expression.

"Headache," she murmured, blindly reaching for her bag. If she could reach her pill bottle she could swallow a couple of pills dry, and maybe, just maybe, the headache would go away.

Mac stared. Her face had lost all color and there was a glazed look in her eyes. "Hell, this is more than some run-of-the-mill headache," he said flatly.

She shook her head, instantly regretting the motion that set off fireworks inside her brain.

"What do you see out there?" she whispered.

He frowned. "Are you sure you're all right?"

"Yes, please just tell me."

Mac turned back to the window. "I see Mr. Rodriguez kicking a bunch of kids out of his store. Probably for reading the magazines. Mrs. Patton's in front of her used furniture store—she's smoking a cigarette. I see a couple men walking down the street. Now they're stopping to drool over some hot-looking brunette walking by. Another woman is stopping to look in Mrs. Patton's front window. Someone ought to tell her that a lot of the furniture in there is what Mrs. Patton finds at garage sales and it's usually what no one else would want. Other than that, nothing all that unusual. The woman is walking away. So's the brunette. Those guys are busy picking their eyeballs off the sidewalk.''

Dana was fumbling with the cap to her pill bottle when she realized the pain had left as abruptly as it had appeared. She dropped the bottle back into her bag. The only sign of her headache was a faint throb, which was infinitely easier to handle than the earlier bone-racking pain.

''Are you sure you're all right?'' Mac demanded.

''Yes.'' Now she was beginning to feel downright testy. How many times did she need to answer that question?

''Sure couldn't tell it by me. A moment ago you looked white as a sheet. I thought you were going to pass out.''

''I forgot to each lunch.''

Mac shook his head and muttered something about women and their ''diets.'' He reached for his jacket. ''Come on.''

''Where?''

''You'll see.'' He whistled to Duffy, who immediately rose to his feet and headed for the door. Mac swung his key ring around his forefinger as he guided Dana out of the office and downstairs to the truck.

He stopped long enough to drop Duffy off at Barney's, then directed the truck toward the freeway.

He kept Dana in suspense as he expertly wove through the heavy traffic. When she later saw a strip of blue in the distance, she turned to him.

''The beach?''

''Just the view,'' he said cryptically.

Mac parked behind a large building and climbed out of the Explorer. He walked around the vehicle to open Dana's door.

''Why have you brought me to the beach?'' She looked skeptical.

''Sea air is the best cure for a headache.'' He helped her out of the truck.

Dana looked at a huge No Parking sign attached to the back of the building.

"Aren't you afraid of your truck getting towed?" she asked.

"I helped the owner out with some ongoing vandalism," he replied. "His way of thanking me was permanent beach parking. Around here, a parking space is like gold. The vehicles allowed to park back here are registered with the local police department. I come down here when I need to leave the real world behind."

"How does coming down here allow you to leave the real world behind?"

Her jaw dropped once they walked around the side of the building and entered the colorful beach boardwalk area. The building was advertised as one of the largest arcades on the West Coast. Judging by the loud sounds spilling out, she'd hazard a guess it was also the noisiest.

Mac smiled as he watched her study her surroundings. He had had a feeling she'd never been down here, and judging by the awe on her face, he'd been right.

"I should have gone back to the office," she said, looking a little guilty.

"Hey, a little time away from real life is good for you," he told her, halting when she stopped in front of a canvas-sided booth that featured brightly colored bead necklaces and bracelets. He picked up her hand and gently tugged on it.

That didn't stop her from pausing at a cart where a man displayed handmade leatherwork. Or another where a wide variety of candles were available for sale.

Dana held one particular candle up and looked at Mac. She arched an eyebrow.

He winced at the candle created to be a perfect replica of a part of a man's anatomy. "Some people have overactive imaginations,'' he muttered, gingerly taking it out of her hands and putting it back on the counter.

With each step she took, Dana seemed to slough off more of her tension. She stayed close to Mac when several bikini-clad in-line skaters rolled past them, and almost crawled up his chest when a man walked by with a python draped around his shoulders.

''Hey Harry,'' Mac called out.

The man raised a hand in greeting.

''Harry likes big snakes?'' Dana asked.

''Actually, Harry prefers mice. Lyle's the one who likes big snakes,'' he replied. ''He's got a couple boas and another python at home.''

Mac then said hello to a sultry-looking woman standing in the doorway of a store that boasted a psychic who could answer all of life's questions.

''You know some unusual people,'' Dana commented, not missing the woman's come-hither smile directed toward Mac.

''Former clients. Sabrina had an ex-boyfriend who refused to admit their relationship was over. She needed some protection for a while. Then he hooked up with a stripper, and Sabrina had her life back again,'' he said.

Dana looked around at the bustling energy surrounding her. ''I'd like to have my life back again,'' she murmured wistfully.

''It'll happen,'' he told her. ''I can't promise it will be like it was before, but you'll have your life back and that's what counts.''

Dana wanted to say she wished she could believe him. It seemed as if this nightmare had gone on forever, although she'd only hired Mac a couple of weeks ago.

They didn't speak for some time as they continued walking. The headache she'd suffered from in his office was nothing more than a faint memory now. When she looked off into the distance she could see the curve of the ascending moon, and lights on the nearby pier starting to twinkle on.

They walked down the boardwalk, their bodies occasionally brushing.

Dana felt hypersensitive with each touch of Mac's arm against hers. As if all her senses had been stripped and left exposed to the air. The roar of the ocean only steps away sounded loud in her ears. She knew if she stuck her tongue out, she would taste the salt in the air.

She chanced an upward glance at Mac. The harsh curve of his jaw told her he picked up on her tension. And echoed it.

"Let's get something to eat," he said abruptly, turning her toward an open-air restaurant. Without asking her, he chose one of the tables under the awning that provided shade during sunny days. This evening, a candle shone brightly from each table.

"And no trying to order just a salad," he ordered. "I want to see you eating real food."

"You seem to think I don't eat without you ordering me to." She studied the menu. "Not even the Chinese chicken salad?"

"I don't care if it's loaded with chicken. It's still a salad. Try again."

Dana knew whatever she ordered, it would taste like cardboard. Remembering the headache that had cropped up earlier, she opted for herbal iced tea.

She laced her fingers together and rested them on the tabletop. Her gaze was steady as she looked at Mac.

And waited.

What was he going to do?

Mac was doing his damnedest not to get involved with

Dana, but it wasn't easy.

Hard evidence had her guilty. Pure and simple. But it was what he felt inside that told him she hadn't orchestrated all that'd gone on. Now he just had to figure out the puzzle of who was doing this to her.

There she sat, looking fragile and cool as a cucumber. Delicate shadows darkened the skin under her eyes, and she looked slightly haunted. A woman any sane man would know enough to stay away from.

He couldn't seem to listen to his common sense.

She was quiet as she dipped her chicken strips in ranch sauce and daintily nibbled on them. She appeared fascinated with the various people walking along the boardwalk. She looked everywhere but at him. Even with the fading light, there was no lack of people for her to watch.

He wondered if Sabrina knew who was trying to ruin Dana's life. It would be worth the twenty bucks to find out what she'd read in a crystal ball or her treasured tarot cards.

He was beginning to think bringing Dana down here was a mistake. He thought she'd needed to find a way to work off the frustration that had been haunting her. He'd always found the shooting gallery a good way, and cheaper than using live ammo.

He shouldn't have touched her. He could have instructed her without touching her, without putting his arms around her and then feeling her slight frame press back against him. That was when he'd felt himself get hard. For a guy who believed in not getting involved with a client, he sure screwed up here.

Now, a shore breeze drifted through the air, the saltiness tempered by the faint fragrance of her perfume.

"You always seem to know what I need." Her soft voice cut through his musings.

He wasn't touching that comment with a ten-foot pole.

She turned back to him. "It's as if a person can come out here and forget everything else."

"Maybe you just need to get out more," Mac said.

She looked out toward the beach. If he wasn't mistaken, he'd swear her expression was wistful.

"I guess I do," Dana murmured, turning back to her food. She picked up one of her seasoned French fries, then put it back down again. "All of this is new to me." She turned back to him. "Do you miss being a policeman?"

Her innocent question brought a faint pang of regret to his heart. Yeah, he missed being with the department. Comes from being an idiot who believed he could change the world, he thought cynically. Once it was finally pounded into his head that he couldn't, he realized he might have a chance to do some good as a PI. If nothing else, he'd tracked down plenty of deadbeat dads who now realized it was a good idea to pay child support if they wanted Mac out of their face.

"Yeah, I miss it," he said finally, ignoring the slight catch in his voice. "But I doubt it misses me."

"But you feel you're doing more good now."

With her quiet statement, he realized that there were quite a few facets that made up the woman known as Dana Madison. He was anxious to learn them all.

It took him five minutes to realize she hadn't taken another bite. He dug into his back pocket for his wallet, pulled out some bills and tossed them on the table.

"Come on," he ordered in a rough voice, standing up and taking her hand.

She didn't protest as he pulled her out of the restaurant. Nor did she ask what he was doing when he headed for the sand. He released her long enough so she could pull off her shoes and trouser hose, then grabbed her hand again before continuing his walk down to the water's edge.

Dana jumped and yelped when the cold water rushed over her bare toes.

Despite the tension simmering between them, Mac couldn't help grinning. "I thought you were used to the beach."

"The water in the Bahamas is a lot warmer," she muttered, swiftly moving around to his other side.

Mac recaptured her hand, and they walked aimlessly up the beach with nothing but silence between them.

As the minutes ticked by, he was relieved to see Dana had allowed herself to relax some. After a while, he pulled her along toward an area set up with picnic tables. He hoisted himself up on the tabletop, then sat her down on the bench, positioning her between his legs.

"You look out there and you can't imagine there's ever anything wrong with the world," he said in a low voice.

"Now you're a philosopher?" she asked.

He found himself playing with strands of her hair that floated in the breeze. It felt as silky as it looked.

That obnoxious Eleventh Commandment was becoming more difficult to abide by all the time.

He never was any good at listening.

As if he'd spoken her name, Dana turned her head to look up at him. The moonlight turned her eyes to silver and threw faint shadows across her face.

Mac ignored his common sense screaming in his ear as he grasped her chin and tipped it upward. She didn't look away as his head lowered toward hers. She deliberately kept her eyes open as his mouth covered hers in a searing kiss.

Dana had thought she'd been kissed before. Now she knew nothing she'd experienced before had prepared her for Mac. His skin was rough as if he hadn't had time to shave that morning. She was used to a man's skin so clean shaven it was like a baby's bottom. He didn't wear expensive cologne. His clothes were untidy, and he just plain didn't give a damn about anything.

But he did know how to kiss a woman.

He was all wrong for her. Yet her blood heated to a boil as his mouth shaped itself against hers. She melted against him, and, reaching up to slip her arms around his neck, opened her mouth to him.

She moaned softly as his hand cupped her breast, his thumb unerringly finding her sensitive nipple.

"You're trouble with a capital *T,*" he said huskily, dragging his mouth across her cheek to find her ear. He tugged gently on her earlobe.

Finally able to bring herself to her senses, she pulled away, almost falling backward. Mac grabbed her arms, halting her fall just in time. She tried to regain her breathing but it still sounded rough to her ears. She unconsciously lifted her hand to her hair. It was disheveled and curved against her cheek. She hadn't even realized he'd tunneled his hands through it. What else wasn't she aware of? She tentatively checked the buttons marching down the front of her blouse. They were still in their proper place. She didn't look at him as she thrust trembling fingers through her mussed hair. "I'd like to go back now," she said in a low voice. She licked her lips, then wished she hadn't. She could still taste him.

She rose to her feet and waited for him to do the same.

Dana's thoughts ran wild as they walked back to Mac's truck. She hadn't expected one kiss to turn her inside out.

She thought of Mac as trouble and now she knew she was right. He was trouble. He was everything she'd never dealt with before. He also had her thinking there was nothing more important in life than kissing him.

He didn't say another word until he helped her out of

the vehicle and walked with her to her car. He stood by while she disarmed the alarm and opened the door.

"Dana."

She looked over her shoulder.

He stepped closer and brought his hands up to cup her elbows. The kiss he brushed across her lips was featherlight and just as potent as the soul-stealing one he'd given her earlier.

"I won't apologize," he whispered.

"I wouldn't expect you to," she whispered back. "Not when I wanted it as much as you did."

Mac's obvious surprise over her candid reply gave her the opportunity to slide inside her car and pull the door shut.

As she drove away, she again ran her tongue over her lips.

The memory of his taste was already not enough.

Chapter 6

Mac's kiss haunted Dana just as her nemesis haunted her. While the latter left her with a feeling of darkness and dread, however, Mac's kiss carried a more powerful sensation that cut her off at the knees.

For the next week, she threw herself into her work. She thought it would bring her the sense of completion she used to feel, but that feeling eluded her.

One afternoon, her assistant cornered her and demanded to know what was going on. "Honey, you need to slow down a little," she scolded. "Take some time with that gorgeous guy of yours. I don't think he'd complain if you did."

"He has a busy schedule, too," Dana responded. Damn, she'd managed to forget Mac for all of five minutes and now Marti brought him back.

It hadn't been easy for her to keep him from filling her thoughts. By the time she'd gotten home the night of their kiss, she felt as if she'd been tossed onto a Tilt-A-Whirl.

Since then, sleep had eluded her. And she'd learned that concealer could only do so much to hide the damage.

"I'll leave tonight as soon as I finish going over this correspondence," she promised.

Marti gave her a look of disbelief. "I've heard that one before. It would be good for you if you actually did it."

Once her assistant left, Dana promptly forgot her promise. There was too much to do.

By the time she finished, her eyes were gritty from staring at the computer monitor. She grabbed her briefcase and left the office, making sure the front door was locked behind her. Anticipation of a long hot bath quickened her steps toward the elevator.

For the first time in the past few days she even felt a hint of appetite. Stopping by her favorite Chinese restaurant for some take-out seemed like a good idea.

Once in the parking garage, Dana walked toward her vehicle, her keys out and a finger on the button to disarm her car alarm.

"Dana, baby."

At the sound of the unfamiliar voice, she spun around. "Who's there?" she demanded.

"It's me, baby." A man stepped away from the shadows. "Ready and waiting."

She backed away. "Stay away from me," she warned, holding out her hand. "George! George!" she shouted for the security guard who patrolled the garage during the evening hours.

While the man walking toward her was dressed presentably in suit and tie, the stark desire on his face frightened her. He looked at her as if he knew her intimately.

"I don't know you." She spared a quick glance over her shoulder. She didn't want to find herself trapped against a car without a way to escape. "Stay away from me."

The man looked puzzled. "What's wrong with you? You

called me, remember? You told me to meet you here.'' He continued walking toward her.

Fear raced through her body. ''I told you to stay away from me! *Mac!*'' She screamed the name of the person she unconsciously trusted more than anyone. *''Mac!''* She spun around and started running toward the exit. She stumbled once on her high heels, but managed to regain her balance and keep on running.

A squeal of tires greeted her as the now familiar Explorer sped toward her. The vehicle had barely braked to a stop when Mac was out the door. Duffy leaped out behind him and ambled over to Dana. The dog took one look at the stranger approaching them and issued a warning growl.

''Back off, Carter.'' Mac was doing some growling of his own.

The man looked puzzled, then angry. ''She called me,'' he insisted.

''How could I call him? I don't even know who he is,'' she whispered, clinging to Mac.

He put an arm around her shoulders. He wasn't going to take his eyes off the man.

''Someone's playing you for the fool you are, Carter,'' Mac said in a harsh voice. ''Do us all a favor and get lost. Ms. Madison is a pawn in this game just as you are.''

''Bull. You're the one who's the fool. Fine, take her,'' he sneered, speaking to Mac even as he stared at Dana. ''I only stuck around as long as I did because she's a hot number in bed.''

Mac's hold on Dana tightened. ''Get out of here before I decide to beat the crap out of you.''

Carter didn't need to look at Mac's face to know he spoke the truth. He turned away and fled. A few moments later, a Cadillac raced past Mac and Dana.

''That was Gary Carter?'' Dana whispered, struggling to

tamp down her fear. "Why did he say I called him? I didn't."

If Mac doubted her, he didn't show it. "Come on, let's get your car and I'll follow you home," he said in a rough voice, propelling her toward his truck.

She looked up at him. Her eyes were liquid blue pools shimmering with tears. "I'm not sure I can drive," she confessed.

Mac took her face in his hands and studied it carefully. Her fear washed over him like a flood. A few low words of profanity fell from his lips as he pushed her into the passenger seat. No time was wasted as he deftly secured her seat belt and walked around to the driver's side. Duffy was urged into the back seat before Mac climbed in behind the wheel.

"You haven't eaten yet, have you?"

"I don't think I could eat anything," she confessed.

"You'd feel better if you did."

"Food doesn't cure everything," she muttered, as he drove for the exit.

"No, but it will take care of the shakes you've got."

"I thought whiskey was for that."

"Alcohol is only an escape, not a remedy. Trust me on this." He made a stop at the guard shack at the exit. "Silver Cadillac probably going too fast. Crazy driver," he told the guard. "You see him leave?"

The man nodded. "Sure did, after he gave me some mouth about the parking rates. Since he didn't want to ruin that fancy paint job by crashing through the gate, he paid."

"If you see him again, would you let me know?" Mac handed him his business card.

The man took the card, glanced at Dana, obviously recognized her and nodded. "I'll let the others know, too. We'll keep an eye out for him."

"Great, thanks."

"After what just happened, you can't think he'd come back," Dana said, as Mac gunned the engine, moving smoothly through traffic.

"He probably won't, but you can't take a chance by assuming." Mac looked over his shoulder before changing lanes. He fiddled with the controls. Warm air swirled around Dana.

She looked out the window. She pressed her fingertips against the glass. The cool sensation felt strangely comforting.

"It's starting up again, isn't it," she murmured.

"If I take you home after we eat, you won't be able to go out tonight unless you call a cab."

A low *woof* sounded in her ear as Duffy hung his head over the back of her seat.

"Hey, stay in the back," Mac ordered.

"It's all right." She twisted around and curled her fingers in the dog's thick fur. Duffy licked the side of her face.

"You say that now, but there comes a time when he turns into a major nuisance. St. Bernards are notorious for drooling, and unfortunately, that was one of the traits he inherited from his mom. His engaging black Lab personality came from his dad. With a pedigree like that, I made sure he had his little operation as soon as he was old enough," he said wryly. "If I could help it, no poodle in the neighborhood was going to claim Duffy had sullied her reputation."

Dana tentatively patted the dog's head. Duffy whined in appreciation and batted her hand with his head in a plea for more. She grew braver, dug her fingers into the thick fur and scratched his head.

"Now you've really got a friend for life." Mac pulled into a parking lot and stopped. "Hope you don't mind the casual atmosphere. There aren't many places that accept the Duff here. You put a tie on him, he tends to start chewing on it.'' He climbed out and walked around to the passenger door. After he'd helped Dana out, he whistled to the dog, who happily clambered out of the rear seat and followed them to the entrance of the fast-food restaurant. Mac tied his leash to a cement block next to a patio table.

''Double cheeseburger, no bun?'' he asked the dog, who woofed an affirmative. ''If you'd rather stay out here, Duffy will make sure no one bothers you,'' he assured Dana, who was looking furtively around the parking lot.

''A cheeseburger is fine with me, too, but I think I'll take mine with a bun,'' she replied. ''And a diet cola, please.''

He nodded and went inside. He was out in no time, carrying a tray filled with their food. He handed Dana hers, then placed Duffy's food on the flattened wrapper on the ground. The dog wasted no time in consuming his treat.

Dana worked on hers more slowly. She nibbled on her burger, worried her jittery stomach might rebel. Luckily, the food stayed down. She picked up a French fry and nibbled on that, too.

She was grateful Mac said little. He asked her once if she wanted any of the ketchup packets, but then concentrated on his own food and offered Duffy a few French fries.

Dana was surprised a little later when she looked down and realized her food was gone. She could only attribute it to Mac's quiet and undemanding presence. Not that it made him easy to ignore. She doubted he could ever be ignored. She took a sip of her drink and carefully set the cup down.

''I didn't call that man,'' she said quietly. ''The things I learned about him were because I'd made some enquiries. And I was very discreet when I did it,'' she insisted.

''You didn't need to do it, to begin with. That's my job,'' he reminded her. ''No matter how discreet you are, someone's going to end up connecting you with him, and that's not what you want.''

She bit her lower lip. She'd never given in to anyone. Never allowed anyone to take charge. Now she had no choice.

''All right, what do I need to do?'' she whispered.

Damn, couldn't she ask a simpler question? Mac chewed slowly on his French fry, needing the time to think it over.

''We do nothing.''

''How can you say that?'' she argued. ''No, we have to do something.''

''*You* do nothing. I make sure Gary Carter stays away. After tonight, if he's smart, he'll do just that.''

Dana shook her head, still trying to comprehend what had happened. ''He believed he knew me.''

''That's his problem. We know different,'' he reminded her.

''It's my problem, too! The man insinuated we were having an affair.'' Her voice grew shrill with anger.

''Think about it, Dana. Gary Carter only knows what he's been led to believe. That you're the woman he's been with. We both know different,'' he said on a final note. ''Someone's been playing with his head just as much as they've played with yours.''

Dana felt her food start to travel up her throat. *Who could hate her this much?*

She carefully folded the papers into a neat square and placed them on the plastic tray. She looked away from him. ''I need to go home,'' she said abruptly, still refusing to glance at him.

He took one look at her pale features and nodded. ''All right.'' He gathered up the papers and tossed them in the trash, leaving the tray on top of the table. He unhooked Duff's leash from the pillar and led him back to the truck.

The silence inside the vehicle was heavily charged as Mac drove Dana home. She didn't like the emotions bubbling inside her. She felt fidgety and unsettled. A vision of being imprisoned inside a volcano came to mind.

Dana usually prided herself on keeping her emotions well in check. She prided herself on her honesty. Now someone wanted to destroy everything her father, and now she, had worked hard to build. She flip-flopped between screaming and crying.

She swallowed the lump threatening to choke her. She was glad when her house came into view. It was amazing she still viewed it as a haven, when it was where the nightmares had begun.

Mac parked in the driveway. He draped his hands over the steering wheel and stared at the dark windows. "I thought I told you to set up timers on your lamps in all the rooms," he said brusquely. "You should even hook one up to your stereo system." He opened his door and climbed out.

Dana had her keys out of her purse and was out of the vehicle before Mac could reach her.

"I forgot. I'll take care of it this weekend." She suddenly felt tired. Earlier thoughts of a long hot bath were replaced with a longing for her bed. "Do you think anything else will happen tonight?" She hated the quaver in her voice. She'd hoped she wouldn't display any fear.

She looked up when Mac touched her arm. The nearby streetlight cast a harsh light on Mac's face that made it appear carved from granite.

"You have to help me out here, Dana. I made those suggestions as additional safety measures," he said. "I bet you even forgot to turn on the alarm before you left this morning."

"It's not as if the neighborhood is in a bad area or has

no protection whatsoever," she muttered, not willing to admit she *had* forgotten.

He muttered a curse. "You better stay out here while I check the house." He took her keys out of her hand and strode up the walkway.

Dana stood by Mac's truck, her arms wrapped around her body for protection. She watched him unlock the door and step inside, saw his tall form swallowed up by the darkness. She waited for a light to come on, but the house remained dark. She strained all her senses to hear the tiniest whisper of sound, to see even the faintest of shadows. But she detected nothing. Or Mac was so good he was undetectable. She looked over her shoulder when she heard Duffy whining.

"He'll be back soon." She whispered a reassurance to the dog as if hearing the words would reassure her, too. It wasn't easy when her mind was conjuring up dark possibilities of what could happen to Mac in the house.

She breathed a sigh of relief when Mac appeared in the open doorway and made an "all clear" gesture. She wasted no time in reaching his side.

"It's safe in there?" she whispered, squinting to try to see past him into the inky blackness.

"It all looks fine to me. I didn't get any feeling that someone had been in here," he replied in a normal voice.

Dana took a tentative step farther inside. She groped for a light switch. She felt better when light flooded the hallway.

"Timers on the lamps," Mac reminded her.

She turned to face him. She wanted to beg him to stay because she didn't want to be alone. Yet she hated herself for feeling helpless.

"Hey." A roughened palm cupped her cheek. She lifted her eyes. Mac's usual harsh expression was gone. "I'll be right outside. You yell, I'll hear you and be here in seconds. Okay?''

She nodded mutely.

Mac's thumb rubbed gently across her lips. They automatically parted under his touch, and her tongue appeared to taste the salt of his skin.

Mac groaned. ''Sweetheart, things like that won't get me out of here all that fast,'' he said roughly. ''Considering I'm here to protect you, I think it's better I leave while I can.''

Don't go. Her eyes telegraphed her need.

He hesitated, but refused to break his Eleventh Commandment. Instead, he pressed a hard kiss against her lips. ''Lock the door, set the alarm,'' he ordered as he walked out, closing the door after him.

Dana grabbed the table as her knees gave out. How could a man's touch affect her so much?

''It's because of everything going on,'' she muttered, forcing her knees to lock.

Dana stopped by the kitchen long enough to pick up a bottle of water and carry it into her home office. She checked for phone messages and, after finding none, switched on her computer. Within no time, she was logged on to her files at work. She used to be able to bury herself in her work and forget the world around her.

It wasn't as easy to do when the world insisted on intruding.

She was wearing her favorite party dress. The blue one with lace that her mommy bought her for her sixth birthday. It was the most beautiful dress in the world.

And her hair had been curled and tied back with a ribbon. She sat in front of her mommy's mirror because she wanted to see how pretty she looked. Except, something wasn't right. When she looked in the mirror her reflection wasn't smiling. But she knew she was smiling.

"Why are you smiling, Dana? You're ugly," her reflection told her. "You're not pretty like me. Daddy always loved me best. You should go far away because no one wants you here."

"No," Dana protested, not understanding why her reflection would be speaking to her. "You're lying!"

The smile on her reflection's face wasn't a pretty one. It was a scary smile. Dana wanted to run away from the face looking at her, even though the face looked just like hers.

"Go away. You're not real," she told her reflection.

The smile disappeared as quickly as it had appeared, and the girl's face contorted into a horrifying mask. She looked down at her pretty blue dress and pulled at the lace around the collar. Soon it was shredded. She then pulled off the white buttons and tore at the sleeves.

"Stop it!" Dana screamed. "Don't ruin my dress!"

Her reflection opened her mouth and screamed back. Her scream was terrifying to Dana, but what really scared her was the blood pouring down the side of her head. She cried out, but it was as if no sound emitted from her mouth. She closed her eyes and covered her ears with her hands, but it didn't stop the screaming nor the memory of the girl's bloody face. She ran from the room but her reflection's screams followed her.

"No!" Dana shot up in bed. Her mouth felt sore as if it had been stretched wide from her screams, and her heart beat rapid tattoos against her chest. She looked down and found her fingers clutching the sheet as if it were a lifeline.

Had she dreamed her screams or had she screamed for real? She listened for the sound of Mac pounding on her door. Surely if she'd screamed, he would have heard her. Her eyes darted toward every shadowy corner of the room. Images of monsters she hadn't feared since she was a child hovered just out of reach. It would have been so easy to reach out and turn out a light to banish those monsters. But she didn't want to take her hands out from under the safety of her covers.

She wished Mac were here. She knew if he held her, she wouldn't feel such terror.

She slowly lay back down, but sleep refused to return. She kept her eyes wide open and counted off the seconds until dawn.

Dana was awakened later by the insistent buzz of her alarm clock. She rolled over in bed feeling a painful pounding deep within her head. She hurt so much she wanted to cry.

As she lay there praying the hammering inside her brain would go away, she thought of her dream. She remembered reading how many dreams had a hidden meaning. She dreaded to think what last night's dream might have been trying to tell her. Even more, she feared the scene in her dream was actually something that only spoke to her when she was asleep.

Could that mean there was two sides to her nature? Suddenly, she felt afraid. What if none of this would end until one destroyed the other?

Chapter 7

Dana's headache refused to go away even after the two extra-strength aspirin she took as soon as she crawled out of bed. She called her office and told them she would be coming in late. When Marti asked her if she was all right, she assured her she was fine. She just had an appointment she'd forgotten about.

She made a breakfast she couldn't eat and sat at the kitchen table staring at her plate and the cup of coffee she couldn't bring herself to drink.

"What's wrong?"

She looked toward the back door which now stood open. She swore it was still locked when she came into the kitchen.

"Just a bad headache," she said. "How did you get in?"

"Since you still haven't put in better locks, I guess I'll have to do it." Mac rummaged through the cabinets until he found a coffee mug. He filled it up and drank some. He eyed her plate. "Not hungry?"

"I told you. I have a headache," she explained. She pushed her plate toward him. "Be my guest."

He ignored her sarcasm. He settled down in the chair to her right. The eggs and toast were gone in a few bites. He looked around with a hopeful gaze. "Any more?"

"Only if you cook it yourself."

Mac shrugged, got up and whipped up some scrambled eggs. This time, he portioned some of the eggs off onto another plate and added buttered toast.

"You have any jam? No, wait, I'll get it myself." He looked through the refrigerator and brought out jam and a carton of orange juice.

Dana stared at the second breakfast Mac had prepared. The idea of eating even a fraction of what he'd put in front of her was daunting.

"It won't hurt you. Just try it one bite at a time," he advised. "I may not be the best cook in the world, but I can promise you you won't get food poisoning."

She managed a faint smile and under his coaxing finished a good third of her breakfast.

"How's the headache?" he asked afterward as he stacked the plates in the sink.

"I'm just grateful it wasn't a migraine." She watched him move around the kitchen. She wondered just how many times he'd been here, since he seemed to find some things a little too easily. Something shifted deep within her as she realized he looked all too right here. Conversation hadn't been necessary during the meal, and the silence between them was a comfortable one.

How could she think of him this way when she knew they were completely wrong for each other? She broke her gaze away from him and glanced up at the clock.

"I'm going in late," she told him. "You really don't need to stick around. Thank you for breakfast."

Mac arched an eyebrow. "You're not the type to be late to work."

"When I have a headache the size of Texas, I do." She hesitated. Should she tell him about her dream? She didn't want to talk about it. She was afraid if she talked about it, it would somehow become real. But then, she could also hope talking about it would banish the terror. "I had a bad dream last night," she said in a rush.

She waited for him to make light of her statement. Bad dreams weren't anything new. Unless it was something like the one she'd suffered. Then it was pure hell.

Mac sat down at the table. "Tell me about it," he quietly urged.

Dana took several deep breaths. She cast about in her mind for the best way to begin, then decided there was only one way to do it.

"I was six years old," she said slowly. She kept her eyes fastened on her hands, moving restlessly on the tabletop. "And I was sitting in front of my mother's mirror admiring my new dress. The odd thing was, while I was smiling, my reflection wasn't. Then my reflection spoke to me. She said I didn't need to smile because I'm ugly. She said I wasn't pretty like she was. That Daddy always loved her best." Her breath hitched. "She told me I should go far away because no one wanted me." She choked back a sob.

Mac reached across the table and covered her hands with his. His comforting touch gave her the courage to continue.

"I told my reflection to go away. That she wasn't real," she said between soft gasps as the memories flooded through her. "But she didn't go away. Instead she looked terrifying. She looked down at her dress and it started to shred as she tore at it. I screamed at her and she screamed back." She looked up, the horror of her dream mirrored in her eyes. "She wouldn't stop, so I ran out of the room, but I could still hear her. That's when I woke up."

Mac moved over to the chair next to her as he reached in his pocket and pulled out a handkerchief. "It's clean," he assured her as he mopped the tears from her cheeks. Tears she wasn't aware of shedding until then.

"I woke up feeling so scared," she uttered in an aching whisper.

He pulled her into his arms, pressing her face against his shoulder. "It's okay," he soothed. "Like you said, it was a bad dream."

"What if it has a deeper meaning?" Her voice was muffled against his shirt front. "Some people say what you dream means something. What if my reflection is another side of me?"

"Is that what Abby told you?"

"It's too early to call her."

"It isn't now." After making sure she was calmer, he got up and walked over to her phone. He tapped out a number and waited. "Hey there, Ab. Yeah." He chuckled. "Can you see Dana Madison today? Something happened." He nodded a couple of times as he listened. "Okay, we'll be there." He hung up. "She'll see you at ten."

"I planned to be in my office by then," she protested. After telling him about the dream, she felt a little better. And a little silly that she had allowed it to bother her so much.

Mac picked her phone back up and punched out another number. He whistled under his breath as he waited for someone to answer.

"Marti Cameron, please," he said crisply.

"What are you doing?" Dana started to stand up, but he pointed at her with a silent order to sit.

"Marti, Mac McKenna here. Oh, she called, did she?" He gave her a sideways glance. "Forgotten appointment. Yeah, I guess it's as good an excuse as any. I thought I'd show her how to play hooky.'' He chuckled at something Marti said. ''Actually, she's looking as if she's ready to kill me, but I think I can change her mind. Sure will. Thanks.'' He hung up.

''You can't do that!'' she sputtered.

''Do what?'' He was the picture of boyish innocence.

Dana threw up her hands. ''Make it sound as if we're lovers! All I had to do was call Marti and tell her I had a doctor's appointment.''

Mac leaned against the counter, crossing his arms in front of his chest as he watched her pace the length of the kitchen. If he wasn't mistaken, he'd gotten her so worked up she'd forgotten about her headache.

''Maybe I'm mistaken, but I can't imagine Marti is the gossipy type. At least I didn't tell her you were seeing your shrink.''

''Marti doesn't gossip, but that isn't the point. She still can't help but think the worst.'' How could she make him understand that what her employees thought of her was important to her.

''Be grateful she is. It makes it all the easier.'' He glanced at his watch. ''You've got just enough time to get dressed before we have to leave for your appointment.''

She looked down at her blue fleece robe that was tightly belted around her waist. ''I can drive myself.''

''Sure you can, but think of it as my doing my job.''

Instead of giving him the argument he obviously was prepared for, she settled for a quick nod. She stopped just as she reached the doorway.

''Mac?''

He turned around.

She managed a brief smile. ''When do you sleep?''

''I catch winks here and there. You don't need to worry,'' he assured her.

''Then I guess all I can say is thank you.''

He smiled. "Just to prove what a nice guy I can be, I'll even do the dishes while you get dressed."

Mac was grateful to have some time to himself.

Dana had looked haunted as she recounted her dream. Hell, that was no dream. That was some nightmare determined to scare the hell out of her. It sure scared the hell out of him.

What was the significance of her dreaming about an alternate Dana. It sounded like something out of *X Files*. His first thought was that maybe she did have a split personality and it was starting to assert itself in a dream.

Not all that many years ago, he would have looked at all of this in black and white and seen it for what it was. Not for what it could be. Now he knew better. Too many things weren't what they appeared to be.

But Dana was what she appeared to be. It was someone else who wanted him to believe she wasn't. Now all he had to do was find out who it was.

He shouldn't have held her in his arms. Sure, she needed comfort, but he was definitely thinking about something other than comfort.

She's a client. You don't fool around with clients.

"It's a good rule, McKenna. See if you can remember it for more than five seconds at a time," he muttered, filling the sink with hot water. He squirted a healthy measure of dishwashing soap into the water, and continued muttering to himself as he washed the dishes and frying pan in a haphazard way that splashed water onto the counter.

He doubted his method of washing dishes would measure up to Dana's standards, but hell, they were clean. He swiped them with a dish towel and put them away. He even attempted to mop up the water on the counter.

"You didn't have to do the dishes," Dana said, walking into the kitchen. She winced as she looked at the sodden dish towel tossed on the counter.

"Figured since I ate your food, I should do the dishes."
He was surprised she'd taken his advice. She'd dressed in
jeans and a silky looking T-shirt the color of cantaloupe.
She'd pulled her hair back into a neat braid and wore minimal makeup. "You ready to go?"

She grimaced. "As ready as I'll ever be. Although I
could have waited until my regular appointment."

Mac shook his head. "Personally, I don't think you
should wait. Maybe Abby can give you some answers."

Abby was in the outer office talking to her receptionist
when Dana, Mac and Duffy walked in. Abby glanced point-
edly at Duffy, then at Mac.

"He didn't want to stay out in the truck," Mac explained. "Besides, it's not as if you're in some big building." He ordered Duffy to lay down. The dog ambled over
to a corner and plopped back on his haunches. He gave
Mac a doggie grin. Mac sighed. "There's nothing worse
than a smart-aleck dog."

Abby shook her head. She turned to Dana. "There are
times I think the dog is smarter than the owner. Come on
back, Dana." She turned toward the door leading to her
private office.

Dana hung back.

The psychiatrist sensed her unease and smiled. "It's all
right."

"My head knows it's all right," she admitted, following
the doctor at a slower pace. "After all, it's not as if this is
my first visit. It's the rest of me that's not handling this
very well."

Mac picked up a magazine and chose the couch near
Duffy, who was now lying down, a ball of fur. Mac offered
Dana a look filled with encouragement.

Once inside Abby's inner office, Dana took possession

of the chair and settled back into the plump cushions, while Abby took the nearby chair and turned on the tape recorder for their session.

"I told Mac there was no reason to come in ahead of my regular appointment," Dana told her. "It's not as if what happened was going to suddenly disappear before then."

"From what Mac told me, you had a nightmare that left you feeling unsettled," she prompted.

"It was a nightmare that scared the hell out of me. It was so strong and clear that I think there was a message in it," Dana confessed. "You can blame that on my taking Psych 101 in college."

"Sometimes dreams have hidden messages because when you're asleep your subconscious is more open and thoughts that you would keep hidden have a chance to surface," Abby explained. "Did you feel any undue stress before you fell asleep? Drink any alcohol or perhaps take a new prescription drug?"

Dana shook her head. "Nothing out of the ordinary." She didn't see the need to mention the encounter with Gary Carter in the building's parking garage. She couldn't imagine any connection between her nightmare and Carter. Nor was she about to discuss what was going on between her and Mac. Not when she was still trying to figure it out for herself.

"Do you recall how you were feeling or what you were thinking when you went to sleep?" Abby asked in the low voice that Dana found soothing.

"All I seem to think about anymore is the turns my life has taken in the past few months," she replied.

Abby tucked a dark curl behind her ear. Dana idly noticed the deep rose shade of the woman's nail polish and how graceful her hands were.

"Why don't you tell me how your dream began," Abby suggested.

Dana could feel the tension building inside her. She took several deep breaths but still had trouble formulating her words.

"Look at the window," Abby suggested. "It's daylight and nothing can harm you now. What you're doing is telling me a story."

Dana looked out over the small fenced yard behind Abby's office. A small flower garden with a bird bath set in the middle and a wooden bench nearby was clearly meant to relax its occupants. She started to feel her tension dissolve as she looked at the colorful scene.

"I was six and I was wearing my new blue dress..." she began.

Dana told her story in a slow, halting manner. With each word, she could feel the tension form a tight curl inside her body. Only by looking out the window and not thinking about what she was saying could she manage to tell the story a second time. By the time she finished, she collapsed exhausted against the back of the chair.

"What did you feel when you first woke up?" Abby asked.

"Frightened," she said simply. "Afraid that my reflection was trying to take over my life."

"And you've never had any portion of this dream before?"

"No." Dana shook her head. "I was surprised that I'd even remember anything about my sixth birthday."

"Why is that?"

"I had an accident around then. I fell and cut my head and was unconscious for a few days."

"Were you wearing the blue dress then?"

Dana was silent for several minutes. "I honestly don't remember. I didn't even remember the accident after it happened. But now that I think about it, I don't recall wearing the dress again.''

''An easy answer would be that you might have ruined the dress back then. Something happened that triggered the memory in your subconscious, but even now it was easier to blame it on someone else. Even if that other person looked just like you.''

''Or I do have a split personality and my dream was telling me what I've feared all along,'' Dana commented.

''Or it was nothing more than a dream,'' Abby suggested. ''I know you won't want to hear this, but nothing is ever clear-cut. We won't be able to come up with a definitive answer in just this one session. But we can make a start.''

''Right now, I'll take anything I can get.''

When Dana finally left Abby's office, she felt drained.

Mac immediately rose to his feet and walked toward her. He looked over her head toward Abby. ''Is she all right?''

''You don't have to talk about me as if I'm not here,'' Dana grumbled.

''That's up to Dana to tell you,'' Abby replied. ''Dana, I'll see you next week.''

Dana nodded and pushed her way past Mac. He wasted no time in grabbing Duffy's leash and following her out of the office.

''What happened?'' He was pulled to a stop when Duffy paused to inspect a bush.

''I told her,'' she said shortly. She stood by the Explorer's passenger door. ''I really need to get to my office.''

''I told Marti you'd be out for the day,'' he reminded her as he unlocked her door. He didn't move away. ''Are you sure you're all right?''

Dana didn't mention she'd gotten a look at herself in a mirror when she left Abby's inner office. There was no missing the haunted look in her eyes and the tension lines around her mouth.

She wanted to lie and tell him she was fine. But how could she tell him that when all he had to do was look at her and know differently?

She swallowed with difficulty. "I'm scared," she whispered. "Really scared. I think of books and movies where a woman has herself made up to look like someone else in order to take over their life. What if there's a woman out there who wants my life? What if that woman is really living inside me?"

Mac wrapped his arms around her and held her against his chest. She rested her cheek against his shirt front. The spicy scent of his skin tickled her nostrils.

For a man who likes to show the world his bad-boy image, he can make a woman feel very safe, she thought to herself as she curved her arms around his waist.

How long had it been since she'd felt this safe? What would she do when this was all over? Would she lose all her fears and go on as she had before? She doubted she could ever go back to the life she was living before. Nothing could ever be the same again. A good part of it was due to the mysterious goings-on in her life—but a large part of it was Mac.

She didn't want to think about the day when she'd say goodbye. Instead, she held on to him tighter.

"Feel mad at the world?" he murmured.

"I feel mad at not being able to do anything about it," she admitted.

He drew back. "Then let's do something about it." He studied her clothing. "First off, we need to stop by your house and have you change into something a lot more casual."

"This is casual," she argued.

"Not for what I have in mind."

"And what is that?"

"The chance for you to fight your demons."

Chapter 8

Dana dropped her arms to her sides. "I can't do this."

"Sure you can," Mac told her. "Just do what I told you and you'll do fine."

She lowered her voice and looked around. "I feel silly."

"No one is even looking," he assured her. "Come on. Hit me."

When he drove her back to her house and told her to change into a pair of shorts and T-shirt, she had no idea Mac meant to take her to a gym. He'd asked if he could leave Duffy in her backyard, and she'd agreed since Mac promised to clean up after the dog. She only hoped Duffy wouldn't decide her flowers looked tasty. So now she was standing in the middle of the most depressing building she'd ever seen. And feeling more than a little foolish with the boxing gloves Mac had made her wear.

This wasn't the kind of fitness club she was familiar with. There wasn't any state-of-the-art exercise equipment available for its members, a swimming pool or even aero-

bics classes held every hour. This place was a real honest-
to-God gym, complete with the sharp tang of sweat in the
air that had her wondering if this was what men's locker
rooms smelled like. The stained brick walls were decorated
with old posters advertising boxing matches that dated back
to the early sixties. She stared at the practice boxing ring
where two men were sparring. She winced as one man's
head whipped back when a blow was struck near his chin.
Punching bags and free weights finished the sparse decor.
The huge room was dimly lit, and she could tell the men
who worked out in this place were serious about their bodies. She doubted a juice bar would ever find its way in
here.

She was the only woman in the cavernous building and
she'd never felt more out of place. Mac had carried a gym
bag in with him and left her long enough to change into a
pair of sweatpants that had been washed to fragile softness
and a sweatshirt that stopped short of his midsection and
had the sleeves torn off. He looked as if he belonged here
among the men who dressed the same way. She knew the
other men probably saw her navy bike shorts, tank top and
hundred-dollar cross-trainers as proof that she didn't belong
here. She sensed if she hadn't come in here with Mac,
someone would have asked her politely to leave.

Mac took her over to one corner that boasted a padded
floor, and proceeded to tape her hands then fit her with a
small pair of boxing gloves. Afterwards, he did the same
to himself.

With clinical precision, he showed her how to stand, how
to keep her body relaxed. And then, standing behind her
and with his arms around her, he demonstrated several
punches and even taught her a couple of basic kick moves.

"I want you to punch me in the stomach," he ordered.

She was appalled he would ask such a thing of her.
"No!"

"Sweetheart, trust me, there's no way you can hurt me. You're not strong enough. I want you to just go ahead and punch me." He patted his midsection, which looked hard as a rock.

Dana did as he instructed. Her gloved hand bounced off his abdomen.

Mac hooted with laughter. "Is that wimpy tap the best you can do?" he jeered. "Honey, a fly could hit me harder than you can. Come on, baby, show me what you've got. Show me what you're feeling right now."

She hit him again. This time hard enough to send a shock wave up her arm. He didn't even flinch.

"You've got someone making your life a living hell, and all you can do is tap me." Mac's voice turned hard and cold as ice. His eyes were just as Arctic. "Don't wimp out now. Do what you want to do to your enemy. Make her suffer the way she's made you suffer. *Dammit, do it!*"

Dana wasn't sure what happened, except that Mac's taunts seemed to open a door inside her mind.

The disgusting things she'd found inside her house. The woman pretending to be her. Even the fear her mother wouldn't recover this time. It all flooded through her like a tidal wave. Once started, it couldn't be stopped.

She was blind to everything around her. She didn't see Mac standing across from her. She saw her enemy. The little girl in the mirror shrieking at her.

Dana screamed just because it felt good and she went after Mac with the vengeance of a mythical harpy. She ducked her head and punched him in the stomach and kept on punching. She cursed him and kicked him. She flailed at him with her hands, awkward in the large gloves. By now it didn't matter. She was fighting back and she wasn't going to stop until her nemesis fell in a bloody heap. She was oblivious to everything but the fury that ran through her veins.

Dana had no idea how long her attack lasted. Only that she stopped because she couldn't catch her breath, and sweat and tears stung her eyes. Her arms trembled violently and her legs felt as if they would give out on her. She started to take a step, and would have fallen if Mac hadn't grabbed her. She clutched at him the way a drowning person clutched a life preserver. Tears streamed down her cheeks, and she couldn't have said a word if her life depended on it. She felt as if she'd shattered into a million pieces and had no hope of ever being put back together again.

"It's okay, Dana." His low voice rumbled in her ear. "Just let it all out. You'll feel better for it. I promise. "

But it wasn't okay, she wanted to scream at him. Instead, she just clung to him as she cried for all that had happened. For the loss of an innocence that had allowed her to think the world was a bright and wonderful place. For the realization that dark and ugly-minded people populated the same universe she did.

Dana had no choice when she hit that emotional wall. It was either let it all out or be so consumed by it that she'd never recover.

By the time the tears slowed, she felt exhaustion overtaking her.

"You did good," Mac said into her ear as he continued to hold her.

She chanced a few glances around the large building. No one was looking her way. "I can't believe no one saw me make a fool of myself." She yanked up the hem of her tank top and used it to wipe her eyes and nose.

"Anyone who saw anything would have seen a brave woman fighting her demons." He picked up one of her hands and untied the glove. He repeated the action with her other hand. Then he unwound the wrappings from her hands. She looked dully at his hands. She had no idea when he'd managed to take care of his own. Then she saw the beginning of a bruise on his midsection.

"I did that?" She was horrified that she'd actually hit him hard enough to damage the skin.

"Yeah, you should be proud of yourself." He smiled at her.

"Proud that I hurt you?" She couldn't believe she was hearing right.

"I didn't think you could do it." Mac pulled a dingy-looking towel out of his gym bag and wiped his face with it. "How do you feel now?"

Dana took a few minutes to perform an internal evaluation. *Cleansed* was the only word she could use to describe what she felt was going on inside her.

As they left the building, she noticed a few looks directed her way. If she wasn't mistaken, each one held a hint of respect.

Perhaps she wasn't the only one with an internal battle to fight.

Mac was stunned by the ferocity of Dana's attack. He'd goaded her in hopes he'd get her to let loose with a couple of punches. He hadn't expected she'd light into him like a wild animal. It had taken some fancy footwork and quick action to protect himself from her punches and kicks. With her emotions running so high, she hadn't even seen him. Instead she'd seen whatever haunted her, and that was what she'd fought. Mac just happened to be in there. He winced as a couple areas of his body made themselves known. He'd have more than a few bruises in the morning. But they were worth it.

The shadows he'd seen in Dana's eyes that morning were gone. Her hair was damp with sweat and any makeup she wore was gone. He'd bet everything, she was dying to get home and take a shower. That's why he took her to one of his favorite Mexican food joints instead.

It was small, Mexican music blared from a radio in the steam-filled kitchen and there were no menus other than a chalkboard listing two choices of what the cook had decided to whip up for that day.

Dana looked around with fascination. She leaned across the tiny round table. "No offense, but are you sure the Board of Health hasn't condemned this place?" she whispered.

"They quit cooking rats years ago. Hey, I'm just kidding," he said swiftly. "You won't find better food anywhere in the city. They make their own tortillas, guacamole, and a salsa guaranteed to burn your stomach from the inside out."

A dark-skinned waitress smiled warmly at them and greeted Mac by name. She left a bowl of taco chips and salsa on their table, and left to get their drinks. Mac accepted his beer and tipped the bottle upward, drinking half before putting it down.

Dana dipped a tiny corner of a chip in the salsa and brought it to her lips. Her eyes widened and teared up as she quickly ate the chip then drank her water in hopes of cooling the volcano in her mouth. She agreed with Mac's suggestion that they eat the *carnitas*.

"How do you find these places?" she asked.

"This was my beat when I was in uniform," he replied, using a chip as a scoop for the fiery salsa. "The partner I had then was the owner's son."

"Was?"

He nodded jerkily. "Manny and I caught a kid breaking into a video store a couple blocks from here. The kid spooked, tried to fight back, and before we knew it he'd buried a knife in Manny's heart." He took a deep shuddering breath. "I can still see the look of shock on Manny's face as he realized he was dying." He rolled the beer bottle between his palms, a characteristic gesture. "His was the first cop funeral I attended. And, unfortunately, not the last."

"And you refused to forget his family," she said.

"More like they refused to let me crawl off in a corner," he admitted. "The day after Manny's funeral, his mom showed up with a plate of enchiladas and ordered me to eat every one of them. The next day, his dad and two brothers showed up with a couple bottles of tequila and we drank to Manny's memory." A faint smile touched his lips. "I'd never been so sick in my life. If it hadn't been for them keeping at me, I probably would have quit the force then and there. Not because I was afraid of getting killed, but because I was afraid of losing another partner. Manny's mother, Lydia, told me it was up to me to go on. To do what I'd planned to do, which was work my way up to detective. Subsequent promotions meant I left the neighborhood, but I never forgot them." He looked around. "I come here a couple times a month for dinner. Lydia fusses over me and scolds me for not eating right."

"And you do not eat right!" A heavily accented voice interrupted.

Dana guessed the woman setting the plates before them could be anywhere between forty and sixty. She had the ageless beauty many women try to obtain with expensive creams and surgery. But the sorrow reflected in her expressive dark eyes said her life wasn't an easy one.

"Finally you bring a woman for me to feed." She wrapped her hand around Mac's neck as she dropped a kiss on his cheek. "I am glad to see you have chosen one who is not only lovely but looks as if she has intelligence." She smiled at Dana.

To Dana's surprise, a dark red color circled Mac's neck and moved up his face.

"Lydia, this is Dana Madison. A client," he muttered.

Lydia's laughter was clear and musical. "Of course she is, *mi hijo*." She pinched his cheek. "Now you will eat everything on this plate," she told him. She turned to Dana. "And so will you." She stepped closer. Her smile was gentle as she tipped Dana's chin up to better study her. "Mac will make things right for you. When that happens, your eyes will light up like the stars in the sky. And smiles will be easier for you. Mac is a good boy. A little stubborn, perhaps." She waved her hand back and forth. "But I think you can deal with that. Now eat before it gets cold. If you eat all your food, I will bring you flan."

"Best damn flan in the country," Mac complimented. *"Ow!"* He rubbed the back of his head where Lydia had smacked him.

"What have I told you about your language?" she scolded before walking back to the kitchen.

Dana ducked her head as she picked up one of the *carnitas*. Her lips tipped upward as she pretended to concentrate on her food.

"Do not laugh," Mac ordered under his breath.

His scowl did nothing to intimidate her. Her shoulders trembled with suppressed giggles.

"First I get beat up, then I get laughed at," he muttered. "Big tough private detective."

At least, that was what he thought she said. He wasn't about to ask her to repeat it. He settled for spooning fiery salsa on one of the *carnitas* and crunching down on the spicy food.

Lydia was right. He'd never brought a woman here. Maybe because he felt the Esteban family was the family he never had. If he'd brought a woman to the restaurant before, Lydia would have been ready to plan a wedding. Why he'd brought Dana here, he wasn't sure. Part of him said he was proving that when this was all over he wouldn't be able to just walk away from her. He wouldn't be able to leave her.

Just as Manny's family hadn't walked away from him or blamed him for Manny's death. As he'd blamed himself.

"I won't have a stomach lining after all this." She waved her hand in front of her open mouth. "There's steam coming out, isn't there?"

Mac grinned. "More like fire."

"Augh!" she groaned, then laughed, looking more relaxed than she had all day. "First you try to turn me into Stallone, then you succeed in turning my stomach into a volcano. You don't do anything in half measures, do you."

He gingerly rubbed his midsection. "Next time, I'm wearing body armor."

"That wasn't a gym you took me to. That was a room filled with major testosterone. Were they all boxers?" she asked, picking up one of her *carnitas* and taking a bite.

"Some are. A lot of cops also go there. It's not a place you'd find written up in a local magazine. Mainly because the owner prefers to keep his place low-key."

"I don't think he has anything to worry about." She brushed an unruly strand of hair away from her face. "I'm not trying to be a snob, but I can't imagine women rushing in to use the equipment."

"Their loss."

When Mac looked at Dana now with her hair tousled, no makeup, and even a little smelly from her workout, she looked more beautiful than she did when wearing her designer clothing and made up to the max.

Oh yeah, he was really keeping his distance with this client.

"Don't you ever think about taking a day off to play?" Mac asked when they later left the restaurant. Lydia appeared again with two large brown bags, which she pushed into Mac's hands after instructing him one of them was for Dana. She hugged the younger woman and told her to return any time, and that she didn't need to bring Mac with her. Mac grumbled a bit about how he wasn't appreciated, but he smiled when he kissed Lydia on the cheek.

"I have too much work to do to even think about taking a day off," Dana explained

He unlocked the truck and placed the bags carefully in the storage area.

"But you took today off and nothing happened. The sky didn't fall and you didn't turn to dust." He helped her into the passenger seat and walked around to the driver's side.

Dana secured her seat belt. "You forget that I've basically stepped into my father's shoes. And it hasn't proven to be all that easy. Our established clients still tend to think of me as Jeremy's daughter, not as the owner. I've had to work hard to gain their trust in me. Then when my mother had her stroke, I spent any remaining time at the hospital with her."

"That's a lot of pressure for one person," he murmured.

"You should talk. Look at all you do. You have more integrity than a hundred men," she pointed out. "Yet underneath that bad-boy exterior you're pure marshmallow."

Mac winced at her description. "If you don't mind, I'd really appreciate it if that piece of news didn't get out." He climbed behind the wheel.

"Don't worry, your secret is safe with me," she assured him.

The moment Dana entered her house, she felt the tension knotting up between her shoulder blades. Reality struck a hard blow as she recalled why she'd wanted to leave the house that morning.

Duffy pawed at the patio door, woofing a demand to be

let inside. She walked over and slid back the door. He paused long enough to lick a thank-you kiss across the back of her hand before bounding over to Mac.

"No matter what you do, it isn't easy to forget, is it?" he commented as he put down the brown paper bag Lydia had given him.

Dana unloaded the containers and placed them in the refrigerator. Then she pulled out a pitcher of iced tea and filled two glasses, pushing one toward Mac. She filled a bowl with water and set it down on the floor for Duffy.

"Did Abby think your dream had a meaning?" Mac asked, following her into the family room. He chose the couch while she curled up in a chair.

Why did he have to bring that up? Dana didn't want to remember her nightmare. She'd been able to push the memory to the back of her mind for the past couple of hours. She wanted to pretend it hadn't happened and that she and Mac had spent the day together.

Except that their "day out" had been spent at a psychiatrist's office, a gym where she tried to punch the stuffing out of Mac, then a restaurant where the owner treated him like a beloved son.

She circled the rim of her glass with her fingertip. "Dr. Moore said the dream could have a hidden meaning or it could be nothing more than a nasty nightmare due to eating dill pickles before bed," she replied.

"You ate dill pickles before you went to bed?"

"No, I was just using it as an example. You know how some say if you eat certain foods before you go to bed it can cause nightmares?" Encouraged by his nod, she continued. "Or maybe watch a scary movie or read something in a book."

"Is that what you were told when you were a little girl?" he asked.

"Actually, I was told if I ate chocolate cake before I

went to sleep I'd dream about the land where chocolate was made. I used to wake up feeling so disappointed that I didn't dream about Chocolate Land.''

"It sounds as if your parents wanted you to have nothing but good dreams," Mac said quietly.

"Yes, I guess they did." She set her glass on the nearby table. "Since I was the beloved only daughter of doting parents, I should have been a spoiled-rotten child who cared for no one but herself."

"So what happened?" he asked, curious to find out more about her.

One shoulder raised in a careless shrug. "Perhaps it had to do with my father insisting I do chores to earn my allowance. I had to keep my room clean, make my bed, and as I got older I was given a few more chores. My father loved to say you had to earn your own way."

"No getting any toy you wanted? Private schools? Trips to Europe every summer?"

"I'm sure I had more toys than I knew what to do with. I attended a private school, but that was because my mother seemed to be afraid I wouldn't be safe in a public school. The trip to Europe was a surprise after I graduated from college," she replied. "My parents tended to be overprotective when I was little. When I got older, I once asked my father if he ran a background check on each of my friends and their families. I was honestly afraid he was going to say yes."

"Any reason why he seemed paranoid? Was there a kidnapping threat when you were little? Maybe one of your friends was kidnapped?"

Dana thought about it. "No, not that I remember. Yet, there was one afternoon I'd gone to a friend's house. She only lived down the street from us. But I hadn't told anyone where I was going. When I got home, Daddy was ready to call the police and my mother was having hysterics. That was the first time he'd ever yelled at me. By the time he finished, we were both crying.'' Her brow furrowed. ''Odd, I haven't thought of that time in years. He later said that we lived in a neighborhood of wealth and he didn't want anything to happen to me.''

''You were very close to your father, weren't you.''

She nodded. ''My mother said we were two of a kind. If I played with my dolls, I'd put them in an office setting. My mother's health was fragile long before she had her stroke. Our time together was having tea parties, or I would help her with her flower arrangements. She was happiest when she looked after her flowers.''

''No offense, but it sounds as if you had a pretty lonely childhood.'' Mac finished his iced tea and put his glass on the floor.

''I think it was more I was a loner,'' she corrected him. ''About every six weeks or so, my parents would go off somewhere for a long weekend. I didn't see anything relaxing about those times for them, since they both usually came back quiet, almost distant. Harriet, our housekeeper, would make elaborate plans for us. We'd stay up all night eating popcorn and watching movies. Sometimes I was allowed to invite a couple friends over for a slumber party.''

''But what about now?'' Mac asked her. ''Do you still stay up all night eating popcorn and watching videos, or have slumber parties?''

She offered him a wry smile. ''They're not exactly high on my priority list.''

''Maybe you should bump them up.''

''I have a life, Mac,'' she reminded him. ''Maybe even a double life.''

''Is that what Abby said?''

''She hasn't seen me enough to come to any decision.'' She shifted, now sitting cross-legged in the deep cushioned chair.

What was Dana going to admit? That with each passing day she was feeling more lonely? That these frightening episodes had left her looking over her shoulder?

"Excuse me," she mumbled, bolting out of her chair. She hurried into the bathroom and closed the door behind her, then splashed cold water on her face and patted it dry. She stared at the mirror, but it only brought back memories of her nightmare.

Had something happened to her as a small child that caused her parents to be overly protective? If so, could that have something to do with what was going on now?

It wasn't until she started to replace the hand towel on the rack that she noticed it. Her hand froze in mid-air, the towel slipping from her nerveless fingers.

"Mac." She spoke his name in a hoarse whisper. She cleared her throat. "Mac! *Mac!*"

"Dana?" A fist pounded against the door. "Let me in."

"It's unlocked," she said. She still hadn't moved, and stepped aside just before the door flew open.

Mac grabbed her by the shoulders. "What's wrong?"

She jerked her head toward the bathroom counter.

He moved around her and swept his gaze over the area. At first glance, nothing looked out of place. Until he realized, just as she had, that a figurine stood behind the frosted glass container that held hand cream.

Mac pulled a handkerchief out of his back pocket and carefully wrapped it around the figurine as he picked it up.

Dana looked ill as she stared at the figure fashioned in a blatant, erotic manner.

"That is so sick," she gasped.

"'Slut of the Year.'" He read the words engraved along the base of the statue. "I'll see if a friend of mine can get any prints off this."

She shook her head. "How could this have happened? I

set the alarm before we left the house," she insisted. "It wasn't there this morning. I know it wasn't!"

Carrying the statue in one hand, he wrapped his other arm around her and steered her out of the room.

"Nothing matters," she babbled. "No matter what I do, this won't go away."

He set the statue down on a table and grabbed her shoulders. "Yes, it will," he said fiercely. "There was a good reason why this happened now. Things have been too quiet lately. This was done to shake you up."

"Mission accomplished," she said bitterly.

"Only if you allow it to." He looked torn. "I want to get this in. Are you going to be okay?"

Dana was barely listening to him. "I'm always okay. Don't you know that?" she murmured. She looked as if she was ready to cry.

Mac wrapped his arms around her and seized her mouth in a kiss that literally took her breath away. He consumed her the way a dying man ate his last feast. As if there were no tomorrow.

With a muffled curse, he pulled away. He spun around, hands on his hips as he filled his lungs with much-needed air. He reached for the statue and carefully picked it up so he wouldn't accidentally smudge any fingerprints.

Dana, not doing much better, held on to the nearby table as she tried to regain her senses.

"You've got a good right hook and a potent mouth," he muttered. He snapped his fingers at Duffy, who'd been dozing in the kitchen. "Set your alarm after I leave," he ordered as he headed for the door.

Dana made her way to the door and threw the dead bolt. It took her three times to get the code right before the green light flashed, silently announcing the alarm was set.

For the next hour, she sat in a chair staring at the wall. She was still reeling from his kiss.

She prided herself on being a rational human being. Yet, Mac McKenna only had to look at her and she went weak in the knees. If he'd suggested they move to her bedroom, she would have willingly gone.

She'd heard danger added an erotic edge to a person's senses. She wondered if that was the spice between them.

She was certain Mac could turn out to be more dangerous than whoever was out to get her. More dangerous because she knew he could steal her heart.

Chapter 9

"After today, it's kinda nice to have a quiet night," Mac said out loud. He shifted his position in an effort to stretch his legs. His abdomen still ached from Dana's lucky punches. His way of making it better was to snack on Lydia's homemade taco chips and salsa.

Dana, he thought, *tasted hotter than the hottest salsa Lydia had ever concocted.*

Experience told him the statue left in her bathroom was a deliberate taunt. He hadn't thought there would be any fingerprints, and there weren't.

Talk about lousy timing. He'd gotten her to relax. To stop looking haunted. Then this happened. He muttered a curse.

Duffy whined and bumped his nose against Mac's back.

"You don't have to go out, you faker. You just want to go down the road and see if that poodle is out in her backyard," Mac told him. "Face it. She's not for you, tough guy. She's class with a shapely bod and saucy little tail."

Which had him thinking again about Dana. Not that thoughts of her had ever left his mind after that kiss they'd shared earlier in the day. "I'm surprised you didn't look for someone spicier. Like a glamorous golden Lab or maybe a demure collie." He put his hand back and scratched the top of Duffy's head. The dog happily slobbered on his shoulder. "We really need to do something about that drool problem of yours."

Mac thought about getting out and taking Duffy for a short walk. Maybe they would run into that cute little poodle. Since the St. Bernard had seen her during a walk a week ago, he'd been pulling Mac toward the snooty pooch's house in an attempt to glimpse at her. He didn't have the heart to remind the dog a love life was out of the question.

He straightened up when his cell phone rang.

"You didn't slip the poodle your number, did you?" he asked, picking up. "McKenna."

"A typical masculine greeting. I think I should respond with something you'd easily understand. What are you wearing?"

He knew the voice. He just didn't know it in this sultry mode.

"Nothing too daring. Just a pair of sheer boxers in a sassy shade of red," he replied. "How about you?"

"Nothing much, just a sexy little number I picked up the other day. The color is called 'candlelight' because a candle can shine right through it," she said in a husky voice that brought to his mind a large bed covered with silk sheets. "While it falls to my feet, there's only these tiny straps and a barely-there bodice. I'm sure you would like it. Maybe even like it so much you'd want to tear it right off me."

He was positive his jeans shrunk a good four sizes.

"Wouldn't want to ruin good material," he croaked. He ignored the dog's paw batting at the back of his head.

"I'm sorry you aren't here to see it," she purred. "I'm sure you'd like it."

"Yeah." He glanced over at the house. He couldn't see any lights burning. He didn't expect to see any, since it was almost two a.m. The master bedroom was in the rear, so there wasn't any chance he could see it from where he was parked. And you didn't need a light to talk on the phone.

"Then the least I could do is take it off. But I'd much rather you did it."

Now he was running out of air.

Mac fixed his gaze on Dana's house as if he could see through the walls to the woman within. As if he could see her lying in bed with her phone to her ear as in a low voice she described her nightgown in explicit detail. Then erotically described how she would take it off. Sweat glistened on his brow as he visualized what she was saying. By the time she finished, he was positive he was ready to die. But he'd die a happy man.

"Sweet dreams, Mac," she murmured.

It took him several minutes to realize she'd hung up. Another few minutes passed before he could breathe normally again. He even feared he was going cross-eyed. That potent mouth conjured up some pretty hot words.

He dropped his cell phone on the passenger seat. He warily eyed the instrument as if it had suddenly come to life on its own.

Phone sex wasn't something Mac had ever tried. After tonight, he realized just how dangerous it could be.

He was suddenly certain that the woman he'd spoken to on the phone wasn't Dana. It had taken him a couple of minutes to hear the differences; it had sure as hell sounded like her.

Questions chased through his mind. Who was it? How

had she known about him? Why was she now calling him? And how had she gotten his number?

He knew it would take some time to try to figure some of this out, but one thing was clear. Someone had decided the rules of the game needed to be changed.

Now she wasn't toying only with Dana; she had extended her dark little games to Mac.

"You're going to lose," he murmured, continuing to look at Dana's house as if his gaze alone could protect her. "You're going to lose big-time."

"How can my staying out of the office for one day generate so much work?" Dana muttered, pushing a pile of paperwork away from her.

For the first time, she had no desire to do any work. She glanced out the window and wished she was outside in the sunshine instead.

"Are you sure you don't want me to straighten up those files?" Marti asked. She placed several inter-office folders in Dana's In Box.

Dana shook her head. "Right now there's nothing earth shattering for me to work on and this keeps me out of mischief," she joked.

"As if you've ever had to be kept out of mischief," Marti retorted. "All right, I offered and I'm smart enough not to offer again. Just remember that K comes after J," she reminded her as she left the office.

"I always wondered about that." Dana laughed. She returned to the papers. She knew she would have to check every sheet of paper to make sure they were in the correct folder along with putting the folders in alphabetical order.

Her thoughts were troubled as she wondered how her enemy had gotten into the offices. She'd already checked with the security desk, but she couldn't find out any answers from them. She thought of the times she'd come in after hours when no one manned the desk. It would have been just as easy for someone to come in and get upstairs. Considering how easily her house had been broken into, she feared her office security system had also been bypassed.

As she worked she found herself unable to stop yawning.

"You couldn't tell I had a good night's sleep last night." She muttered to herself as she stifled another yawn.

After the night before, she knew she needed it. But when she'd fallen asleep, a stray thought had crept into her mind. A tiny voice asked what it would be like if Mac was in the bed with her.

"I'm certain I wouldn't have been sleeping," she told herself.

"I want to talk to your mother."

Dana's head snapped upward. For a moment she wondered if she hadn't conjured up his presence merely by thinking about him.

"Good morning to you too," she said in the same abrupt tone he used. "Don't tell me, you charmed my receptionist into letting you sneak back here."

He grinned. "I didn't need to charm anyone. You introduced me to your staff, remember? After that first time, they seem to think we're involved."

"Because you did everything but stand on your head to make them think that way," she pointed out.

"That was one thing I could never do. Guess my head isn't flat enough," he mused. "Actually, all I had to say is that I wanted to surprise you. Your receptionist told me to come on back." He walked in and sat down in the chair across from her. He glanced at her paper-covered desk. "What'd they do? Save it all up for you?"

"It looks like it, doesn't it? Now you know why I say I don't dare take a day off."

She hoped he wouldn't guess she'd been thinking about

him. She'd taken on this task in hopes she could keep her mind off Mac for a while.

Little did she know her efforts would be in vain because he would show up.

"You are not talking to my mother. I already told you she's not well. She still has a lot of problems with her speech."

Mac leaned back in the chair, propping his ankle on his opposite knee.

"I promise not to do anything to upset her. But we need to start thinking that she might know something you don't. Same with your mother's housekeeper. I told you in the beginning this case had to be handled my way. You should be grateful I'm telling you in advance instead of my just going out there."

"I've made sure all of this has been kept from her," she argued.

"Your housekeeper knows and for all you know, your mother just might know something," he told her. "Moms have a habit of knowing everything even if you don't think they do. I know mine always did."

"This is not about some stupid little secret," she said relentlessly. "I can't allow it. My mother's fragile health couldn't take any of this." She took a deep breath to calm herself. "I don't see why you would need to talk to her anyway."

Mac refused to back down. "For all you know, you could have been having that nightmare since you were six, and you've just blocked it."

Dana could feel the nausea traveling up her throat. Only by sheer will was she able to avoid disgracing herself. "That's not possible," she protested, her voice scratchy with fear.

He looked at her directly. "Are you sure?"

"No, I'm not sure, but surely something would have been said to me about it when I grew older."

"Not if your family didn't see any need to tell you. If they were afraid it would upset you." His expression was grim. "Take your choice, Dana. Either you go with me to make sure I don't put the thumbscrews to your mother and the housekeeper, or I do it my own way."

She stood up. "I should have punched you a lot harder yesterday."

Where was the man she'd called a marshmallow just the other night? Why was he pushing this so hard?

She stacked the files in a neat pile. Without saying a word to him, she reached inside her bottom desk drawer and pulled out her bag. She glared at him as she stalked past him.

"Marti, Mac and I are going out to see my mother," she informed her assistant. "I'll be back before you leave for the day."

The older woman turned to Mac and smiled. "Don't rush back. The only problem we've had is finding a bunch of files out of order, and I can have one of the clerks finish those."

Mac shot Dana a telling look. "Files out of order is never any fun."

Dana ignored him and walked down the hallway. Her back was ramrod straight, her head held high as she headed for the elevator. With his hands stuck in his jeans pockets, Mac sauntered lazily behind her.

The elevator door slid open, revealing an empty car. Dana stepped inside and stabbed the button marked Garage. Mac leaned against the wall, his hands still stuffed in his pockets.

She refused to look at him, but her senses couldn't ignore him. Her skin felt jumpy, she felt out of sorts and she was seriously thinking about some primal scream therapy.

Mac broke the silence first. "Must have been frustrating to come in and find a bunch of files out of order."

She didn't reply. She continued staring at the row of numbers overhead as the car descended.

"Odd that happened, since you seem to be almost anal on having everything in its proper place."

Silence reigned.

When the light indicating they'd reached the garage lit up and the doors started to slide open, Dana started to take a step. Mac's hand appeared, slamming the Close Door button. Her head snapped upward.

"What are you doing?" she demanded.

"Were you going to call me and tell me about the files?"

"We've had temps in here for the past few weeks. One of them could have done it," she replied, knowing she sounded as if she couldn't believe her own words.

He shook his head. "You can't tell me you seriously think that."

"Of course I think that," she said. "It's the most logical reason. There is no proof that someone deliberately mixed up the files." Dana threw up her hands. "Fine, believe whatever you want."

"Which is why I'm the expert."

She resisted the urge to roll her eyes. She pulled her keys out of her briefcase. "I'll drive." She left no room for argument as she walked briskly toward her car.

Dana didn't speak during the drive to her mother's house. She was too caught up in fearing the worst for her mother. Would Moms be awake? Aware of her surroundings? Dana trusted Mac not to put undue stress on her mother, but did he honestly understand just how fragile the older woman was at this time?

She already had a pretty good idea how Harriet would treat Mac. She'd succumb to his bad-boy charm and ply him with hot coffee and muffins.

Dana parked the car near the front of the house. She climbed the steps to the front door without bothering to see if Mac was following her.

"Dana, what a surprise!" Harriet exclaimed, hugging Dana. She glanced beyond her. "I see." She chanced a quick glance at Dana's tense features. She turned to Mac. "You must be the private investigator."

"John McKenna." He held out his hand. "I go by Mac."

"Hello, Mac." She put her hand in his. "I'm Harriet."

Mac knew in those few seconds that Harriet had taken stock of him and approved of what she saw. And he knew that if she didn't approve, he probably would have been booted out before he could get past the front door.

"Has something else happened?" Harriet asked, looking from one to the other.

"No, but if you've got the time, I'd like to talk to you about a few things." He flashed her a winning smile.

The woman looked to Dana for confirmation. Dana nodded.

"While the two of you are talking, I'm going to go upstairs and see my mother," Dana murmured, heading for the stairs.

"I've got a coffee cake just out of the oven and coffee just brewed. Come on back to the kitchen. We can talk there," Harriet commanded as she started off for the rear of the house. She didn't look back.

'Yes, ma'am," Mac said meekly.

"I wish you would talk to me, Moms." Dana's voice trembled with unshed tears. "I feel as if you're hiding from me and I don't know why you would do it." She gently squeezed her mother's hand. The skin felt cool, dry and papery under her touch.

She reached for the tube of hand cream always kept on

the nightstand. She squeezed a healthy dollop onto her palm, then rubbed the rich cream between her palms and tenderly smoothed it over her mother's hand and partway up her arm. She repeated the action with the second hand. The delicate scent of gardenia rose up to tickle her nostrils.

"Remember Kenneth Adams, Moms?" she asked, going on as if her mother had replied. She always prayed her mother would hear her words even when she slept. "I ran into him last week at Belson's Market. I'd gone in there for some of that pepper cheese Daddy used to love so much. Kenneth asked how you were doing. He said he and Loretta are planning on seeing you at their Labor Day barbecue. He said Loretta is spending a couple weeks at a spa in Arizona. Translate that to, she's off somewhere having some plastic surgery. Remember how much she always hated those dark bags under her eyes? I bet the next time we see her those bags will be gone." She continued stroking her mother's hand between hers, even though the limb remained unresponsive under her loving touch. She continued her bright chatter as her mother lay there with her eyes closed.

By sheer force of will, Dana didn't break down in tears. She knew her mother wasn't in a coma. The doctor had assured her of that. That didn't explain why she was always asleep when Dana was there.

"Was my mother awake this morning?" she asked the nurse, who'd kept a discreet distance during Dana's visit. Dana personally thought the woman didn't appear very friendly, but she knew if any of the nurses proved to be a problem, Harriet would straighten it out immediately.

"Mrs. Madison and I had a lovely conversation while she had her breakfast," the nurse replied in a low voice. "You have to understand, she still tires easily. But she is doing much better."

Dana nodded. Perhaps she was asking for too much too

soon. She noted a faint hint of blush had been applied to Alice's cheeks and her hair had been brushed. But she also saw the faint spidering of blue veins against her thin eyelids, and her lips appeared slightly dry even after Dana had applied lip balm only moments before.

She knew no matter how much Mac argued, she couldn't allow him to see her mother. Alice Madison had enough to do just in getting well.

"Do you think Dana's mentally unbalanced?" Harriet poured Mac a second cup of coffee and sliced another piece of coffee cake for him.

He consumed the first in three bites. "Nope." He savored the spices in the still-warm cake. Without a doubt, it was the best coffee cake he'd ever eaten. He feared if he didn't give the housekeeper the answer she wanted to hear, she'd whisk the food away from him. For a man who was known for his interrogating skills, he was quickly learning Harriet could give the FBI lessons. All she had to do was feed a man and he'd tell her everything she wanted to know—and then some.

"Then why did you ask me if she ever had emotional problems as a child?" The older woman poured herself a cup of coffee and took the stool next to him.

"I like to cover all my bases," he defended himself. "So far, I haven't been able to find one logical reason for anything that's happened."

"Dana is a woman in the vulnerable position of recently taking over a successful company. Jeremy Madison was an excellent businessman, but he also made his share of enemies because of how successful he was. I wouldn't be surprised if one of them didn't transfer those feelings to Dana," Harriet said. "I'd like to know why you haven't found out anything yet. This case doesn't seem all that difficult. Dana said you're very good at what you do.'' Her expression told him she thought otherwise.

Mac regretted his insistence on talking to the house-keeper. What should have been a friendly, businesslike chat had turned into a round of wills. So far, they were even. So far, Harriet had told him what she deemed necessary and nothing more. To make matters worse, she'd softened him up with homemade coffee cake, and coffee that tasted like real coffee and not the mud he brewed each morning. Now he felt even pulling out his credentials and citations from the police department wouldn't impress the woman.

''If there's something going on, I'll find it and take care of it,'' he assured her.

''You should have done that already.'' Harriet's pursed lips boded ill for Mac.

He quickly curved his arm around his plate, for fear she would take it from him. She smiled knowingly.

''It took a lot of prodding to get Dana to tell me what was going on,'' Harriet said. ''It all sounds frightening. You need to find out who's terrorizing her. If you weren't watching over her at night, I'd insist she come back here and stay.''

''This person is pretty clever at what she does. She seems to know just what buttons to push,'' he explained. ''Right now, it would be nice if she'd get bored and head for new territory.''

Harriet arched an eyebrow. ''Do you honestly think that would happen?''

''No,'' he said truthfully. The late-night phone call still had him feeling unsettled.

Harriet must have seen something in the shift of his expression. ''If you hurt my girl, I will hurt you,'' she promised.

He knew she would, too. ''I haven't hurt a client yet.''

''That's not what I meant and you know it.''

Mac sipped his coffee. "I don't believe it's right to get emotionally involved with my clients." *Sure, McKenna, that's why you kissed her.* "Of course, considering most of the people I deal with, I wouldn't care to." She was fixing him with a steady gaze that was downright unnerving. He eyed her with a narrow gaze. "Are you sure you're not my mother in disguise?"

Harriet was still chuckling when Dana walked into the kitchen. Dana waved Harriet back to her seat as she headed for the coffeepot and poured herself a cup. She eyed Mac's plate, which now bore only crumbs.

"You better have left some coffee cake." She spotted it and cut a slice for herself, then carried the plate and coffee mug over to the counter. She chose the stool by Harriet.

"How was your mother?" Mac asked.

"Asleep." She looked pensive as she drank her coffee. She turned to the housekeeper. "Is there a chance—" she paused, hating to put it into words "—a chance she's being drugged with something that makes her sleep too much?" she asked.

Harriet looked shocked. "Of course not, dear. In fact, we talked for some time this morning when I took her her breakfast."

"Then why is she asleep whenever I come here? I feel as if I should call first to see if she's awake for my visit. But then I'm afraid she'd be asleep, anyway, when I arrive." Dana looked ready to cry. She took a moment to compose herself before she turned to Mac. "I can't let you see her. There's nothing she could help you with. Not with her in this condition. If you want answers, you can get them from either me or Harriet."

His gaze momentarily softened as he looked at her. "Don't worry," he assured her in a low voice. He stood up and picked up his jacket. "Harriet, it was nice meeting you, and anytime I can take you away from all this, give me a call.''

"Wait a minute.'' Harriet wrapped the rest of the coffee cake in aluminum foil and handed it to him. She noticed Dana's look of surprise. "Don't be greedy, dear. I can always bake another one for you,'' she said, wrapping her in a hug and kissing her on the cheek. "He's good for you, dear. Hang on to him.''

"It's just business,'' she whispered back, even though she knew she didn't sound all that convincing.

Harriet smiled. She knew she was lying.

As they walked outside, Dana stopped and looked up to her mother's bedroom window.

Mac drew her into his arms. "Want me to run a check on your mother's nurses?'' he offered, adding with a slight grin, "No charge.''

She managed a weak smile. "It's been so long since she and I have been able to talk. There've been so many times when I've been here and prayed she would open her eyes and talk to me. At first, even when she had trouble forming words, she would try to communicate with me. Now I feel as if she wants nothing to do with me. And I have no idea why.'' Her voice was muffled against his shirt front.

He tunneled his hand under her hair, rubbing her neck in a soothing circular motion. "I've heard it said that sleep is an excellent healer. For all you know, one day you'll come over here and she'll greet you at the door.''

She sniffed. "Wouldn't that be wonderful? I've already lost my father. I don't want to lose my mother, too.''

Chapter 10

Dana's sleep was invaded by the nightmare two nights later.

As before, she was six years old, wearing her favorite blue dress. The dress she had to admire by sitting in front of her mother's mirror. And just as before, her reflection taunted her with the cruel words that no one loved her, that she wasn't pretty. Then the taunts were followed by that otherworldly scream. Except this time, the words thrown at her were dark obscenities, and her reflection's face was completely covered with blood.

When Dana woke up she was convinced she was screaming along with her reflection.

Unable to return to sleep, she pulled on a robe and walked through the dark house. She stopped in the living room long enough to partially pull back a drape. She now knew where Mac parked his truck. While she couldn't easily see it from the window, she had the comforting knowledge that he was there.

Call him.

She didn't think twice as she returned to her bedroom and picked up her cordless phone.

"Yeah." Mac's low voice vibrated through her being.

"Mac?" she whispered.

"Dana?" His voice sharpened. "What's wrong?"

"I almost feel silly now. It's not as if I'm a small child who's convinced there are ghosts in the closet." She tried to make light of it, but her voice broke at the end. "I had that nightmare again."

"Oh, honey," he murmured. "Exactly the same?"

"Pretty much."

She held on to the handset as she left the bedroom and headed for the kitchen. There was enough moonlight streaming through the window that she didn't need to turn on a light. She took a carton of milk out of the refrigerator, poured it into a saucepan and set it on the stove.

"Maybe a glass of wine would relax you," he suggested. "Having some might help you get back to sleep."

"I think I'd be better off with a cup of hot chocolate. The few times I've had a glass of wine before bed left me with a horrible headache in the morning." She found the tin of Swiss cocoa she favored. "I'm sorry I disturbed you. I guess I just needed to hear another voice." Her laughter was shaky. "Maybe I should double-check for those ghosts."

"Considering everything, I think it's natural you'd feel spooked. If all you wanted was a voice, you could have turned on the television," he said, not unkindly.

"It's not the same," she protested, adjusting the flame under the pan. "They can't tell you everything's all right," she said.

Silence hovered on the other end. "Want me to come over?"

Mac. In her kitchen at three in the morning. Her in a

nightgown and robe. The atmosphere would be as intimate as a bedroom. She heard a soft *woof* in the background.

"Is that Duffy?" she asked.

"He's in lust over a poodle three houses down from you," he explained.

"I thought Duffy had 'the operation.'"

"He did, but I learned long ago that doesn't stop him from having crushes on cute little girl dogs that ring his chimes."

"It sounds more like Duffy is obsessed with poodles."

"He's always liked petite girls." Mac chuckled. "Duffy has a wide romantic streak in him."

She started rummaging through her refrigerator and pulled out a package of hamburger. "I may not have a cute little dog, but I can offer him a hamburger."

"We'll be right over." The line clicked in her ear.

Dana wasted no time in turning off the alarm and unlocking the back door. She had a hunch Mac would come in that way. She turned down the heat under the milk pot and started shaping a hamburger patty. It wasn't long before the door opened and Mac and Duffy walked in. The dog loped over to Dana and rubbed his face against her robe.

"Hey, back off," Mac ordered, pausing long enough to reset the alarm.

Duffy looked at Dana and whined.

"You have to wait until it's finished cooking," she told him.

"You didn't have to do that for him." Mac leaned against a counter and watched her turning the meat patty over.

"Of course I did. I thought he'd prefer a hamburger for a late-night snack. Would you like some hot chocolate?" She turned the hamburger patty over and picked up the milk pot.

"Sure."

Dana fixed two mugs and placed them on the table. Once the hamburger patty was finished cooking, she set it aside to cool.

Mac picked up a chair and turned it around. He started to pick up the mug, but she stayed his hand. She opened a cabinet and pulled out a bottle of Irish Cream liqueur.

"Want a little extra?" She held up the bottle.

"Sure. You won't have wine but you'll add some liqueur to your hot chocolate?" He held up the mug.

Dana poured a healthy dose in each mug. "This doesn't give me a headache," she explained. Before she sat down, she placed the cooked hamburger patty in a bowl and cut it up in pieces. She set it down on the floor. Duffy immediately headed for the bowl and wolfed down the contents.

Mac sipped the hot drink and nodded in approval. "This is good." He waited to speak until Dana had drunk some of her hot chocolate and seemed more relaxed. "Any reason why you think your nightmare returned? Anything happen earlier tonight that might have triggered it?"

She cradled her mug in her hands for what comfort it could offer her.

"As you know, I came home at a reasonable hour. I had a salad and grilled chicken breast for dinner. I watched television for a while, took a shower, then went to bed. I read for about an hour, then turned off my light. I don't think I was asleep for very long before it began."

Considering her warm nightgown and robe, she looked as if she were cold. Her hair was tousled waves, as if she hadn't bothered brushing it when she got up. There wasn't a trace of makeup on her face and the fragrance coming from her skin was light and powdery.

"It's starting to eat you up," Mac said in a voice that inferred he knew what he was talking about. "Now that it's made its way into your head, it's refusing to leave. "

"You're making it sound like some sort of nasty parasite," Dana commented. She turned her head to look down at Duffy, who dozed peacefully sprawled on the floor. "But then, if that was the case, all I'd need is some medication. Of course, it still might be all I need."

Mac shook his head. "That won't get rid of it."

"Speaking as one who knows?" she murmured as she picked up the two mugs and carried them over to the sink.

"Every cop has nightmares about something. Don't ever let one of them tell you different. Leaving the force doesn't make them go away, either." Mac rested his arms along the back of the chair and watched her movements as she rinsed out the mugs and Duffy's dish.

Anyone looking in the window would think of them as a couple who'd decided to have a late-night snack. The dog lying nearby added to the domestic picture. They probably looked like something out of *Good Housekeeping* magazine.

"Why do you think you dream about that blue dress?"

Dana paused in her movements. "I honestly don't know. Maybe I saw a little girl wearing a blue dress and absently thought of mine for some reason."

"And why the blood?"

She frowned as she took her thoughts backward in time. "Funny, I didn't remember it until just now. Maybe it's because I've been talking about it. I was wearing the dress when I had my accident."

Mac turned to her. "The one you mentioned before?"

Dana nodded. "As I told you before, I don't remember very much about what happened."

"Close your eyes and think back to that time," he pressed. "Maybe something will come to you that you didn't remember before."

She obeyed his suggestion and tried to relax. "I was climbing on a chair so I could reach a toy. I fell and hit my head. I still have the scar.'' She absently rubbed her scalp near her hairline. ''The fall pretty much knocked out the memory of those first six years.'' She laughed softly. ''When I was in college, I asked my mother if the memory block was because I'd suffered some sort of shock. I had myself convinced it could have been due to some traumatic event while potty training or something. She was horrified I would think such a thing and told me I'd hit my head and that was all there was to it.''

Mac stared at the wall, not seeing the colorful pictures. His mind was too busy sorting information. ''I'm not an expert, but from what little I know, I don't remember hearing a knock on the head like that would cause amnesia,'' Mac commented. ''At least, it normally wouldn't happen unless something that preceded the injury was disturbing enough to make a person want to forget it.''

''Considering the worst punishment I ever received was no dessert, I can't imagine there was ever anything that distressing in my past.'' Her features clouded over. ''Just my present.''

''But why couldn't your past be trying to tell you something about your present?'' Mac asked.

Dana was startled by his question. ''You think the two are somehow connected?''

''Why not? Any other reason why you would dream of yourself when you were six? Maybe you're having this nightmare because something deep inside you is trying to tell you something. Trying to point out something happened to you during that time. Which just might have something to do with your accident.''

Dana kept shaking her head as if just doing so would mean there was no truth to his words. As if she didn't want to believe it could be that simple.

Mac mentally cast about for anything that could help

them. Could it be that one little thing that was the answer to everything?

"What could Harriet tell us about that period in your life?"

"She didn't come to work for my parents until afterward. I can't imagine she would know anything about it, unless my father or mother happened to mention it to her. And I can't think why they would do that."

Dana's eyes looked bruised with fatigue. She covered her face with her hands. "All we've done is raise more questions," she said. "This is so frustrating, Mac! What do we know so far? Not enough to find out who's doing this."

She looked around the kitchen and off to the family room. "From the day I saw this house, I knew I'd found exactly what I was looking for. I was an answer to a realtor's prayer. The moment I entered I felt as if I'd come home. I had hoped for something that would give me even a fraction of the comfort and security my parents felt with their home. I felt it here." Her shoulders lifted and fell. "The feeling is gone," she whispered sadly.

"Only if you let it." Mac stood up and walked around the table to her. "Come on, Dana. It's time for you to try to go back to sleep."

She looked up at him with mute appeal. Eyes a deep blue shimmered with unshed tears.

He tugged on her hand and pulled her to her feet, then guided her down the hallway until they reached her room.

When he entered the room, he pulled her robe off and tucked her into bed as carefully as if she were a small child. After he draped the covers over her, he made ready to leave.

"Mac." She grabbed hold of his hand. "Please, I don't want to be alone."

He knew that she didn't mean anything by asking him to stay. She just needed to know he was there.

He sat down on the edge of the bed and tugged off his shoes. He laid down next to her and pulled her into his arms. His palm cradled her head, holding it against his shoulder.

"It's okay, Dana. Go to sleep. I'm here now," he said softly.

He lay back on the pillow with her curled up next to him. He soon felt her body grow lax as she drifted off to sleep.

He lay awake, listening to the silence surrounding them. Just before he fell asleep he was aware of Duffy stealthily climbing onto the bed and stretching out along the end.

"She may not be too happy to see you up here, buddy," he whispered.

Duffy gave a doggie shrug and plopped his head back down.

Mac had a fleeting thought before he fell asleep that this was just too family-like. And way too nice.

The first thing Dana noticed when she woke up was the sound of the shower running. The second was the heavy weight on her feet.

She lifted her head to find Duffy. The dog was still asleep, his body moving up and down as he dreamed. His body twitched from doggie dreams.

She wasn't sure, but she thought she smelled coffee.

"Duffy?"

"Sorry about that. I guess he thought you needed a chaperon."

Dana turned her head. Mac stood in the bathroom doorway wearing nothing but a towel hitched around his hips. His hair was still damp and stuck out in spikes, and he was unshaven. He hadn't fully dried off, and water droplets clung to the mat of curling dark hair on his chest.

She hoped she wasn't drooling.

"Do I smell coffee?" she asked hopefully.

Not the greatest of opening lines, but she wasn't used to waking up with a dog half lying on top of her and a nearly naked man coming out of her bathroom.

"I put it on before I took my shower. Want a cup?"

"Definitely."

"Hey, Duff, quit dreaming about the poodle. Off the bed. Now." Mac waited for the dog to climb off the bed before he left the room.

Dana couldn't take her eyes off Mac as he walked away. She felt a whimper crawl up her throat. Now she knew with great certainty that a damp towel did wonders for a man's naked body.

She knew it was thanks to Mac that she'd woken up in a more positive frame of mind. Even the memory of her dream didn't seem to hold the terror it had before.

She found her robe on the floor where Mac must have dropped it the night before.

When she entered the bathroom she found it still steamy from his shower. She rushed through brushing her hair and teeth and washing her face before Mac returned. She had no idea how he managed it, but the room even smelled like him. She was just coming out of the bathroom when he walked into the bedroom carrying a coffee cup in one hand and a duffel bag in the other. She arched an eyebrow as she accepted the cup he held out to her.

"You must have given the neighbors an eyeful," she commented.

"I slipped out to my truck before I took my shower to get my bag, then forgot to bring it in here," he replied.

She gratefully gulped the brew. She welcomed the rush of caffeine in an effort to energize her body. She averted her eyes from his near-naked form. She started to sit down on the bed then quickly straightened up. She pretended she meant to walk over to the window and open the drapes.

He grinned at her discomfort.

"I guess I better get dressed," he said, holding up the bag.

"I'll start breakfast," she muttered from her spot by the window, where she looked out as if something in her backyard was utterly fascinating.

Dana didn't turn around until she heard the bathroom door close. Then she escaped to the kitchen and refilled her cup. She pulled out a frying pan, and had scrambled eggs ready and bread in the toaster when Mac walked into the kitchen.

"It looks good." He accepted the filled plate she handed him. "Thanks."

"When I think back about it, I feel a little silly that I allowed a bad dream to upset me so much," she began. She set another plate of scrambled eggs on the floor for Duffy, who inhaled them. "I'm an adult. I should know nightmares can't hurt you."

"Nightmares can be pretty nasty," he pointed out. "The one you've been having is coming across as more than real. You just have to remember that anything that isn't real can't hurt you."

She snatched up his explanation with both hands. "True, but sometimes I think they're right when they say it's easier said than done."

Mac shrugged. He looked off into the distance as he spoke. "I wouldn't worry too much. It happens to all of us. Shadows grow too big and too dark. As a result, we find out we can't easily overcome them."

Dana knew Mac was speaking from personal experience. She wondered if he was remembering watching his partner Manny being killed. She knew it was something from his past that brought the darkness to his voice and etched the pain on his features.

She reached over and grasped his hand. It took a moment

for him to respond. When he did, he looked down at her hand covering his, then up at her face. His faint smile banished the darkness.

He brought her hand to his lips. As he lowered it, he glanced at the clock on the wall and winced.

"Sorry for not offering to do the dishes, but I've got an appointment," he told her, getting to his feet. He snapped his fingers in Duffy's direction. The dog immediately got to his feet and walked over to his master.

Mac paused before heading for the door. He stared at Dana, the expression on his face not giving a hint as to what he was thinking. But she could see the tension in his body. His eyes didn't move from her face.

"Mac."

He turned around and moved toward her. When he stood in front of her, she looked up at him with mute appeal. He circled her wrists with his hands, then pulled them upward, arranging them to loop around his neck. When they were settled to his satisfaction, he lowered his face to hers and covered her mouth with his.

His mouth was so gentle on hers, it was like the faint whisper of a butterfly against her lips. He coaxed her response with a sexy finesse he hadn't displayed before.

If her knees had buckled before, now they downright melted. Along with the rest of her, as his tongue tempted her tongue into play. His fingertips caressed her breast with a featherlight touch that brought a strangled moan to her lips. She clutched his forearms so she wouldn't collapse to the floor.

Mac released the loose knot that held her robe closed and slid the heavy fabric down off her shoulders, until it lay in a pool around her feet. His breath was warm against her cheek as he used his finger to trace the prim collar on her nightgown.

"Do you realize what a turn-on this thing is?" he rasped

in her ear. His tongue started doing things to the delicate shell that she was positive were illegal—they felt much too good.

"No." Her voice was high-pitched and breathy to her own ears.

Again he ran a finger along the collar. "This is something a proper schoolteacher would wear. It covers you from top to bottom so a guy can't see anything. That kind of outfit gives a guy fantasies," he murmured in her ear.

Her head was spinning. "What kind of fantasies?" she asked, once she felt confident she could form the words.

He gently bit down on her earlobe. "Fantasies where I'm unbuttoning it one button at a time." He matched action with his words.

By the time he undid the fourth button, cool air brushed across Dana's skin, but only for two seconds before the warmth of Mac's hand replaced it. She closed her eyes and savored the sensation of his thumb rubbing against her nipple in a circular motion. She gasped as he pressed down, causing a lightning bolt to streak down to her womb.

Now there was no way her legs could hold her. Luckily, he swung her up into his arms before she completely melted. She buried her face against the curve of his neck as he carried her toward the rear of the house.

He laughed softly when he entered the bedroom. "You don't like unmade beds for more than five seconds, do you?" He used one hand to throw the covers down to the end of the bed.

"I didn't know." Her words were muffled against his skin.

"Just like this nightgown, a made bed needs to be unmade." He set her down on her feet.

"So I need to be unmade, too?" she asked, wondering if her dizzy feeling was due to Mac's lips feathering across her temple.

She could feel the pleasant vibrations of his laughter against her skin.

"Oh, yes, very unmade." He dispatched the next few buttons with ease. Before Dana could blink, her nightgown was pulled over her head and dropped to the carpet.

Dana watched Mac's eyes turn a deep molten green as he gazed at her nudity.

"You are so beautiful."

Those four simple words spoken with husky sincerity made her blood heat even more.

"There's only one problem," she said, feeling more confident by the second.

"What's that?"

"*You're* wearing too many clothes." She couldn't unbutton his shirt with the same ease he'd used with her nightgown, but it, too, soon dropped to the floor. Her fingers faltered a bit when she started to unbuckle his belt. When he moved to help her, she brushed his hands away and finished it. Her gaze lowered as she pushed his jeans down past his hips—then widened.

Mac shrugged. "I'd forgotten to put a set of clean underwear in my bag."

She smiled as she moved closer to him. "I wouldn't worry. It saves time."

Dana shrieked when she suddenly ended up on the bed with Mac lying over her. He levered himself onto his elbows so he wouldn't crush her.

"Do you realize how badly I want you?" he rasped.

She encircled his hardness with her hand. "Maybe you should tell me," she purred. "Just so I don't misunderstand."

Mac jerked at her touch. He rubbed his forehead against hers as he groaned. "Not a good idea, sweetheart. I don't intend for this to end before it even begins."

"Oh, I think that's a wonderful idea." She slid over him.

"And don't worry about anything ending too soon—I'll make sure you enjoy every minute," she whispered, punctuating each word with a kiss.

"Then the least I can do is offer you the same promise," he told her. He began by brushing his lips across her nipple, then opened his mouth over it, sucking deeply. "Milk and honey," he murmured.

Dana gasped as white-hot sensations shot through her body. "You know just where to begin, don't you?" she said huskily.

She allowed her hands to roam, and he did the same.

"Like velvet," Mac told her as his mouth inspected the soft area behind her knee, then moved down her leg with agonizing slowness.

"It tingles," she replied as she watched him caress her ankle. "Mac!" She moaned with delight when he flipped her over and dropped gentle kisses along her spine.

"Did you know you have four freckles back here?" he whispered in her ear once he reached her nape. He'd swept her hair to one side so he could investigate there, too. "And hair like silk."

"Mac," she moaned, shifting her hips under him. She twisted enough to turn onto her back. "You are a very cruel man." She lightly raked her nails down his chest. She lifted her head and pressed kisses against the faint lines on his skin.

"I'm telling you I think you are the most beautiful woman in the world, and you think I'm cruel?" His lips nuzzled her ear, then found the sensitive skin just behind it. One hand swept downward along her hip. His fingers tangled in the dark blond curls and beyond. He exhaled heavily when he felt how moist she was. She rotated her hips against his two fingers, silently asking for more.

Dana's breath caught in her throat as an electric current ran through her veins. "Don't stop saying it," she breathed, gripping his arms. "In fact, don't stop, period." She trailed her hand downward.

Mac caught her hand, then pressed it against himself.

He muttered a soft curse as he left her for a moment. She cried out her dismay but smiled when he returned to her.

"When you're looking like heaven on earth, there is no way I would leave you for any longer than five seconds," he told her, sliding along her body. He moved into the inviting cradle of her hips and settled into the welcoming heat.

Dana curved her hand around him, guiding him to her center. He paused, looking down at her.

What would she say if he told her he felt as if he'd come home? That nothing had ever felt so right.

"Perfect," he told her, carefully lowering his body.

She laughed with sheer happiness. "Better than perfect."

Mac buried himself deep within her. Just as slowly, he drew out until only the tip stroked the damp petals. Dana was positive she'd lost track of time as he continued to send her flying.

She looked up at him, seeing the stark desire etched on his face. She was positive she wore the same expression.

"Mac." She whispered his name, unable to say more as she felt the contractions begin deep within her. She unconsciously tightened around him, then moved faster, lifting her hips to meet his. She felt the urge to fly as he thrust her farther into the heavens.

Dana refused to close her eyes, although she was positive lights exploded in front of her as she exploded. She grabbed his shoulders as the pleasure-pain became unbearable. As she reached the pinnacle she had no idea she screamed Mac's name. He covered her mouth with his, seeming to steal her breath as he followed her into the void.

* · * · *

Dana's street was always quiet this time of day, with its residents either already gone to work or running errands. The woodsy area with its path created for walkers was almost deserted—except for one person.

The woman found it easy to stand at the rear edge of Dana's property without being seen.

Even though she couldn't see into the house, she still made sure she stood close enough to hear. With the bedroom window slightly open to the warm morning air, it was easy enough to eavesdrop on the intimate conversation.

A stormy feeling some might have called jealousy swamped her body. She snarled as she turned and clawed a nearby tree trunk. That a nail broke and her skin was scratched and bleeding didn't matter. She couldn't feel the pain. Not when anger overrode everything else.

It is not fair! It is not fair that Baby Girl is in there doing the dirty deed with that stud detective. What could he see in her? He had to have been disappointed with the end result. That little milksop couldn't give a man pleasure no matter how much she tried.

She glared at the house as if her savage gaze could set it on fire and incinerate the occupants.

She doesn't deserve a man like him. He needs to find out just what kind of woman he needs.

Tempting thoughts of going in there and doing away with Dana had her starting to move forward. It would be so easy to accomplish.

All was quiet now. She knew they must be in there basking in the afterglow of what sounded like some pretty hot sex. The fact that she had first felt Dana couldn't satisfy him, then was convinced Dana had, didn't matter. Her thoughts flip-flopped all the time. She didn't see anything wrong in it. Whatever she thought at that moment was what she truly believed.

She'd barely taken two steps, when a dog's deep bark

sounded from inside the house and shook her out of her murderous thoughts. In moments, a large dog appeared at the sliding glass door leading to the patio. As he saw her, he jumped up on his hind feet, pawing at the door in hopes he could open it himself.

For a moment, she was stunned by the sight and feared the dog would accomplish his objective.

She was surprised Dana had allowed the mutt into the house. Dana must have been more desperate for a man than she'd thought.

She laughed when she realized the dog wasn't able to get out. All he could do was bark and jump at the glass door. Her secret was still safe.

No problem. I can come back anytime I want to take care of you, Baby Dana.

Chapter 11

The bone-chilling cold that suddenly struck her had to have been some kind of warning.

Dana felt it a few seconds before Duffy started barking. She wasn't sure why she sensed there was a connection between the two, but the idea refused to go away. It frightened her.

Duffy's angry barking told her something was out back that the dog didn't like. She could hear him jumping up against the patio door in an agitated manner as he fought to get outside.

Since Mac was in the bathroom, she started to go over to the window to see what was bothering the dog. She'd just started to reach for her robe, when Duffy stopped barking. Just as abruptly, the chill left her body.

"What's up with him?" Mac frowned as he came out of the bathroom.

"Maybe he saw a cat," Dana replied, not believing her own logical explanation and not understanding why she felt this way. She wrapped her arms around herself, briskly rubbing her arms with her hands.

The chill had left but not the fear.

She pasted a smile on her lips. It wasn't difficult to do, when Mac stood there in all his glory.

Minutes ago she'd felt safe in the circle of his arms. In turn, she'd held him as he trembled with aftershocks. She'd listened to his muttered prayers for her beauty and response to him. She'd combed her fingers through the dark hair matting his chest. She'd felt the strength under the layer of roughened skin. And reveled in it. She didn't think she could ever tire of touching him.

Dana realized she'd never thought of herself as a woman who would enjoy the kind of raw elemental sex she'd just experienced with Mac. Her earlier encounters were sterile compared to the heights Mac had carried her to.

She wanted to fly again. She wanted to feel safe again, and the only way she could was in his arms.

Her need must have shown on her face, because Mac stopped in mid-stride.

"You really know how to make a guy crazy," he admitted. "Right now, I'd like nothing more than to take you back to bed, but I need to see what's going on with Duffy." He reached for his jeans and pulled them on.

Dana sat back on the bed, holding her robe in her hands.

Mac looked over his shoulder just before he left the room. "Stay here," he instructed.

"I won't leave," she promised. She could feel her heart climbing up into her throat as she strained with all her senses in an attempt to know what was going on.

"What's going on, boy?" she heard Mac ask the dog. "You see a cat or something? Come on, let's take a look."

Dana swiftly put her robe on and tied it tightly. She suddenly couldn't keep her promise. She had to know. She hurried out of the room and down the hallway to the family room. By the time she reached it, Mac was already outside. Duffy was running back and forth along the length of the back fence. Several times he stopped and jumped up, throwing his large body against the wooden posts. She winced as the fence shuddered against the blows.

Mac also checked the length of the fence, but he did his investigating by looking over it. He'd walk several steps, stop and peer over. After he checked out the entire rear section, he walked over to the side that wasn't bordered by another house.

He was frowning when he returned—a frown that deepened when he found her sitting on the couch.

"I thought I told you to stay in the bedroom."

She ignored him. "Did you find anything?"

"As you said, maybe it was a cat." He picked up Duffy's leash and whistled for the dog. "I'm going to check out the land just behind the house. And don't leave," he ordered, as he snapped the leash on the dog's collar. "Set the alarm after I go."

Dana ran to the door and punched in the code the moment Mac and Duffy were gone. She stood at the patio door, her palms pressed against the glass as she waited for occasional glimpses of the top of Mac's head.

She had no concrete evidence, but she knew whatever had sent Duffy into such a frenzy was now long gone.

When she saw Mac returning to the house, she quickly turned off the alarm.

"Did you find anything?" she asked the moment he stepped inside. He opened the patio door so Duffy could go outside.

"Trampled grass that looked fresh, but I don't know if someone was just there or was there an hour ago," he replied. "Maybe someone was out there taking a walk."

"Or maybe someone was out there watching us," she whispered, still looking through the glass door.

Mac stood behind Dana with his hands resting on her shoulders. He gently pulled her back against him, crossing his arms in front of her as if offering her his protection. She reached up, curving her fingers over his arms. They watched Duffy amble around the yard, occasionally stopping to sniff a bush or mark his territory. He acted as if nothing had upset him.

Dana closed her eyes and allowed herself to bask in the warmth of Mac's embrace. She turned her head so she could rub her cheek against his chest. The crisp hairs tickled. She sighed when she felt his cheek resting against hers.

"Are you sure?" he murmured, easily guessing her need. "I didn't mean to, but I think I was a little rough with you. I don't want to hurt you."

She tipped her head back and flashed him a smile that was pure female. She was a woman who'd been made aware of just what she had to offer a man.

The right man.

It only took her smile, not any words, to convince him she was more than sure.

Mac didn't waste any time before returning to the bed.

"You're going to be even later getting to the office," he advised, even as he made damn sure she wouldn't heed his warning.

She looped her arms around his neck. "I don't see why anyone would complain. After all, it is Saturday."

Mac should have felt guilty. After all, he'd just made love to a client. Made love to her more than once. He'd broken the commandment he'd made the day he'd opened his office. He'd known it would never be a good idea to get involved with a client. Yet, here he'd gotten involved with Dana, in spades. He'd always walked the straight and narrow with a client. Why had he changed his rules now?

He'd even managed to keep his commandment when he

helped out Kandy Kane. He'd found the man who'd beaten the stripper so badly she hadn't been able to work for months. After her attacker was arrested, a grateful Kandy not only added a bonus to his fee but also invited him to frolic in a large waterbed with a fake fur covering. Considering Kandy had a body that had most men salivating, with luscious curves that earned her the big tips, it hadn't been an easy decision. But he'd done it. He'd walked out of her apartment, cursing himself every which way. But he knew he'd done the right thing.

Thou shalt not mess with gorgeous clients. Admittedly, he generally used a harsher expression than *make love*. Except the crude term didn't apply where Dana was concerned.

She was warm and openly responsive as she moved into his arms. And she smelled like baby powder, which he'd discovered came from the body lotion she kept on a glass shelf over the bathtub.

If he was going to break his own rules, he couldn't have done it with anyone more special.

He couldn't remember anyone else ever feeling so perfect in his arms.

Damn, he felt complete with her—something he hadn't thought he could ever feel.

She now lay on her stomach next to him. He smiled as she drew lazy patterns on his chest. "Are you having fun?"

"Yes, actually, I am." She watched the dark hairs wrap around her finger. "What were you like as a little boy?"

He absently rubbed the spot between her shoulder blades. He needed to touch her. To feel the silken surface of her skin.

"I wasn't anything special. Just a typical pain-in-the-ass kid who got into fights, played baseball and cut school when I could," he replied.

"I bet your mother wasn't too happy with you playing truant." She kept on drawing aimless designs on his chest.

"My mom wasn't around to be happy or unhappy," Mac admitted, staring at the ceiling. If he was going to say things he hadn't thought about for a long while, he couldn't look at her and lose himself in eyes the color of cobalt. He found they tended to make him say things he normally wouldn't.

She was one dangerous woman.

"Your parents were divorced?" she pressed.

He let out a loud breath. "My dad eventually divorced her. She just up and left one day. She said she couldn't handle my dad's job. She didn't like knowing he was going out there and could get killed at any time. He worked Narcotics. A lot of times he worked undercover, which meant he'd be gone for months at a time and he couldn't contact us. We had no idea when he'd be back. He'd also been shot and knifed more than his share of times. One of the times he was in the hospital, she packed up her things and left. We never heard from her again." He spoke to the ceiling.

"Oh, Mac." Dana's voice was soft with pain. "She left your dad and left you too? How could she do that? You must have felt devastated."

He watched the sunlit patterns on the ceiling. It was easier than looking at her. "She didn't feel any guilt about it. Dad was ticked off more than anything else. Probably because he thought he had to find someone to look after me when he was on a case. I showed him I didn't need anyone. I could take care of myself."

She guessed there was more to the story, but he wasn't ready to tell her. "How old were you when she left?"

"About ten," he said in a flat voice. "As Dad always said, I was big for my age, and as long as I didn't burn down the house, he wouldn't need to worry about me."

Dana rested her cheek against his chest, wrapping her arms around him. He combed his fingers through her hair. From this angle, he could see the scar along her hairline she'd talked about. He gently traced it with his fingertip.

"No one said anything about you staying home by yourself?" she asked. "Teachers at school? Other policemen? If your father wasn't home all the time, someone had to have been there to take care of you."

"Some of the wives brought by meals when Dad was undercover. I had the entire precinct making sure I toed the line." Mac's laughter held no mirth. "They all knew my dad's parenting skills were pretty limited and they didn't want to see me thrown into the System. My ex-wife used to say I was too much like my old man."

Dana shot up. Her mouth dropped open in shock from the bombshell Mac dropped. "You were married?"

"For three-and-a-half years." He wrapped his hand around the back of her neck and brought her down to him again.

"Do you ever see her?" she asked.

"Not since the divorce papers were signed, and that was quite a few years ago. She's happier married to a masonry contractor who works regular hours. They've got four kids and six cats, and she drives carpool."

"It sounds like she didn't want to do her fair share to make things work, " Dana said softly.

"I don't think either of us did," he admitted, tangling his fingers in her hair and brushing it away from her face. His fingertips encountered the scar again.

He frowned as he looked down at the narrow ridge that disappeared into her hairline. What was it about the faint mark that seemed wrong? Sure, it bothered him like hell that she was hurt so badly it left a permanent memory of her accident. He didn't want to think how a little girl must have suffered that day. No, it was more than that that left him feeling unsettled.

She reached up and kissed the hollow of his throat. "So I guess he wasn't there for your football and baseball games."

Mac thought of the dark-visaged man who put terror into many a drug dealer's mind. The man who had a boy hating him with a vengeance for letting his mother go and for never being there for him. "Actually, I was on the baseball team. Except, my dad thought baseball was for wimps." *Even when I pitched a no-hitter against the school's biggest rival.*

"Everyone needs someone," she whispered. "That kind of pain is too sharp for anyone to handle by themselves." *That's it!*

He shifted his body so he could better study the scar.

"You said you fell and cut your head?" he asked, using his fingers to part the hair from the mark.

Dana rolled away, taking the enticing warmth of her body with her. She shook her head so her hair settled back into place.

"It was a nasty punishment for my doing something I wasn't supposed to. I climbed up on a chair because I wanted a toy on a shelf. I overbalanced and fell. I hit my head on a corner of one of the shelves. I was told I bled everywhere, since it was a head wound. I only remember waking up in the hospital with a bad headache and feeling the stitches." She leaned halfway over the bed and picked up her robe. She shrugged into it and tied the belt as she knelt on the tumbled covers.

"But you also said that after the accident you couldn't remember anything that happened before you fell. So how do you remember falling?" He sat up and pushed the pillows up behind him.

"I don't know. I guess because I was told I fell. Why

do you want to know about something that happened years ago?'' she asked.

"Just curious. What do you remember about falling?'' Mac took the stray loop of hair and tucked it behind her ear, letting his hand linger against the warmth of her neck.

Dana frowned as she cast her mind back to that time. "To be honest, I don't remember anything about it. My parents told me what happened, after the doctor told them I couldn't remember how I fell. All I remembered was waking up in the hospital and crying because my head hurt.''

"So they were there when you fell. I'm surprised one of them didn't see you and catch you in time,'' he said casually.

She shook her head. "Maybe they were across the room and couldn't reach me in time. Maybe they called out a warning that startled me. That could have been when I fell. Why are you asking me about this?''

"I told you. I'm curious.'' Mac's smile didn't reach his eyes. "Call it a legacy from being a cop. We like to see things settled. Everything tied up in a neat little package.''

His brain started spinning as he tried to figure out why Dana's parents might have lied to her. Years of work-related injuries taught him one thing, and that was what caused certain scars. One thing he knew was that the narrow scar along her hairline hadn't come from connecting with the edge of a shelf. He knew the difference, since he had a couple of scars like hers on his body.

Dana didn't like the intense expression on Mac's face. "What aren't you saying?'' she demanded. "Why are you so curious about something that happened years ago?''

"I've seen scars like that before and they don't come from hitting a shelf,'' he said quietly.

A cold trail of fear traveled down her spine. She licked her lips. "What do they come from?''

Mac was silent for several moments. He kept his gaze level. "It's a knife wound."

Dana couldn't keep her eyes from his face. She didn't doubt his words. But she still wanted to tell him he was mistaken.

If it was the truth, that meant her parents had lied to her.

"I'm going to take a shower." She climbed off the bed and stopped by her dresser for underwear and a change of clothing. When she went into the bathroom, she closed the door with a soft *click*.

She ran the water as hot as she could stand it. The spray pelted skin that felt ultrasensitive after Mac's lovemaking.

How could a child end up with a knife wound? If her parents had lied to her about her accident, were there other things they lied to her about?

She ducked under the water to wet her hair, then squirted shampoo into her palm. She lathered up and vigorously scrubbed her scalp as if she could scrub away the scar.

Her fingers lingered over the narrow ridge of scar tissue. She forced herself to think back to that day. She had wanted her favorite doll, but it had been put up on the shelf. She was too impatient to wait until someone could get it down for her. So she pushed a chair over to the shelves and climbed up. When her mother came in and found her on the chair, she called out to Dana. Dana panicked and fell.

Be honest with yourself, Dana. Mac is right. How could you remember falling? Wasn't it what you were told?

All she did was come up with more questions.

Wasn't it said that people start acting completely differently after a blow to the head? Could that have happened to me and just not shown up until now?

She panicked as the shower stall seemed to crowd in on her. She quickly rinsed off and climbed out. As she dried herself off, she told herself she was better off not thinking about any of this. After her accident, her parents had urged her to forget it had even happened. It was easy enough to do when her wound healed and left nothing but the faint scar. She wished she could go back to that time and forget it all over again.

Dana took her time drying her hair and putting on some makeup to hide the shadows that darkened her eyes. She did everything possible to help her put a little bit of distance before going back out there.

When she finally did, she found the bed neatly made up and no sign of Mac. Then she heard the shower running in the guest room.

A search of the refrigerator revealed she didn't have much left. It didn't seem to matter to Duffy, as he happily tried to nose his way past her to see if there was anything there for him.

"You're out of luck," she informed the dog. "There's not even anything here for your master and me."

"He figures anytime a refrigerator door is open, it's meant for him." Mac's hair still glistened with water droplets as he entered the room. "Come on, I'll take you grocery shopping."

"That must be an exciting prospect for you," she said drily.

"Only if we can find some of those ladies in white uniforms giving out free snacks." He tossed his keys up into the air and caught them. "You do it at the right time, you can make a meal out of it."

Dana nudged the large dog to one side and closed the door. She presented Mac with a stony stare. She wasn't going to let him charm her out of her bad mood just yet. "Just as long as we don't talk about scars anymore."

"And here I was going to show you the cute one on my butt."

She didn't smile. "I can see that you think there might

have been more to my fall off that chair. I don't know if there was and I don't want to know."

Mac grew still. "Sometimes you're better off if you know the truth."

"My parents have never lied to me. Just leave it alone, Mac. I mean it." She privately resolved to remain firm on the issue. Now she knew she wasn't eager for answers that could change her perception of her family. She'd already lost so much, she didn't want to lose any more.

He shrugged.

Dana felt a small victory at Mac's capitulation, but she had a good idea it was still far from over. If she knew her PI, he'd find a way to tackle it from another direction.

Mac eyed the mega grocery store with a wary eye. There wasn't any way this place could be called a mere grocery store. Not when they had video rentals in one corner, a pharmacy in the other, along with a florist and even a popular fast-food franchise inside.

"All they'd have to do is sell furniture and you'd be all set." He pushed the cart for Dana while she consulted her list and put things in the basket.

"I don't come here as often as I used to," she admitted. "Probably because there was a store not far from the office and it was easier to stop by there after work."

He grinned when she added a box of large dog biscuits to the basket. Duffy would definitely be her friend for life.

Mac never thought of grocery shopping as a fun activity. Truthfully, he avoided it all costs. His idea of grocery shopping was stopping long enough to fill the cart with a variety of frozen dinners, coffee and any junk food that appealed to him.

Dana had different ideas when she shopped. She took the time to carefully examine every item before she dropped it into the cart. But he did like watching her small frown as she made her examinations. At the same time, he was never so grateful as when they were in the checkout line and her items were being scanned. Dana wrote out a check and handed it to the cashier. A moment passed before the woman smiled uncertainly.

"I'm sorry, Ms. Madison, but I have to call the manager about this," she said, picking up the phone next to her register.

Dana was surprised. "I've written checks here for larger amounts than this," she said. "Is there a new policy?"

The checker didn't reply as she turned away to speak softly into the phone. A minute barely passed before a man wearing a white shirt and tie approached them.

"Ms. Madison." He also spoke softly as he steered them away from the checkstand. "I thought you understood the last time you were in here that we can no longer accept your checks."

"What are you talking about?" She kept her voice low. "Are you saying something is wrong with my check?" She felt the heat of Mac's body behind her, and it gave her comfort. She had a horrible feeling this wouldn't be pleasant.

The man hesitated before explaining. "I'm sorry, Ms. Madison, but in the past two months, four of your checks have been returned by the bank due to insufficient funds. While you were fairly prompt in making them good, the management does have a policy about this type of situation when it happens too often. As you know, I explained that to you when this last happened. Naturally, if you pay cash or use your ATM card…" His voice fell off under her glacial stare.

She felt light-headed as the words rang inside her brain. "I have never bounced a check in my life," she said slowly and succinctly. "And I haven't been in this store for at least three months. There has to be a mistake."

The manager glanced past her to Mac, who stood silently by her side. The man flushed. "I'm afraid there's no mistake, Ms. Madison. In fact, I was the one to assist you the last two times when you came here to settle the problem."

Dana couldn't hear anything over the roaring in her head. "I don't care what you're saying. I know I wasn't here."

"Dana." Mac's quiet voice cut through her protests. "Never mind." He pulled his wallet out. "I'll take care of the groceries. We'll settle this later once we get a few more facts."

She refused to budge. "No, I want this settled now." She fixed the manager with a steely stare. "I have not been in this store for months. There is a mistake here."

Mac pulled out his ATM card and quickly took care of the bill. Once finished, he took Dana's arm and literally pulled her out of the store.

"What are you doing?" She tried to dig in her heels, but he wasn't having any of it.

"Dammit, Dana, either you go along peacefully or so help me I will throw you over my shoulder and carry you out of here," he told her with clenched teeth. He somehow managed to steer the shopping cart with one hand and keep a firm hand on her arm.

Dana had no choice but to stumble along or fall on her face. She ran beside him in order to keep up with his longer stride. Her breathing grew labored as she fought back angry tears.

"Why did he say all those horrible things to me?" she demanded as they stopped at the rear of the Explorer.

"He said all those horrible things because you bounced checks in his store. People tend to get testy when too many checks are returned due to insufficient funds," he replied, popping the back of the vehicle open and stowing grocery bags there. He pushed her onto the passenger seat and walked around to the driver's side. "For him, it was nothing personal. Just business."

"I don't care if it is just business. I didn't do it!" she yelled.

Mac twisted in the seat and grabbed her shoulders. "Listen to me." He spoke in a harsh voice guaranteed to grab her attention. "If it wasn't you who bounced those checks, it was someone who pretended to be you. That means they also have to look enough like you to pull it off, in case anyone working here is familiar with you. Someone has a major grudge against you, Dana. They're doing everything possible to have you embarrassed and they're doing a good job of it. So just remain calm, and we'll figure this out."

"So now we know for sure I have a look-alike running around pretending to be me," she said bitterly, flopping back in her seat. The frown on her face and arms crossed in front of her chest were indications she was more than frustrated, she was furious. The bright spots of pink dotting each cheek seemed to grow in intensity as her temper flared higher.

Mac remained quiet as Dana cast curses on the person who'd orchestrated everything that had happened to her so far. He stifled a sigh. He could see he wasn't going to be able to get through to her until she had a chance to calm down.

Mac didn't see it as a good sign.

This woman was doing a hell of a number making Dana's life a living hell. He'd even bet she'd been in the woods behind Dana's house that morning. That was why Duffy went crazy.

He switched on the engine and set the vehicle in gear. "We've got some work to do."

Dana didn't say another word during the drive back to her house.

Mac couldn't blame her. It looked like someone had been

spying on them, and had managed to blacken Dana's name at her grocery store and probably even her bank if she'd found a way to access Dana's accounts.

And now it looked like her parents had lied to her. The people she'd always trusted. It wasn't like his family, where his mother lied by saying she loved him, then left him behind. Or Faith claiming to love him—until she decided she didn't want to be married to a cop anymore and went out looking for a replacement before she'd even dumped him. Or the few other women in his life who'd always left because they couldn't handle his darker side.

The lies told to Dana were more serious because it looked like there was much more to her accident than they ever wanted her to know.

How did you get answers when one person involved was dead and the other unable to communicate?

"Where do you keep your bank statements?" he asked the moment they entered the house. He set the grocery bags on the kitchen counter. Duffy immediately balanced on his hind legs with his front feet planted on the counter's surface as he burrowed his head in the bag that held the box of Milk Bones. "And your boxes of checks. Anything that has to do with your personal finances. Are they kept here at home or at your office?"

"In my home office."

He headed for the office. "When was the last time you balanced your account?"

She closed her eyes, thinking back. "It's been a few months. What with Dad's death, Mom's illness and so much going on at the office, I haven't found the time."

"Then I suggest we don't waste any time checking it out." He started opening desk drawers until he found the file he was looking for. He pulled out several fat envelopes with the bank's return address printed in the corner. He also found other envelopes stuffed in the file folder. He held them up. "Personal knowledge of these kind of envelopes tells me they're bounced check notifications."

"It can't be. I have overdraft protection," Dana explained, bewildered by what she was seeing. "If there were problems the bank would have called me."

Mac didn't bother asking permission, he just started tearing envelopes open and studying the contents.

"Three checks written out to Kitty's House. Shop known for its marital aids and daring leather clothing," he explained.

Dana choked.

"Two of these were written to Ned's Place. Funny, I thought his was a cash-only business," he muttered, continuing to sort out the checks.

He made two piles of checks, one for the usual household payments and the other for places he knew Dana would never frequent. By the time he finished, they both realized what had happened to Dana's overdraft protection. It had been maxed out. He pulled out a check paid to Dana's mortgage company and one written to an adult bookstore. He wasn't an expert in handwriting analysis, but the two signatures looked identical to him. He chose six checks at random and stuffed them into an envelope. He knew someone who could study the handwriting and see if there was any difference in the signatures.

"I don't need this." Dana rubbed the spot between her eyebrows. She left the room.

"You could help me here," Mac called after her.

"From what I can see, you're doing just fine on your own," she snapped. "Since coffee would only make my nerves even more jangled, I'm going to have a small glass of wine."

I probably shouldn't drink any more wine. I always seem to wake up with a headache when I do have some.

Mac shot out of the chair and reached the kitchen just a few steps behind Dana. He took the wine bottle out of her hand and lifted it to the light. He shook it slightly and watched a faint cloud settle down to the bottom.

"What now?" she cried.

"That's what we need to find out. It's something I should have thought of before when you said it was starting to give you migraines," he said, stashing the bottle in a paper bag.

Dana pressed her hand against her stomach. She felt as if a gallon of acid had just been dumped into it. "Mac, you're scaring me."

"Believe me, right now *I'm* scaring me." He put the bag to one side. "You said nights you had a glass of wine you'd wake up with a bad headache. Was it because you had a restless night? Trouble sleeping?"

Dana thought back and slowly shook her head. "Actually, once I turned out the light, I never seemed to remember anything until morning. But I always woke up with a bad headache. I was beginning to think I'd developed some kind of reaction to the wine when I had the same problem with this new bottle."

"Let me check this out first," he said. He stuffed the envelope containing the six canceled checks in his jacket pocket and picked up the wine bottle. "While I'm doing this, I want you to go down to the bank and close out any of your personal accounts. You don't need to give them a reason. Just do it. Ask for a cashier's check. Then find yourself another bank and open your accounts there. Do you keep all your important papers in a safety deposit box?"

"Not all of them. Some I keep here," she replied.

"Take everything with you. Don't leave anything here. Empty out the old safety deposit box and get a new one. You might even consider doing the same with your business accounts. In fact, have your accountant audit all the accounts. Just to be on the safe side.'' He looked around. ''Do me a favor and also check all your office's computer files. Maybe now you'll reconsider the idea that a temp messed up those files.''

Dana heaved a deep sigh. ''Something tells me I'm not going to like what I find.''

But she wasted no time in booting up her computer. From the moment she checked her first file and discovered it had been accessed a few days earlier, she knew what she would find. Each file gave her the same story.

''The only thing she hasn't done is interfere with my mother,'' she muttered.

''She's done a real number on your bank accounts.'' He stood behind her and looked over her shoulder at the computer monitor. ''The first thing we're going to do is encrypt your system. You'll need a password for every file. Not an easy one, either. And you are not to write it down anywhere. Keep it in your head and don't tell anyone. Not even me.''

Dana buried her face in her hands. She hadn't expected control of her life to be so viciously taken out of her hands.

''Is she doing what I think she's doing?'' she whispered.

''Only if you're thinking she's taking over your life, step by step.''

Chapter 12

Mac wasted no time in encrypting all of Dana's computer files. When he finished, she followed his instructions. She thought of a password she prayed no one else would guess. Now all she could do was hope that her enemy wouldn't somehow break into her mind and discover one of her last secrets.

"I don't want to leave you alone any more than I have to. And I need to get these to a couple of experts I know," he told her, gesturing with the bag holding the bottle of wine and the envelope filled with the canceled checks. "I called the neighborhood's security patrol. I told them who I was and asked for additional drive-bys. I told them you have a stalker. I know, I know." He noticed the look in her eye. "I've said more than once I don't think all that much of them. But they do patrol the area and they might see something we don't. I told them your stalker is a woman who's pretending to be you. I asked them not to make any contact but to call me. If she shows up here

again, she might not be so lucky. What else do you need
to do before you can go with me?''

She shrugged. The lump in her throat wouldn't allow for
speech.

Mac pulled her into his arms and kept them tightly
wrapped around her. He rested his chin on top of her head.
''Would you believe me if I told you we're closing in on
her?''

''No.'' Her voice was ragged with resignation. ''She
seems to keep finding something new to taunt us with.''

He leaned back so he could kiss her. His mouth lingered
on hers.

''She's not going to win, Dana,'' he whispered against
her lips. ''She's starting to make mistakes. She's pretended
to be you and written checks out of your bank account. A
big one there. Her emptying your bank accounts is another
big one. People who know you are seeing her. No matter
how much she resembles you, there's going to be someone
who will see the difference—and that's when it will start
to fall apart.''

''That's understandable if she's going to take over my
life.'' She inhaled the spicy scent of his skin. ''But you're
not going to let her, are you?''

''She doesn't have a chance,'' he vowed, kissing her
again. ''Let's finish what you need to do here, then we'll
get out.''

Dana nodded. ''It shouldn't take long.''

Mac followed her back into her office and took possession of the chair by Dana's desk.

She sat down and went through her checking account
statements. She looked ready to cry when the ending balance came out the same no matter how many times she
rechecked it: zero.

''I had no idea,'' she groaned. ''And I should have. After

all, she's been in my house more than once. Why wouldn't she have taken my money, too?"

"Where's your box of checks?" Mac asked.

Dana pulled it out of her bottom desk drawer. She checked each book.

"The third one down is missing," she announced. "Since I just put a new book of checks in my checkbook, it would have been some time before I noticed it." She turned to her computer and went on-line. "Twenty of the twenty-five missing checks have already been cashed." She sat back, shattered by the alarming information. "You're right. She could have gotten into the company files, too." She reached for her phone.

Mac listened to Dana talk to the company controller. After a brief apology for disturbing him on the weekend, she asked that he begin a company-wide audit first thing Monday morning. Judging from Dana's responses, Mac guessed the man was questioning her reason for the out-of-the-blue request. She explained she feared there was money being withdrawn by an unauthorized person. It took her some time to assure the shaken man that she knew it wasn't due to him or his handling of the accounting department.

After she finished her call, she looked at Mac. "Let's get this over with."

With Mac standing behind her as a silent guard, she went to her bank and began the process. She cashed in a bond that allowed her to settle the balance due on the overdraft protection, and left a token amount in the checking account to cover any outstanding checks. She emptied her safety deposit box and left the building as quickly as possible.

Mac was with her every step of the way as she performed the tasks that she hoped would offer her some protection until they found the woman.

She doesn't want to just overturn your life, Dana. She wants to destroy you.

Dana had no idea where that thought came from, but the reality of the statement echoing through her head struck her hard. It seemed the woman was getting more blatant by the moment.

If she truly wanted to destroy Dana, how far would she go?

Dana feared it could come down to a fight for her very life.

Mac abruptly made an illegal U-turn and sped in the opposite direction.

"I thought we were going to the crime lab," Dana said.

"We're still going there, but I need to check something out first."

"Why are we here?" she asked, when he parked in front of the Madison home.

"We've got more questions, right? Let's see if Harriet can give us some answers."

Harriet's smile dimmed when she identified her visitors. "What's wrong?" She grabbed his arm and dragged them both inside. "What's happened?"

"Nothing yet," he replied. "I just have some questions I hope you can answer."

"How is Moms?" Dana asked.

"She's doing fine, dear. So much better that the one I worry about is you. Come on back to the kitchen." She led them back to the room redolent with the domestic fragrance of cinnamon and other spices. She waved for them to sit at the breakfast bar while she gathered up cups and plates.

Mac's mouth watered as she set a cup of coffee and large cinnamon roll in front of him.

"What do you need to know?" Harriet asked, sitting down with a cup of coffee of her own.

Dana looked to Mac. Her eyes telegraphed that she knew what he was going to ask. No matter how much it hurt any of them, the questions had to be answered. It was time to know the truth.

Mac quickly chewed and swallowed. "What do you know about the time when Dana fell and cut her head open?"

"Only what I've heard from her parents," the housekeeper answered. "The scar along her hairline was pretty red and angry looking then. Alice told me about Dana's fall and how her early memories were wiped out afterward."

"So they told you I fell and struck my head on a shelf?" Dana cut in.

The older woman frowned. "Yes, of course. Was there a reason why they wouldn't tell me? I didn't start working for the Madisons until they moved here months after Dana's accident."

"Moved here after my accident?" Dana shook her head. "No, I've always lived here."

"So Dana wasn't practically born in this house?" Mac sipped his coffee, wishing his at home would come out this rich and flavorful.

Harriet patted Dana's hand. "No, in fact, they lived in another town. About twenty or thirty miles north of here, if I remember correctly. They advertised for a live-in housekeeper, and I was looking for some stability. I got that and more. Alice and Jeremy invited me to feel like a part of the family from almost the beginning."

Mac digested the information. "Do you remember where they moved from?"

She named the town. "Why are you asking about something that happened so long ago? Why do you think Dana's accident has something to do with what's happening to her now?"

"You tell her," Dana said in a choked voice. "I can't."

Harriet looked from one to the other. "Tell me what?"

"When Dana's parents told you about her accident, do you remember exactly what they said about it?"

"Oh my, this was so long ago," she murmured. "From what I recall, Alice said Dana was climbing on a chair to get a toy and fell off the chair. She hit her head against a corner of one of the shelves and cut her head open. The poor baby ended up with some stitches and had to spend a couple days in the hospital. She didn't remember any of what happened. Alice never said why they moved here not long after it happened."

Harriet turned to Dana. "What happened, honey?" A horrifying thought suddenly came to her. She glared at Mac. "If you're thinking that this head injury did something to her that didn't surface until now, you are very wrong. This girl does not have a split personality," she said with finality.

"Nothing like that," he told her. "I happened to get a good look at Dana's scar. I can tell you for a fact that scar didn't come from connecting with a sharp piece of wood."

She looked confused. "What do you mean it didn't happen that way? Are you saying Alice and Jeremy lied about it?"

"Yes, I am," he said bluntly.

"But why? If Dana didn't hit her head, how was she so badly hurt? You can't think one of them did it?"

"I never thought they did. Perhaps they were protecting someone. The person who did hurt Dana," he replied. "Her scar came from a knife wound. Someone went after her with a knife and sliced the skin." He went on to explain. "If she'd hit the corner of a shelf, the scar would have been wider, probably even a bit jagged. Dana's scar is a clean line. Like this one." He rolled up his sleeve to reveal a thin line across his forearm. "I got this when a teenager high on drugs thought he could slice and dice me."

Harriet's gasp gave him the answer he expected. She didn't miss the similarity.

"But why would they tell such a lie?" she whispered. She looked around as if she feared they would be overheard.

"The most obvious reason would be that they didn't want people to know Dana had been attacked with a knife. The question now is, who did it?" He took a deep breath. He didn't look at Dana as he voiced his request. "I want to talk to Alice Madison, Harriet."

"No!" Dana cried out.

Harriet sighed. "She's not supposed to have any stress, Mac. There had to be a good reason for them to lie about it. I refuse to believe Jeremy or Alice had anything to do with this," she said swiftly, in case that thought occurred to him.

"Even if neither of them wielded the knife, that doesn't mean they don't know who did. We need to find that out. For Dana's sake," he said in a low voice. "Someone wiped out her checking account. There's a good chance that person could be skimming money from the business accounts. Dana's having an audit run on the books. I promise you I will be tactful. I won't do anything to upset her, but if there's a way we can get some answers, we need to do something as soon as possible."

"There has to be another way," Dana argued, grabbing Mac's arm.

He shook his head. "There isn't."

"Her speech is still a little difficult to understand," Harriet said slowly. "I won't let you see her alone."

"Fine by me."

"It isn't fine by me." Dana glared at Mac.

He took her hand in his, curving his fingers around hers. "That woman was standing outside your house while we were there," he said softly. "We need to find her."

Harriet glanced at the phone as she stood up. "I should call Barbara and see if Alice is awake, but the woman can be a little too overprotective at times. We'll just hope this is a good time for Alice."

As Mac followed Harriet up the stairs, he could see that while Dana might not have been born with a platinum spoon in her mouth, she still didn't lack for anything. He would have thought a house filled with antique furniture would be dark and forbidding, but they'd managed to keep it warm and homey with the use of fresh flower arrangements and large windows that allowed the light to come in.

When they reached the master bedroom, Harriet knocked once on the door and stepped inside.

"Yes, Harriet?" A woman wearing navy pants and a white blouse stared curiously at Mac, who stood behind the housekeeper. She noticed Dana standing next to him and nodded a silent greeting.

"Hello, Barbara. I've brought Alice some company," she informed the nurse. "I just made a fresh pot of coffee and cinnamon rolls. Why don't you take a break while we visit with Alice."

Mac stifled a grin as he listened to the housekeeper's less-than-subtle bulldozer approach to getting the nurse out of the room.

"I'm not so sure that's a good idea," Barbara said uncertainly, looking from one to the other.

"Of course, it is." Harriet took her arm and steered her out of the room. "You girls work very hard. I know Ms. Madison appreciates all you do. But we're here now, and if there's a problem I will call you immediately. Go down, have your coffee and a cinnamon roll. Don't worry, I baked all the calories out." She winked at her before closing the door on the astonished nurse.

"She cooks. She shuttles people around like pieces on a

chessboard. You really need to marry me now.'' Mac grinned.

"Harrumph! If you're going to marry anyone, marry my Dana,'' she told him, guiding him toward the rear of the room.

"Harriet,'' Dana protested softly, but she was ignored.

Mac couldn't miss the difference of atmosphere in the room. Classical music played softly in the background and the colors were meant to be soothing, but none of it could disguise the room for what it was. A glorified hospital room.

The head of the bed had been raised so the occupant could see her visitors as they approached her.

Mac's first thought was that Alice Madison seemed to be a good twenty years older than he knew her to be. Snowy white hair was brushed back from a face that was just as pale, but unlined. Her eyes were open and watching them. Though dimmed from pain and illness, they were still the same brilliant cobalt color as Dana's.

"Harriet?'' The name was slightly slurred.

"Hello, dear.'' Harriet dropped a kiss on her cheek. "I do believe you're looking better today.''

"He?'' Alice Madison looked past Harriet. A faint smile touched her lips as her gaze rested on Dana. For a moment, fear clouded her features, but it disappeared quickly.

"Hello, Moms,'' Dana said softly.

"Alice, this is John McKenna. He's a friend of Dana's.''

Alice looked fearful again.

"No,'' she moaned.

Mac kept Dana's hand tightly clasped in his. He'd remained behind Harriet. He sensed the woman wouldn't feel comfortable if he came any closer.

"Mrs. Madison, I am not here to frighten you.'' He spoke in a low soothing voice. "I'm here to help Dana.''

"She—'' Alice looked frustrated as she tried to form the

words. She grabbed Harriet's hand with a surprising show of strength, and stared at Dana with wide eyes. "She's not Dana." The words came out slightly garbled but clear enough for Mac to hear.

"Not Dana?" He knew the woman was too frail to lie to him. "Mrs. Madison, this is Dana, your daughter."

Alice moaned and shook her head.

"Mrs. Madison." He thought he'd try a different tactic but worried the woman's agitation would make matters worse. "Can you tell me what really happened when Dana hurt herself?"

He wanted to hit himself when he saw the tears gather in the older woman's eyes, but he knew he had to find out one way or another. Whatever knowledge Dana had from that time was securely locked away in a corner of her brain.

"She didn't cut her head on a shelf, did she," he pressed in a soft voice. "You told people that because you didn't want the truth to come out."

"She—she did it. She hurt her." Alice spoke haltingly. She had to stop every few words to regain her breath. "She wanted…to…cut her face."

Mac felt the chill steal through his veins. He heard Dana's soft gasp, then felt her grip tighten on his hand.

"Who wanted to cut Dana's face, Mrs. Madison?"

"Da—" she gasped. "Darcy."

Dana cried out.

"Darcy." Mac repeated the name, feeling a blow directly to his midsection. Now it all made sense. Why a woman could get away with pretending to be Dana. Why people who knew Dana were convinced they were talking to her, not an imposter. No wonder Dana was so afraid she had lost her mind. She had no idea someone was running around with the same face. "I'm going to take a wild guess here that the Darcy you mentioned is Dana's twin sister."

Alice nodded. Her chin trembled with the emotions she'd held in so long.

"She—" She waved her hands in an attempt to make her point as she fought for air in order to finish the sentence. "She hated—Dana's face."

"So she tried to cut her face off," he said slowly. The stricken look on Alice's face was answer enough. Dana's soft cry was filled with pain. He released her hand and wrapped an arm around her shoulders. He curved his hand around her cheek as she pressed her face against his chest.

Alice now cried freely. Harriet hurried over to Alice and gathered her in her arms. She hitched herself up onto the side of the bed and rocked Alice back and forth as if she were a small child. Alice clutched at the housekeeper with grasping hands, holding on to her as if Harriet could protect her from whatever demons had haunted her all these years.

Mac stood there trying to assimilate all he'd heard and make sense of it.

"What happened to Darcy? Where is she now?" He had a sneaking feeling he knew some of this. Just not all. "And if she's Dana's twin and alive, why didn't Dana ever know about her?"

Alice's face contorted in fear. She started to rise up, then fell back. The shock had caused unconsciousness.

Harriet looked up. "Oh, Alice," she murmured. "Why couldn't you tell me?"

"Moms!" Dana ran to the other side of the bed. She picked up her mother's hand and brought it to her cheek.

"I'm sorry," Mac began. "I didn't mean to…"

Harriet offered a weary smile. "I know you didn't. Alice has always had trouble handling pressure. I know you want more information about this Darcy. I will see what else I can learn."

"After hearing this, we have to agree that this Darcy is the one making Dana's life a living hell," he said.

Dana looked up, still stunned by her mother's revelation. "Why was I never told I have a sister? Where has she been all this time?"

"We'll find out," Harriet promised. "But for now, your mother needs to rest. I will call you as soon as I learn something. I promise."

Dana looked reluctant. "I need to stay with her."

"No sweetheart, you should go," Harriet informed her. "I will call you."

As Mac and Dana reached the ground floor, the nurse was just approaching the stairs. She glanced at them warily.

"Harriet wanted to stay with her a little longer," Dana explained, as she and Mac headed for the door. "I think they want to be alone."

Mac expected Dana to explode after the awful secret she'd just learned. Instead, she quietly secured her seat belt and sat back. When she finally broke her silence, her words were quiet and filled with pain.

"It's not every day you discover the people you've always trusted have lied to you almost all your life."

Dana remained in the truck while Mac took the items into the crime lab. She assured him she would be all right, and that for now she needed to be alone. She had her eyes closed and was resting her head against the seat when he came out some time later.

"You didn't take very long," she greeted him.

"Turned out to be pretty easy." He climbed in behind the wheel. "The wine had enough sedative in it to knock you out for the night. One of the side effects of that particular drug is headaches. With you already having migraines, it was much too easy to trigger them when you had some wine."

"I was drugged?" she repeated on a higher note.

"Good thing you just quit drinking it instead of dumping

it out.'' He pulled the envelope out of his jacket pocket. He slid two checks out of the envelope and placed them side by side on the padded armrest. "I was also able to track down someone to study the six checks. The handwriting is so similar, it took him awhile to find the differences.''

"But he found something. He found proof I didn't write all those checks.'' Her excitement grew as she looked at the two checks. She still couldn't see any differences in the handwriting. Except, she knew she hadn't written one of them.

"He found proof,'' Mac confirmed. He put the checks back in the envelope and stuck the envelope in the glove compartment. He started up the engine and drove out of the parking lot.

"How could they keep such important information from me?'' Dana stared out the window but didn't see the stores and strip malls they passed. She cast her mind back in time, but every time she thought of that day she hit a mental wall.

Mac shot a quick glance at her as he drove. "Did you ever see pictures of yourself as a baby in one of those fancy carriages or a wind-up swing? You wearing nothing but a diaper as you're learning to walk and you fall more than you take steps. Maybe toddling around the front while your parents look on in parental pride?''

She shook her head jerkily. "Kind of hard to have pictures of something that didn't exist. Mac? Why did she hate me so much? What could I have done to her to deserve such hatred? We never even had a chance to know each other.''

"Right now, I can't give you an answer. But I'd say it had nothing to do with you and everything to do with her. For some reason, your sister tried to slice your face off because she didn't want anyone to have *her* face.''

Dana reared back. Her eyes burned like blue-black marbles as the color fled from her face. Her lips tried to form words but none could come. She scrambled for the door latch.

"Stop, please stop," she gasped.

Mac took one look at her white features and immediately pulled over to the side of the road. He'd barely stopped the truck when Dana freed herself and almost fell as she climbed out. Mac got out and stood nearby as she dropped to her knees and retched. He dug out a bottle of water he had in the back seat and broke the seal. He carried it over to her, handing her the bottle and his handkerchief.

She rinsed her mouth and then took several swallows. As she started to climb to her feet, he took her arm and helped her up.

They didn't speak another word as he drove back to her house.

When they walked into the kitchen, the telephone was ringing.

Mac glanced at her caller ID box. "It's Harriet."

Dana shook her head and walked out of the room. She didn't stop until she reached her bedroom. It was starting to get dark, but she didn't bother turning on a light. She knew the timer would switch on a lamp in a couple of hours, anyway. She curled up in a tight ball on the bed, grateful for the enveloping darkness.

She didn't move when the bed dipped slightly and Mac sat down next to her hip.

"She wants us to come out there tomorrow," he said quietly. "She found something she thought we would find informative."

She didn't move when he brushed his hand across her cheek.

"More lies?" Bitterness tainted her words. "That's all I've heard so far. Why should I go out there to hear more?"

The bed shifted even more as he lay down beside her. He wrapped her in his arms. "Because you need to know." He kissed her brow. "Go to sleep, Dana."

Mac remained with her until her slow, even breathing told him she'd succumbed to slumber. Even then, he stayed with her longer because he was reluctant to release her.

He would have stayed there but he needed to check some things out.

After he fed Duffy and put the dog outside, he made himself a quick sandwich and settled in Dana's home office. He did a quick search of all her desk drawers until he found what he was looking for. Dana had pointed it out earlier, and he'd made a mental note to check it out later. Later had arrived.

Everything a person needed to know about Dana was written down in a small notebook. He even found insurance policy numbers.

"No wonder Darcy could access all her accounts," he muttered.

"What have you found?"

He looked up to find Dana standing in the doorway. She'd draped a blanket around her shoulders, and looked small and defeated. She walked in, the blanket dragging on the floor, and sat down in the chair set in a corner.

"While it's an excellent record, it turned out to be helpful for someone who wanted to know everything about you," he said.

She rubbed her eyes and yawned. "I can always put it through the shredder at work."

"Changing everything now will do a lot more good." He tossed the notebook on her desk. He paused. "I found something else." He reached over and tapped a button on her answering machine.

"This is Dana. I'm not at home right now, but I would

like to hear from you. Please leave your name and tele-
phone number. I will return your call as soon as possible."

Dana pushed her hair away from her face as she tried to figure out what was wrong. She frowned as she finally figured out what it was. "That's not me. That's my message, but that's not my voice."

"Close, but not close enough," he agreed. He'd been surprised when he first heard the voice on the machine. He replayed the message several times, noting the difference in nuances and tone. There was a sultry cast that would fascinate any man. The speaker was a woman who was aware of her sexuality and reveled in it.

The woman who'd taped the message on the answering machine was the same one who had called Mac that night.

Mac looked at Dana, whose eyes were shadowed with fatigue and sorrow. Even her shoulders were slumped.

He wanted to see that show of old-fashioned spunk she'd displayed in the past.

He wanted to make her smile for him. And him alone.

He wanted to spend time with her where no one else would intrude.

He vowed that once this was over, they would get away from here and just concentrate on each other. Once there were no worries to haunt them, he was also going to make sure she knew just how strongly he felt about her.

He wasn't about to let Dana go.

How much have they learned about me?

She didn't stand as close to the house as she had before. Not with that dog roaming around outside. Dogs were messy and smelly things. The disgusting creatures brought dirt and other nasty things into the house. Once she had Mac under her thumb, she'd convince him the dog had to go.

The light in Dana's home office was on, and she could

see a hint of two figures against the closed mini-blinds. She could visualize the layout of the room and knew the larger figure was Mac.

She really was growing tired of her game. She needed to find a way to bring it all to a head. If she worked it right, she'd walk away with everything. And those who'd made her life hell for all these years would be the ones suffering.

The anticipation of soon beginning her new life brought a smile to her lips.

A smile that was cold enough to freeze water.

Chapter 13

Dana was hazily aware of Mac cradling her in his arms, and of being carried out of her office. She opened heavy-lidded eyes.

"What are you doing?" Her words came out slightly slurred.

"Putting you to bed." He carefully set her on her feet by the bed.

Dana looped her arms around his neck. "Come with me." She fiddled with his shirt collar.

"You're not awake." He pulled the blanket off and dropped it at the end of the bed.

She moved her hands lower. "I'm awake. And so are you."

Mac groaned.

"I need you, Mac," she whispered, unbuttoning his shirt and spreading it open. She peppered his bare chest with kisses. "You make me feel complete." She pulled him down onto the bed with her.

Mac peeled off his shirt and flung it to the floor. Dana unfastened his jeans, which soon followed. Dana's clothing was removed and tossed to one side also.

His mouth covered hers, his tongue tangling with hers. Dana moaned as Mac slowly explored every inch of her body with his lips. So far, he'd only gotten as far as her shoulder and she was positive she would need to be peeled off the ceiling.

"Mac," she keened, reaching for him with anxious hands.

He adroitly shifted away from her. His mouth settled hotly on a spot just above her left breast. She jerked under the branding touch.

"Let's not rush into anything, sweetheart."

She kept reaching for him, and each time he'd avoid her grasp. Mac finally circled her wrists with his hands and anchored them to the mattress.

Dana moaned and whimpered as Mac feasted on her breast. And she almost screamed when he pulled the nipple into his mouth at the same time as he nudged two fingers into her softness. The electric arc from one area to the other didn't stop as he continued to make love to her in ways she hadn't imagined. Her hips rose up to meet the tantalizing feathering of his fingertips.

Dana wanted to close her eyes and allow the sensations to flow over her. But she had to keep them open because she couldn't believe what was happening wasn't a dream.

With the drapes drawn, the room was a dark cavern where she couldn't see the man stretched out above her. All she could do was experience what Mac was doing to her. She could feel his erection hard against her stomach. She arched up, nudging her knee between his legs. His sharply uttered curse told her she'd gotten the expected reaction. She couldn't hold back a laugh.

"This can go both ways, woman." He used his knee to

nudge her legs farther apart before he settled against her hips.

"Yes, it can." She sighed when she felt his hardness slowly enter her. It was a sigh that turned into a groan when he paused, then slowly retreated. "Mac!" she moaned, clutching him.

He ignored her entreaties and remained inside her. Then Dana tried to take over by clenching her inner muscles. He muttered a curse about uppity women as his body gave in to her temptation. She hugged him tightly, and he quickened his pace until they both succumbed to the skies.

Dana lay back, feeling the relaxation take over as her body seemed to melt into the mattress.

"You sure woke up fast," Mac muttered in her ear. He rolled over onto his side, keeping one arm braced across her waist.

She smiled. "It must have had something to do with the way you carried me off to bed."

"Just doing my job, ma'am."

Dana smiled and snuggled closer.

"Sleep," Mac advised, after brushing his lips across her forehead.

"You were wonderful," she murmured as she closed her eyes and did just that.

She only awoke once, later. The room was dark but not frightening. Not when she could feel Mac's arms around her. She knew exactly when he woke up and sensed she was awake.

He didn't say a word. He merely got up, nudged Duffy out of the room and closed the door. Then he returned to the bed, and once again took her to heights she had no idea existed.

Afterward she lay there trying to catch her breath and reclaim her senses.

It was as she and Mac had fallen into the abyss that she realized something. She didn't want what they had to end.

She'd fallen in love with John "Mac" McKenna.

When Mac gathered her back into the safety of his arms again, she fell asleep. Now she felt as if everything would be all right.

She'd never felt safer.

"Harriet didn't give you any idea about what she found?" Dana asked the next morning after they'd eaten breakfast and together cleaned the kitchen.

"All she said was that we would find it helpful," he answered. He rubbed his jaw with his hand as he stared out into the backyard. "I'm hoping it'll tell us where she's been for the past twenty years and why she's here now."

Dana sighed. "I just want this to be over."

"So do I, honey." He tipped her chin upward and dropped a kiss on her nose. He opened a jar filled with dog biscuits and pulled one out. He tossed it to Duffy, who caught it in his mouth. "Payment in advance, fella. Guard the house."

Dana shook her head. "Some guard dog. He sleeps on the couch when we're gone. And he sheds."

"Yeah, but I bet your couch has never been safer. That's part of his charm. He's supposed to sleep on the couch when we're gone, and shedding is part of having a long-haired dog," Mac said, unconcerned.

Dana fixed Duffy with a glare as the dog walked over to the table and easily rested his chin on the top. "Don't think you're going to start taking your meals at the table," she warned the dog.

Mac tapped his watch crystal. "Time to go."

"Mac." She pressed her hands against her stomach, which was tap-dancing a mile a minute. "Can you think of any reason why my parents concocted such a lie for all these years?''

She knew she was on her way to emotional overload. She'd always felt so smug that she had the perfect family. They were always there for her. They gave her a well-grounded upbringing, and she'd sailed through life convinced she was the apple of her parents' eyes.

Now, in the space of weeks, she found her life turned upside down and learned her parents had kept a dangerous secret from her for twenty years that involved a twin sister she never knew she had.

No wonder she felt as if she wanted to hide in a corner. Instead, she flashed Mac a smile and walked out to the garage with him.

By the time they reached the Madison home, Dana convinced herself she was ready for anything.

''Alice was very agitated last night,'' Harriet said after greeting them. ''I think she was relieved she'd finally gotten it out in the open. She told me about a secret drawer in Jeremy's desk. She said he kept the paperwork there, but she didn't explain what the paperwork was.'' She held up a small brass key. ''This will unlock the drawer.'' She led the way into the office Jeremy Madison kept at home.

Dana stepped in and felt herself catapult back in time. She could almost imagine the faint cherry scent of the pipe tobacco her father preferred. Mac handed her the key, and she pulled out the file drawer Harriet indicated. The lock was flush against one side, and she inserted the key, turning it to one side. When the false side fell back, a thick file folder fell back with it.

Harriet walked to the door, murmuring that she'd get them coffee.

Dana didn't hear anything. She was too occupied, sitting at her father's desk and opening the file. She split the pile of papers in two and handed half to Mac. He took the chair on the opposite side of the desk and began reading.

The first thing she noticed was a birth certificate for Darcy Leigh Madison. Born six minutes before Dana. Her hands shook as she kept turning papers. Medical records for both little girls. Both in excellent physical health, although many times Darcy was noted to be a little too high-strung for her age. Then she found reports written by several nannies who freely admitted they adored little Dana, but they felt Darcy had emotional problems.

"Darcy was three years old when she was first examined by a psychiatrist," Mac announced, reading a typewritten report. "It was recommended by the family physician when she pushed you into the deep end of the swimming pool. You would have drowned if the nanny hadn't heard your screams. When asked why she did it, Darcy said you didn't deserve to have her face."

Dana grimaced at the memory. "Moms once said to Dad, it was a shame we didn't have a pool for entertaining purposes. Then she looked upset, as if she realized she'd said something wrong. I remember he didn't answer her. He just got very quiet. Now I know why."

Harriet came in carrying a tray with three cups and a carafe. She filled the cups, set one in front of each of them, and kept the third for herself.

"So many reports," Dana murmured, finding it difficult to skim even though they all said essentially the same thing. "She was barely a toddler and already the doctors had branded her as some kind of monster seed." Shuddering, she pushed them away. She buried her face in her hands. "I don't know if I can read any more of this."

"Found exactly what we need." Mac held up a sheet of paper. "Three days after your sixth birthday, Darcy decided you would no longer have the face she considered all hers. She attacked you with a steak knife. She even managed to cut you pretty badly before your father was able to take the knife away from her. She threw herself into such a rage that the doctor had to be called, and she was heavily sedated. You were taken to the hospital, and Darcy was admitted to another kind of hospital.''

''When you say a different kind of hospital—'' she licked dry lips ''—you mean a mental hospital?''

He nodded. ''After that day, the doctor felt your life was in danger as long as you and Darcy occupied the same house. Darcy was signed into a private hospital that, gathering from the statements here, cost your dad a pretty penny all these years. Your dad also jotted down notes to himself, as if he felt the need to keep some sort of journal about all this. He wrote that he didn't want anyone to know that his child had obviously blown a fuse in her brain. People they knew in their old town were told Darcy died. Once you moved, she was effectively removed from the Madison family files. You remembered nothing of the incident, so it was easy to keep you ignorant of the fact. Your parents visited her every couple of months. Those visits were particularly hard on your mother.''

''The long weekends they took,'' she murmured. She drank the coffee because she needed the caffeine to keep her going, even though she was convinced it was eating a hole in her stomach. ''Everything a lie.''

''Don't blame them, Dana. They obviously felt the need to protect you,'' Harriet explained.

Dana stared at the papers scattered across the desk. She picked up one sheet and began reading aloud.

'''Uncontrollable rage. She feels a need to be the only one,''' she spoke in a trembling voice. '''Intense hatred. Requires constant supervision. Cannot control herself if the least bit of stress is introduced. Doubtful she will ever be able to maintain a normal life.' Oh, my God,'' she whispered. "They're saying she's nothing more than an animal."

She looked up at Mac. "They just locked her away."

"She was in heavy-duty therapy," he reminded her as he held up one of the papers.

"Someone once asked Alice if she'd ever thought of having more children, and she got the saddest look on her face," Harriet remarked. "She said you were enough for her. She must have been afraid another child might turn out like Darcy."

"There's nothing here to indicate it was genetic," Mac pointed out, holding up a sheaf of papers. "What's important now is to find out how Darcy got out of the hospital and where she is now."

Harriet stood up when she heard a soft knock at the door. She went over and found the nurse waiting. The two had a whispered conversation, then the nurse left.

"Alice wants the two of you to come upstairs," Harriet announced.

Dana shook her head. "I'm not sure I could talk to her now. Not after reading all of this."

"Give her a chance," Mac suggested. "From what I've read, your mother hasn't had it all that easy. The strain from keeping all of this from you was pretty high. For whatever reason, they felt it was necessary. All we have here are doctor's reports and your father's comments. We know nothing of how your mother felt about this."

She reluctantly nodded. "Do you know what really bothers me? What if my mother hadn't recovered from her stroke?" she whispered fiercely. "Would I have ever known about these files unless I found them by accident? Or once she was better would she have destroyed them so I'd never know?"

He picked up a sheet of paper from the pile he'd been perusing. "This shows a trust account had been set up to pay for your sister's care in the event of your parents' death. I'd say your father didn't want you to know.''

His blunt words hurt.

Dana tunneled her fingers through her hair, pushing it away from her face. She was still reeling from the shock but determined to shore herself up.

After all, her father had taught her how to put on a blank face when it was necessary.

As they climbed the stairs, she looked at her surroundings with fresh eyes. Now she knew why there were so few pictures of her as a child displayed. Why her parents had never talked about those first six years of her life.

The home she'd loved so much suddenly felt foreign to her.

When they reached the door leading to the master bedroom, she reached for Mac's hand and gripped it tightly. He looked down and smiled. She wondered if he'd understand if she told him even his smile made her feel safe.

Alice Madison slowly turned toward them when they stepped into the room. The heightened color in her cheeks and frantic way her eyes darted back and forth spoke volumes about her frame of mind.

''I—'' She choked as tears streamed down her cheeks, ''I'm sorry,'' she whispered to her daughter.

''Moms.'' Dana started sobbing. She threw herself against her mother and held on tight.

By the time mother and daughter had had their cry, Alice seemed ready to talk. Mac remained in the background and allowed Alice to tell the story in her own way. Most of it they already knew, courtesy of the massive file Jeremy had kept. Alice was able to bring them up to date as she spoke of her visit to Darcy after her father's death. Alice had difficulty when she spoke of Darcy's fury that she wouldn't be allowed to leave the hospital; she'd verbally assaulted her mother. Alice had left the building a shattered woman.

A few days later, she suffered her stroke.

"Mrs. Madison, we'd like your permission to speak to the doctors at the hospital," Mac finally said.

Alice's lips trembled. "I will talk to the doctor," she replied. She turned to Dana with a smile wavering on her lips. "You were such a sweet baby. For some reason she hated you. We could never figure out why."

By the time they left, Dana's tears had been dried and she was more like the self-composed woman Mac had first met.

"I guess it's obvious that Darcy is behind everything," she said once they were settled in the vehicle. "She must blame me for her being in that hospital all this time. If she found out Moms was so ill, you'd think she'd rather go after her instead of me." She thought for a moment. "Except I'm more accessible." She half turned in the seat. "That's why she's doing this to me instead of Moms. With the business and everything, I would have more to lose, and in the long run, Moms would lose, too. She'd still be striking back against both of us."

"It sounds good to me." He started up the engine. "Can you free up some time?"

She nodded. "I'll do it."

Mac didn't ask her if she wanted to stop for something to eat. He doubted she had an appetite any more than he did.

He cursed himself for not thinking of a sister. There had been nothing in Dana's background to indicate any siblings. But dammit, he should have remembered one hard-and-fast rule. Never assume! Just because Jeremy Madison had done an excellent job of hiding Darcy Madison from the world didn't mean Mac shouldn't have found something.

It had been easy for him to wonder at first if it couldn't have been Dana all along. He doubted her when he shouldn't have. Even reminding himself that anyone would have done the same thing wasn't good enough. He should have known better. Should have remembered too many things weren't what they seemed, and should have dug way beyond the first layers. Should not have refused to believe what was now so obvious.

His mistake could have lost her to him. The thought left him ice cold.

"How about spaghetti and garlic bread for dinner?" Dana asked when they entered the house. "We are going to keep tonight just for us." She pulled out pans and filled one with water. "Dana, the woman. Mac, the man. Duffy, the dog." She looked down at the latter with a faint smile.

Mac recognized the signs. If you made up your mind to not think about something, it didn't exist.

Dana did just what she set out to do. She prepared spaghetti with a sauce with enough garlic that Mac joked a vampire wouldn't come near him for months.

After they cleaned the kitchen, Dana led him into the family room, where she turned on the television. She motioned Mac over to the couch and climbed onto his lap, where she remained the rest of the evening.

Mac looked at Dana warm in his arms and Duffy dozing on the floor by his feet. They looked so normal. As if he'd come home from a long day at the office, and Dana, the same. Would it be wrong to desire this kind of life? He hadn't been able to give it to Faith. Instead, she'd lived the uncertain life of a cop's wife, wondering each day if it would be Mac coming home or the lieutenant coming over to offer his condolences.

It was easier now. Paychecks weren't as regular, but at least he didn't get shot at as much. Still, he knew he wasn't marriage material. Not if Faith, one of the most complacent people in the world, couldn't live with him. How could he dare hope things would be different with Dana?

He forced himself to veer away from the subject. Happily

ever after sounded good in books, but it never seemed to be the same in real life.

"Hey," she protested in a low voice, wiggling a bit in his arms.

He realized he had tightened his hold, and immediately loosened his arms. "Sorry, guess I was elsewhere for a while."

Dana moved about until she could face him directly. She framed his face with her hands. "I didn't like you at first," she confessed.

He laughed. What else could he do? "Yeah, I kind of figured that out."

"I didn't think you were all that fond of me, either," she pointed out.

Mac turned his head so he could plant a kiss in the heart of her palm. "I thought you were coldhearted, opinionated, bossy, and a general pain in the butt because you wanted everything your way."

Dana pouted. "You don't have to be so honest."

"One of my better traits." He smiled. "Besides, you didn't see your expression when you walked into my office. You looked as if you wished you'd walked in there wearing latex gloves and carrying a can of Lysol. You probably even hoped for a decontamination chamber."

"I did not!" she laughed, playfully hitting him in the shoulder. "I just didn't expect a private investigator's office to look so—so rustic."

Mac roared with laughter at her description.

"Or that the private investigator was so virile instead of slimy looking, the way many of them on TV do."

"Okay, the virile comment saved your cute little butt this time. I don't think I could ever get tired of looking at your face," he murmured. "I want to wake up every morning and go to sleep every night seeing it."

She took a sharp breath. "Isn't that dangerous talk for a single man with a dog?"

"Yeah, but it seems you and I've been talking dangerous from day one. Why change things now?" He placed his hands around her throat in necklace fashion. His thumbs met in the hollow of her throat. "I'm no prime catch, sweetheart."

"And I have an insane twin sister." Her eyes darkened. "I can't think beyond that. Please don't say anything more."

Mac hefted her in his arms and stood up. He grabbed the remote control long enough to switch the television off, and turned off the lamp on the way out of the room.

Dana looped her arms around his neck and buried her face against his shoulder. She would take this and be content. She wouldn't dare ask for more.

"Duffy." Her reminder was muffled.

"Yeah, he isn't exactly potty trained." He whistled to the dog and detoured by the patio door to let the dog outside. Duffy shot him a reproachful look over his shoulder as he raced outside. "Damn dog can put across guilt as good as any mom," he muttered, carrying Dana toward the bedroom.

"I want to forget," she murmured against his throat. "I want things to be normal again."

"They will be," he soothed, laying her down on the bed. "The pieces to the puzzle are falling into place. Before you know it, life will be so damn normal you'll wish for some variety."

"No, I won't." She pulled him down on top of her. "Not once."

Mac couldn't sleep. He'd pushed the covers to his waist because he felt too warm, and crooked one arm behind his head. Dana slept peacefully by his side, and Duffy lay stretched out along the end of the bed, breathing evenly, his body twitching.

Was Mac crazy in thinking there could be a future with Dana? Everything about the two of them was opposite. But he still thought about it.

And now it seemed she was backing away by using her sister as an excuse.

Maybe it was for the best. After this was over, they might realize that what they'd shared wouldn't stand up to a normal lifestyle.

For now, he'd settle for her in his arms. Not to protect her, but to protect himself from ghosts that haunted his night.

It was the same, yet not the same. She was wearing her favorite blue dress again. And she was again sitting on the pretty stool. Except there was no mirror for her to look into. All she saw sitting across from her was another little girl in a blue dress who looked like her. She also sat on a matching stool.

"You can't stay here," the other little girl said.

"Yes, I can. My daddy says so."

The little girl smiled, but it wasn't a pretty smile. It frightened her. She wanted to call out for her daddy. She wanted her to go away.

"Daddy doesn't love you, Dana. He really loves me. He wants you to go far away," the little girl told her. "I want you to go away, too. I want you to go away and never come back."

"No, you'll go away," Dana insisted stubbornly.

The little girl stood up. "Be careful, Dana." She spoke in a hard tone at odds with her little-girl voice. "People will think you're just like me. But you don't want to be like me, do you? I bet you'd rather be dead instead of be like me."

Dana whirled away and ran as fast as she could. Except, she couldn't escape the laughter that followed her.

Dana jerked awake. It took her a moment to realize it was the middle of the night. She felt the warmth of Mac's chest against her cheek, listened to the soft rumble of his breath and felt the comforting weight of Duffy's inert body draped across her feet.

It's as if she's trying to get to me in my dreams. She wants me to think I'm just like her, she thought. *I'll just have to prove her wrong.*

As Dana fell back asleep, one bitter thought stayed with her.

Even with all she'd said about putting Darcy out of her mind, she hadn't been able to forget about her after all.

Chapter 14

First thing Monday morning, Dana called Marti and told her she wouldn't be in for a few days. She gave the explanation that she wanted to spend more time with her mother.

"After we finish with my messages, why don't you transfer me to Jack's office, so I can tell him what I'd like him to take over for me," she said, referring to her second-in-command. "It's time I make him work for the money I pay him," she joked. "I'm sure he can handle the wolves as well as I can."

"Good!" Marti verbally applauded. "It's time you realize there's others around here who can do at least a portion of your work."

"I worry about the long-term clients," Dana admitted.

"Every long-term client knew your mother, too. There's always someone who's asking how Alice is doing and asking that they be remembered. And, as you suggested, if they ask about sending flowers, I suggest a donation to the rehabilitation center. You were the one who believed they wouldn't understand if you needed to take a leave of absence because of your mother. You should have given them the chance to prove they aren't all heartless."

Dana sighed. "Control freak, that's me."

After they finished, Marti transferred her to Jack. Dana spent the next hour on the phone going over things with Jack, then hung up.

"Delegating is new for me," she confessed to Mac.

"I don't know. You sounded pretty good. It's nice to know you don't have to carry the whole load yourself, isn't it?" he whispered, then kissed her on the cheek.

Dana sat at the kitchen table looking over paperwork, as Mac did his own work. She smiled as she watched him with his cell phone pressed to one ear, talking away while he paced the kitchen. His end of the conversation told her that he was finding out what was known about her family in the town she was born in.

"Yeah, I want to know anything you can dig up," he said as he refilled his coffee cup. "Call me as soon as you hear anything. Good." He disconnected without saying goodbye. He glanced at Dana. "Are you okay?"

"I'll be better when this is all over," she said honestly.

"Amen to that." He brushed his lips across her forehead. "We've come a long way, Madison."

She leaned against him, her shoulder and head resting against his chest. "Sometimes I feel as if I'm not the same person I was a few months ago. Then I remember that I'm not. I find out my parents lied to me for years, that I'm not an only child and that my sister tried to kill me," she said in a hushed voice. "I suddenly feel as if I'm not who I always thought I was."

"I bet Abby can help you with those feelings," he said gently.

She nodded. "I'm not going to stop seeing her just because it's turned out that I don't have a split personality, after all.'' She held up her hand to halt his protest. ''There were times when deep down I honestly felt it was me. Knowing it wasn't is a big relief, but finding out about Darcy has me wondering if there is a chance I could have even a seed like that inside me…'' Her voice trailed off.

Mac kept his arms around her and rested his chin on top of her head. ''You don't need to worry,'' he assured her. ''Let's make some plans. Let's agree that when this is all over, we'll go away for a nice long vacation where all we'll need is a room with a bed and round-the-clock room service.''

She smiled. ''I'd like that. Can we find a gym, and you let me beat you up again?''

''Anything your heart desires.''

She put her arms around his neck. ''Then my heart desires you,'' she whispered, giving in to her need to kiss him.

''I need to run by my apartment and pick up more clean clothes,'' he told her once they came up for air. ''Do you mind if I leave Duffy here?''

She looked past him toward the backyard, where the large dog was happily sprawled in a shady spot. He'd already settled in as if the yard had always been his.

''I don't think he'd let you take him. You do what you need to do. We'll be here when you get back,'' she promised.

Mac kissed her again. He ran the back of his fingers along her cheek. ''Then I'll make it quick.''

Dana could still taste him on her lips as she fixed herself breakfast. She was sharing her eggs with Duffy, when the phone rang.

''Dana?''

She recognized the voice of her chief financial officer.

''Hank, I didn't expect to hear from you so soon.''

''You know me. I've always been paranoid to the ex-

treme. I've been in here since five doing some unraveling,"
he told her. "The first thing I did was run a quick scan on
our main accounts. After I looked those over, I did a little
more thorough snooping. I don't think you're going to like
what I found."

She groaned. *Not there too.* "Is it that bad?"

"Not as bad as it could be. I'm faxing you some pages
I think you need to see."

"How bad are we talking, Hank?" she whispered.

"I'm sure it could have been a hell of a lot worse if you
hadn't asked me to run the audit now. You better have the
contracts department check their files, too. I think there's
some inconsistencies there."

Dana felt her world tilt on its axis. Later she didn't remember making her way to her office where the fax machine spit out page after page. She gathered up the sheets
and began studying the figures and graphs showing the past
five months. Expense reports she'd supposedly authorized.
Paychecks for an employee she knew didn't exist.

The amount of money disappearing from the accounts
was astounding.

"We have to put a stop to this," she said crisply. "I
think the first thing we need to do is limit the number of
people who can sign a check. Put financial limits on even
that. Two signatures necessary for anything over five hundred dollars. New safeguards for the computer."

"We'll have some people thinking we don't trust them,"
he said. "They've all been with us for years."

She felt a headache coming on. "I know. Then do me a
favor. Tell them the truth. Tell them someone's trying to
ruin the business from the inside out. I know who the person is, just not how she's accomplishing all this. As soon
as she's caught, we'll set up a new checks and balances
system. In fact, ask for their input—what they'd do to protect the files."

By the time she finished her call, she couldn't even look at her breakfast. Right now, all she wanted was extra-strength aspirin.

Her headache hadn't even gone away when she heard her phone ring again. She felt a sinking sensation.

"Ms. Madison, this is Barbara, your mother's nurse—" The woman's voice brought fear to Dana's heart.

"Your mother has been very agitated today. She insists she needs to see you. Would you be able to come by?"

"I'll be there as soon as possible." She practically threw the cordless phone on the bed as she pulled clothing out of her closet.

Dana prayed she would get there in time as she raced toward her mother's house. She fled the vehicle as it stopped, and ran for the stairs. No one responded when she repeatedly punched the doorbell and pounded on the door. She dug her key out and quickly unlocked the door, pushing it open.

"Harriet!" she called out. Only silence greeted her. "No," she whimpered, running up the stairs. She ran so fast into the room that she almost stumbled.

The first person she saw was the housekeeper sitting in a nearby chair and the nurse standing off to one side.

"What's wrong?" she demanded.

"Nice to see you, Baby Dana."

The voice that sounded like her, yet didn't sound like her, interrupted whatever Harriet might have said.

Dana turned to face her mother's bed. She couldn't miss the stark fear on Alice's face. Nor the reason for it.

Now Dana understood why she dreamed of a reflection in the mirror. Darcy was her identical twin. Even if their clothing was different, Darcy's hairstyle and makeup were the same as Dana's.

"Hello, Darcy." She silently marveled at her own calm exterior. Inside, she wanted to scream and throw herself at the woman. Only one thing stopped her from attacking. The sight of a hypodermic syringe Darcy held in one hand. The needle shone silver as it rested against Alice's neck.

"Look at you. You really are a pale copy of me," Darcy said. She didn't look away as she reached to one side and picked up a pile of clothing. She tossed it in Dana's direction. It fell at Dana's feet. "Put them on. And no tricks."

Dana kept her eyes on her sister as she bent down and picked up the blouse and pants. She noticed both were identical to what Darcy wore.

"I thought she was you," Harriet explained. Her eyes glistened with tears as she looked from one to the other. "By the time I realized it wasn't—"

"Shut up!" Darcy snarled, turning on the housekeeper. "She doesn't need to hear a thing from you."

Dana moved slowly, toeing off her loafers and unfastening her pants, pushing them down past her hips. As she changed her clothing, she kept her gaze fastened on Darcy. If the woman made any dangerous moves, Dana wanted to be ready.

What would Mac do in a situation like this?

Dummy, he'd probably make sure not to get in one!

"Why do you want to hurt our mother?" she asked, hoping to keep her voice calm and steady. She couldn't pray for Mac to suddenly appear and save them. He had no idea she was even here. She hadn't left a note.

"What happens to her doesn't matter to me. *Our* mother didn't give a damn about me," Darcy sneered. "This is just to make sure you do what I want. Because if you don't—" She stroked the tip of the needle against Alice's throat. The older woman moaned softly. "Did you know air bubbles in the bloodstream are deadly? It's not even a fraction of what she deserves for shutting me away in that prison." She cast a cold glare at her mother. "She thought she could keep me there forever."

"How were you able to leave?" She hated to speak so civilly to a woman who threatened everyone around them, but she knew she had no choice. After she slipped on the cream-colored silk blouse, she carefully pulled the coffee-colored pants up, tucking the shirt in and zipping up the pants.

Darcy laughed. It was a sound Dana recognized as her own, even if Darcy's held the hint of madness.

"I didn't waste all my time in group therapy, baby sister," she mocked. "I also helped out in the office. All I needed was a sheet of paper with Alice's signature on it, and it wasn't long before I could sign her name as well as she could. I had no idea she'd become ill, but it worked to my advantage. No one questioned her letter requesting that I be released and sent home. After the loss of her husband, she felt the need to have her other daughter with her."

"It was that easy?" Dana was incredulous.

Darcy smiled. "Nothing is ever that easy. But I was able to let them think I would be under a doctor's care during the trip home. Picking up money was never difficult. I had enough to hire someone to pretend to be a doctor. Personally, I think my real doctor, Dr. Fredericks, was happy to see me gone. He was getting tired of firing all the orderlies he'd had to over the years. Just as well. None of them had all that much stamina when it counted. "

Dana could feel her breakfast traveling up her throat. She swallowed before she started to choke.

"So you were the one who traveled to all those bars and motels. And you were the one who had an affair with Gary Carter," she said, just wanting to hear her suspicions confirmed.

"Of course, it was me. It sure wasn't you." Darcy laughed. "Confess, sister dearest, you didn't start really living until I came along and forced you into it." She glanced down and ran a fingernail along Alice's cheek. The woman shuddered as her lips formed soundless words. "I applaud your taste in men. I couldn't have chosen better myself. Is he as good in bed as he looks?"

Dana couldn't play the game any longer. "What do you hope to gain from all this?"

"That's easy. I expect to gain your life," Darcy explained. "Of course, I'll be mourning the tragedy that happened here. Alice Madison killed by Darcy Madison, who will be sent back to that hospital since she is quite hopelessly insane." She ignored Harriet's shocked cry. "And the housekeeper who is fatally injured as she tries to save her employer and dear friend."

"You can't kill us all," Dana insisted, desperate to keep the fatal needle away from her mother's throat. She glanced in the nurse's direction.

"Barbara won't help you, Dana." Darcy flicked an imaginary speck of dust off her collar. "She's been wonderful in helping me see Alice. Poor Barbara. She has a little problem." She mimed holding a bottle. "I help her. She helps me."

"You didn't say anything about killing anyone," Barbara exclaimed. "I won't go along with that."

"Just keep your mouth shut and everything will be fine," Darcy ordered. She turned back to Dana. "Twins should share lives, Dana. That's why I want you to share mine." Her eyes were hard as marbles. "You'll be in that ugly little room, and I'll be here with Mac. I don't think he'll have anything to complain about."

It's not fair! The word screamed inside Dana's head.

She couldn't allow Darcy to get away with this atrocity. But what could she do? She didn't have a weapon at hand.

Who says it has to be at hand?

Her toes searched for her shoes. As she found one loafer, she started to inch her foot inside. Once it reached halfway, she didn't stop to think—she just acted. She kicked upward.

The shoe flew off her foot and headed straight for Darcy's head. Dana took off the moment the shoe started flying. She launched herself at the other woman, hitting Darcy and knocking the hypodermic out of her hand.

If she hoped that would be it, she was sadly mistaken. Darcy's cry of rage deafened her as the woman slapped her hard across the face. Dana ignored the burning sensation on her skin and pushed Darcy away from the bed.

Harriet screamed as the two women ended up on the floor. When a shadow appeared in the doorway, she jumped up and ran to the figure.

"She came to kill Alice. I thought she was Dana," she babbled, grabbing hold of Mac's hands. "Stop her before she kills Dana!"

"Mac!"

The voice was Dana's. But both women were identically dressed. The expression on both faces, the same.

Damn.

"Mac, stop her!' one of them said.

"She's the one you have to stop!"

It was a nightmare come true as he looked from one to the other.

"Dana," he started to say. Then one hit the other so hard, her head snapped back and she fell backward onto the floor. The other woman ran into his arms.

"I don't know what I would have done if you hadn't come," she cried, clutching him. "She made me change into clothes that matched hers so no one could tell us part."

"I noticed." Mac studied her for any signs of cuts or bruises.

She refused to let him go. "She told me how she did everything. I think she would have killed me, too. I was so scared, Mac."

His eyes still traveled over her. Was there a chance Darcy had succeeded, and Dana hadn't?

"Maybe you should have brought Duffy with you," she babbled. "He could have stood guard."

Mac started to relax. He doubted Darcy knew his dog's name.

He held on to her so tightly that she protested she couldn't breathe. He didn't want to let her go. He had come so close to losing her. He carefully put her to one side before walking over to the unconscious woman. He reached behind himself and pulled a pair of handcuffs out of his back pocket. He snapped them on her wrists.

"Harriet, call the police," he said crisply.

Harriet ran for the telephone near Alice's bed, while Barbara headed for Alice.

"I'm so sorry," Barbara whispered to her charge as she quickly checked blood pressure and pulse. "I am so sorry."

It was a blur after that as they waited for the police to arrive. Mac helped a groggy Darcy out of the room, after warning the nurse to stay put. Barbara was so upset about what had happened, she would have promised anything.

Harriet took Dana downstairs for a cup of tea, while Mac dealt with the police. They guaranteed they would drive Darcy up to the hospital and deliver her into her doctor's hands. Mac called the hospital immediately and told Darcy's doctor what had happened and that Darcy was on her way back. He wanted her away from Dana as quickly as possible.

The doctor was upset that his patient had managed to fool him. He asked that Dana be told that from then on extra precautions would be taken with Darcy.

Mac stood near the front door as Darcy was escorted outside to the waiting police car.

"Please, Mac, you can't do this," she pleaded. "You have the wrong one."

He looked at the woman who did look like Dana. But

she'd lied to him so many other times that he knew he couldn't believe her now.

"Don't let her succeed," she cried out before the car door closed after her.

He stood outside, watching the patrol car make its way down the winding driveway until it was out of sight.

He headed back into the house. He needed to feast his eyes on Dana.

When he walked into the kitchen he found her sitting at the breakfast bar with a cup of steaming hot tea and one of Harriet's muffins in front of her. The housekeeper alternately babbled and cried. None of Dana's assurances that she was all right soothed the still-frightened woman.

"It was horrible to see a woman with my sweet Dana's face but such an evil nature," she told Mac as she poured him a cup of coffee and warmed a muffin in the microwave.

"Angelic face, evil nature," Dana murmured. "Quite a combination, don't you think?"

"Interesting way of putting it." He looked at her strangely. "Are you sure you're all right?"

"I feel much better knowing that Darcy's going back to where she belongs." She tore off a piece of muffin and popped it into her mouth.

"I'm just glad it's over," Harriet said, handing Mac the plate with the warmed muffin.

He sat down next to Dana. She sighed and rested her head against his shoulder.

"I was so frightened," she said in a small voice.

"What made you come by?" Harriet asked Mac.

"Pure luck," he replied. "I got back to Dana's house and found some pages her controller had faxed to her. She'd left them on the bed. It seems Darcy was trying to bleed the company dry, too. I didn't find a note saying where she'd gone so I took a chance she'd gotten a phone call and did the star sixty-nine routine. The answering machine here picked up. I left right away. Now I'm glad I did."

"I am, too," Dana said, then whispered, "I need to go home, Mac."

"Let's first make sure Harriet and your mother are all right before we think of leaving," he said.

"I called Alice's doctor," Harriet told him. "He promised to leave immediately, so he should be here any moment. Now about Barbara—" She looked at Dana.

"I'll talk to her," Dana said. "I think she was a victim in this as much as any of us. We'll leave her fate up to my mother."

Mac kept close to Dana, and Harriet kept close to both of them as they waited for the doctor to arrive and then examine Alice.

"Naturally, her blood pressure is elevated, but I can't see anything harmful," he pronounced when he returned downstairs. "She's had a bad shock, and I think the best thing for her would be a good night's sleep. I did give her a mild sedative so she'd get that sleep."

"Then she'll be all right?" Dana pressed.

"Other than being badly frightened, yes she will."

Harriet saw the doctor out, then turned to them. "You two go on now." She pushed them toward the door. "As soon as we try to put this out of our minds, the better off we'll be." She hugged them both.

Dana shook her head. "It will never be out of my mind," she said softly as she followed Mac outside.

"Want to drive back with me, and we'll come by tomorrow for your car?"

She looked relieved by his suggestion. "I don't want to leave you."

All the way back to Dana's house, Mac kept picturing the scene he'd intruded upon. His mouth had gone dry, and his biggest fear had been that the woman he cared about would be badly hurt.

When they arrived, he activated the garage door opener and pulled the Explorer inside. He could hear Duffy barking from the backyard.

"You'd think we'd been gone for months," Mac muttered, as they walked into the kitchen. Duffy stood yelping at the patio door, and Mac gestured for the dog to be quiet.

Suddenly, Duffy's entire demeanor changed. His hackles rose and his teeth bared as he gave a growl that was more than a warning.

"Knock it off," Mac growled back. The dog backed away but his low growls didn't subside.

Dana looked downward. "Maybe these clothes smell like Darcy. I'm going to shower and change," she told him. "I'll feel better when I'm in my own clothes."

"All right."

She started to leave the kitchen, then spun around and hugged him tightly. "I don't know what I would have done if you hadn't come when you did," she whispered before kissing him with the hunger of a woman who'd almost lost her life. She quickly left.

"I don't know what I'd have done, either," he murmured. With narrowed eyes, he watched her departing figure.

After Dana left the room, Mac called the hospital to see if Darcy had arrived yet. He was informed that at that time, the doctor was meeting with her. Mac left a message that he would call the next day.

Darcy was caught and Dana was safe.

He stood at the kitchen sink with a glass of water in his hand. As he drank the water, he looked out the window and watched Duffy roam the backyard. The dog had finally calmed down, but Mac put it down to the dog being put outside.

He was still standing at the sink looking out the window at his dog, when Dana returned to the kitchen.

"There, now I feel human again." She now wore a robe, her wet hair slicked back.

Within moments, Duffy barked and scrambled against the patio door.

"Down, Duffy!" Mac ordered.

The dog dropped down to all fours, but he didn't stop barking.

Dana kept her distance from the glass door. "He's not happy at all."

"Yeah." Mac emptied his glass and set it on the counter. "Are you going to be all right if I go out for a while?"

"Where are you going?" She was alarmed by his announcement.

He picked up his keys. "I need to get to my office. I've got some things I need to check out on another case of mine."

She glided over to him and rested her hands on his chest. "Can't you check them out here?"

Mac shook his head. "I need my files."

Dana wrapped her arms around his neck and pulled his face down for a kiss. "Hurry back," she whispered.

Mac nodded and headed for the garage. He opened the back door and whistled for Duffy. The dog ran over to him and eagerly jumped into the Explorer's back seat.

As he backed down the driveway, four words kept echoing inside his head.

It doesn't feel right.

Chapter 15

Mac was convinced he did his best thinking when he was sitting back in his battered desk chair with his feet propped up on the desk. He used to do some of his best sleeping there, too.

Right now, he was doing some serious thinking.

A sleeping Duffy was sprawled under the desk.

The friend he'd sent up to Dana's birthplace had left a message he'd been successful in digging up information about the Madison family. Mac called him back immediately. He learned that the Madison's neighbors had moved away, but he lucked out in finding a woman who remembered the Madison twins. The politest thing she could say about Darcy Madison was that she was "spawn of the devil." Apparently, everyone was relieved when Darcy was hospitalized.

The man's next words were an unexpected surprise for Mac. He thanked the caller profusely and even promised him a bonus. He had more information than he needed. He didn't mind because he knew all of it was going to come in handy.

After he finished the call, he looked over all his notes. No wonder the family had moved after Dana's accident. Everyone was so afraid that Dana could become like Darcy that the children weren't allowed to play with her. A great deal of speculation swept among the neighbors about Darcy, most of which was that she was just plain evil. And Dana was the one to pay for her sister's terrorizing.

Mac also called Harriet to check on her and Alice.

"We're fine," she told him. "In fact, Alice has come out of this a bit stronger. She feels guilty that she hadn't told Dana years ago about Darcy. She's determined to do whatever is necessary to get healthy again. She even talked to Dr. Fredericks and gave him authorization to talk to you about Darcy. He told her that after this, Darcy would never be allowed to leave the hospital."

"It seems Mrs. Madison bounced back better than the rest of us did," he said, surprised by the news.

"Maybe it's what she needed. She's finally realized that even though Jeremy's gone, she's still alive. She told me the reason she was always asleep when Dana came to see her was because she never knew if it was Dana or Darcy. I had no idea some of the times I thought Dana was here that it was actually Darcy," she said sadly. "How is Dana doing after everything? She did such a brave thing, Mac. I have no doubt Darcy would have killed us all so she could take over Dana's life."

Mac felt a chill.

"She's doing fine." He tapped a pencil against the edge of the desk. *Something is not right.*

"That poor girl," Harriet murmured. "We don't know what made her the way she was, and it's a shame because she never had a chance at a normal life."

"I think she would say that she was the one who deserved everything Dana had." Mac said goodbye and replaced the phone in the cradle, then leaned back in his chair.

It was over. He should be back at Dana's house now, because he didn't want her out of his sight. He was even hoping to talk her into marrying him.

Hell, that's all he'd thought about lately. Except right now, he wasn't thinking of proposing.

He looked down at Duffy, who took up the entire area under the desk.

"I wish you could talk, boy," Mac said out loud. "You know the truth, don't you? Trouble is, I don't think your testimony would be accepted."

He reached for the phone and tapped out a number that he was fast becoming familiar with. "Dr. Fredericks, please."

He doodled on a piece of paper as he waited for the man to come on the line.

"This is Dr. Fredericks."

"John McKenna, Doctor. I was wondering how Darcy is doing."

"She's been distressed since she was returned. I had no choice but to give her a sedative. We find it best to leave them alone for a while so they can calm down on their own. I will be meeting with Darcy tomorrow and doing my evaluation at that time. What I don't like is her insistence she isn't Darcy, but that she's Dana."

Good going, McKenna. You screwed up.

"I can't give you any opinion until I have evaluated her," the doctor went on. "Before, she only talked about wanting her sister's face to disappear. I think because she'd been so determined to take over Dana's life, it was easy for her to believe her own fiction."

"Unless it isn't fiction," Mac muttered. The uneasy feeling had escalated until he felt downright sick.

"Excuse me?"

"What if Darcy succeeded with her plan?" he asked. "What if you really do have Dana and not Darcy?"

"Then I would say we have a serious problem, Mr. McKenna," the doctor said sharply. "Do you realize what you are saying? What this means?"

"Unfortunately, I do."

"Mr. McKenna, Darcy Madison is a very smart and dangerous woman. This kind of statement cannot be taken lightly," the doctor told him.

Mac closed his eyes and replayed the past few hours he'd spent with Dana. Then he thought about Dana yesterday and the day before.

"Dr. Fredericks, you're the only one who knows Darcy Madison," he said. "What I'd like to do is drive up there with her sister. Maybe this time they'll talk instead of fight."

"At this time, your request is impossible, Mr. McKenna. We have very strict procedures that we follow. They're necessary for our patients' mental health. The young woman is extremely agitated now. We need the time to help her settle back in her routine here."

"Your strict procedures didn't do all that much good when Darcy Madison managed to walk away from your hospital," Mac cut in angrily. "Didn't you even think to call Mrs. Madison and enquire about Darcy? She'd been locked up there since she was six. Didn't you think it was odd that her mother would suddenly want her staying with her? Especially with Darcy Madison's medical history."

"As I said before, Ms. Madison is a very clever woman. I was told another doctor would be overseeing her care and that he would contact me," the doctor said stiffly.

"I'd suggest you revise your procedures regarding patients leaving the hospital," Mac said in a hard voice. "Now, as I said, we'll be up there in a couple hours."

"I repeat, it is impossible. I will be reevaluating Ms. Madison in the morning," the doctor pointed out. "If you insist on seeing her so soon, you can see her tomorrow afternoon."

"No, I think this needs to be settled right away." He hung up while the man was still arguing.

Mac took several deep breaths to compose himself. When he felt a little better, he pulled out his phone book. He had some other calls to make.

Duffy whined and rolled over. Mac looked down and smiled.

"It took me a little while to figure it out, but you knew right away, didn't you," he told the dog. "Duffy, you deserve a steak."

"What do you mean we're driving up to the hospital?" Dana demanded. "I can't believe you want me to face her. Mac, she was going to kill me!"

Mac leaned back against the mantel in the family room with his hands jammed in his pockets. The moment he walked into the house, he suggested Dana get dressed because they were driving up to the hospital.

"Think of it as closure," he suggested. "The only meeting you two had was a highly charged one. Maybe if you sit down and try to talk, you might find a way to help her cope."

Dana perked up. "Help her?"

He nodded. "I talked to the doctor about an hour ago. She's insisting she's Dana. I think if she faces you, she'll realize that you aren't going away and have an easier time of coming to terms with who she really is."

She settled on the couch, curling her legs up under her. "I'm sorry, Mac, but I honestly don't want to see her again," she said softly. "Please don't ask me."

"This needs to be done, Dana," Mac said firmly. "If

it's done now, you won't have to see her again if you don't want to."

"You think I should do this just so I can get on with my life? Darling, I can get on with it very nicely," she told him.

"I'm asking you, Dana. For our future."

She looked at him sharply.

She rose to her feet. "Give me half an hour."

Darcy hadn't believed it could be so easy to fool everyone. Mac believed she was Dana; her milksop of a mother believed she was Dana; even that eagle-eyed housekeeper believed she was Dana. She didn't trust the latter. Harriet was old enough to be pensioned off.

She decided this visit might not be so bad. It was going to be so delicious when baby sister saw her walk in with Mac. It would be even more delicious that she would be leaving with him while baby sister stayed behind.

"I know what you're going to say," she said to Mac, taking his arm as they entered the hospital. "You're going to tell me that this will be good for me and I'll thank you afterward."

"This is good for you," he admitted, as he approached the front desk. He gave their names and asked for Dr. Fredericks.

She looked around the waiting room. Still all those drab colors they called soothing. Just being here left a nasty itch between her shoulder blades. She was going to be a great deal happier when she left. Especially since she'd never be back.

"Ms. Madison. Mr. McKenna. I'm Dr. Fredericks." A silver-haired man walked toward them. He looked a little taken aback when he saw Darcy.

"How is Darcy doing?" Mac asked.

"She's still very upset. It would have been better if you

had given her some time to settle back in." He looked from one to the other. "I am still protesting this meeting. It's still too soon for her to face what she's done."

"Some things can't wait," Mac said, refusing to back down.

The doctor frowned, clearly not appreciating Mac's insistence.

Darcy thought this might be a good time to intervene. "Dr. Fredericks, I wasn't so sure this would be good for me, either," she spoke up. "But after listening to Mac and my thinking about it, I understood I needed to come up here. I'd like the chance to talk to Darcy. I want her to know that I don't hate her for what she tried to do." She flashed a warm smile as she placed her hand on the doctor's arm. "Wouldn't my telling her I forgive her help her in some way? And is it possible to see her privately? I would think if she saw you or one of the orderlies, it would only make things worse. Mac will be with me, so I'm not afraid."

The doctor hesitated. "It might, but then again it might not." He looked over at an orderly. "Thomas, would you take them to room three, then escort Darcy Madison there? You won't need to stay inside with them, but I would appreciate your waiting outside the door until their visit is over." He looked at them. "You can have me paged when you're finished."

After the orderly left them in the room, Darcy walked around touching the back of a chair and running her fingertips across the top of a table.

"How depressing," she commented. "You'd think they could do better considering the amount of money people pay to keep their relatives hidden away from the world."

Mac was too busy watching the door. "No matter what you do to dress up the place, it's still a hospital."

Darcy turned when the door opened.

My my, she'd been here barely a day and she already looked terrible. Maybe Mac's idea wasn't such a bad one, after all. She would have the chance to see baby sister pulled down into the dark pit of despair where she belonged.

Dana felt as if she were living in a nightmare. Even more frightening was the fear this was one bad dream she'd never awaken from. Her mouth felt cottony from the sedative the doctor had given her and her head felt unusually heavy.

The orderly was impersonal as he directed her into a room. Then she saw the occupants.

Darcy had won, after all. She stood there wearing Dana's clothes, her hand on Dana's man's shoulder, a smile of triumph on her lips.

"Darcy." She walked forward with her arms outstretched.

Dana automatically stepped back. She didn't want the woman to touch her.

The real Darcy showed the appropriate signs of sorrow for the open rejection.

"Please don't hate me any longer. I'm not angry with what you did," she insisted. "I came here to tell you I'm coming to understand why you did it. Even our mother understands and still loves you."

"Moms?" she whispered, aching to see her mother. Afraid of what would happen to her with Darcy now in charge.

Dana watched Darcy walk over to Mac and stand behind him with one hand resting on his shoulder in a possessive gesture.

"We will do whatever is necessary to help you get better," she said. "No matter how long it takes."

Dana looked from Darcy to Mac. He had to see the difference!

"Dana," Mac murmured.

"No, sweetheart, she needs to understand that there are consequences to her actions." Darcy caressed his cheek with the back of her fingers. "And unfortunately, that means she has to stay here. I just want Darcy to understand she needs to do whatever the doctor says. In time, I'm sure, she'll be much better."

Dana's gaze shifted toward Mac. Could he read her feelings in her eyes? She wanted to scream at him that Darcy had tricked them both. She would have done so—if she weren't afraid the orderly would quickly appear with a nurse and, worse, another one of those hypodermics.

He stared back with the stony gaze she remembered from their first meetings. His gaze rested briefly on the faint bruise coloring her jaw. He gave no indication of his thoughts.

"Dana," he repeated. "Is there a reason why you didn't do something drastic when the cops were hauling you off? Were you so eager for a rest, you had to settle for here?" He waved one hand off to the side to indicate the room, which was as depressing as the reception area.

Darcy turned to him. "What are you saying?"

His jaw worked furiously. "I'm saying your little game is over." He clamped his hand around her wrist. "Thomas." He raised his voice. "Would you and the good doctor come in here, please?"

Dana blindly reached for a chair and sat down.

"What is going on?"

"That's what I would like to know." Darcy was furious. There was no way they could know what she did.

The door opened, and Dr. Fredericks, the orderly and an unfamiliar woman entered the room.

"Dr. Moore?" Dana's eyes filled with tears.

Abby looked at Dana, then at Darcy. "Identical twins tend to make things difficult. I'd say one telling difference here is that this Dana—'' she gestured toward Dana ''—greeted me by name.'' She studied Darcy. ''It must be galling to have failed.''

Darcy's eyes flashed fire. ''I beg your pardon?''

''Dr. Fredericks, Darcy Madison managed to fool us long enough so that Dana, whom she'd knocked unconscious, was brought here in Darcy's place,'' Mac explained.

Dr. Fredericks puffed up. ''That's impossible. I want you to leave immediately before I call the police.''

''No need. I called them before we came up here.'' Mac glared at the psychiatrist. ''I did some checking about you, Fredericks. You charge high prices for nominal care. You're happier with your patients drugged to the gills because then you don't have to deal with them. You take the money, but you don't do anything for them. The money went into your pockets instead of into treatment for the patients. Sounds to me like you flunked your ethics class.''

The man's face turned a deep shade of red. ''Get out of here.''

Mac looked past him. Two police officers stood in the doorway.

''You know the best thing about once having been a cop?'' he said in a low voice. ''You know who to call. You're out of business, Fredericks. As of now.''

The doctor's mouth opened and closed like that of a fish, as the officers approached him. One began reading him his rights.

Mac turned to Darcy. ''Your game is over.''

''You son of a bitch,'' she snarled, lashing out at him with her nails. He manacled her other hand with his fingers.

''Hello, Darcy, I'm Dr. Moore. I came here because Mac asked me to give you some very much needed help. Your mother has set up the paperwork to sign you out of here and transfer you elsewhere. I've arranged for you to be transferred to another hospital immediately." Abby spoke in her soothing voice.

"You can't do this!" Dr. Fredericks shouted even as he was being led away in handcuffs.

Abby shook her head. She looked over her shoulder and gestured. A man wearing a navy polo shirt and khaki pants came over to her.

"Darcy, this is Kevin. He'll be going with us."

"You can't do this," Darcy argued, pulling at Mac's grip.

Kevin took hold of her arm, and with just the right amount of gentle persuasion, managed to lead her out of the room. Her screams and curses lingered in the air.

Abby smiled at Dana, who looked dazed by the entire proceedings.

"Mac called me and told me what had happened," she told her. "I want to see you in my office tomorrow. We'll talk. The nice thing about the hospital receiving the wrong patient is that there are minimal problems getting you out."

Dana pressed her fingers against her lips. Mac crouched down beside her and replaced her fingers with his own.

"Hey, did you honestly think I wouldn't figure it out?" he said quietly. "I'm just sorry I didn't pick up on it right away. If it will make you feel better, Duffy growled and lunged at her right away."

Dana cried out Mac's name and launched herself into his arms. She clutched him so tightly, he soon begged the chance to breathe. It didn't stop her from repeatedly touching his face with her fingertips as if she couldn't believe he was real.

"What about the other patients here?" she asked Abby.

"Dr. Fredericks was the only one at fault. The problem is, he owns the hospital. The authorities will watch over the rest of the staff, but I wouldn't be surprised if the families will need to find a new facility."

Dana looked at Mac. "I want to go home," she whispered.

Mac glanced at Abby. She walked over, examined Dana's eyes, took her pulse and asked her a few questions.

"I'm sure home's the best place for her."

Dana gripped Mac's hand as they left the building. When she was settled in his Explorer, she burst into tears.

"I thought I'd never see you again," she sobbed. "I was so afraid I'd never get out of there."

"Honey, I'm sorry." He gripped her hand tightly. "I should have known it right away. When I saw one of you knocked out, I thought you'd gotten in another lucky punch."

Dana started to laugh but it soon turned back into sobs. Mac unbuckled their seat belts and drew her over onto his lap. He whispered words of love and assurance as he threaded his fingers through her hair. He dropped kisses all over her face as he reacquainted himself with her skin and warmed her with his body heat. And he pressed her face against his shoulder as she cried.

"I almost lost you," he muttered roughly, drawing back enough so he could mop up her tears with hands that turned gentle as he touched her. "I don't know what I would have done if that had happened."

"I couldn't make them believe me," she sobbed. "They wouldn't listen to me."

He pushed her hair away from her face, framing her face with his hands. The idea he could have lost her ate at him like acid.

"It's okay," he soothed. "I'm here and you're safe."

She shook her head. "I should have told you how much I loved you."

"I should have believed you in the beginning. I should have known." He couldn't stop touching her. He had to know she was real. "But it's over now. And I'm not letting you go again. Maybe my old man couldn't make a marriage work and maybe I couldn't before, but I'm going to make *us* work. Do you hear me?'' He shook her gently. ''We're getting married.''

Her laughter mixed with her tears. ''If that's a proposal, I accept.''

''Good thing, because I wasn't going to accept anything else for an answer.''

Epilogue

Two months later

"I still don't think this is a good idea." Mac frowned as they parked in the hospital parking lot. He still had nightmares about the day he had managed to switch sisters and rescue Dana. And he knew she still had nightmares about that time because he would wake up alone and find her in the family room. She would be sitting on the couch rocking back and forth, while Duffy whined and tried to comfort her in his lumbering doggie way.

They married as soon as possible because they wanted immediately to begin their new lives. Dana restructured her company so she could delegate more work and took a leave of absence so she could spend more time with her mother. Thanks to the extra attention and a reason to recover, Alice was doing well with her rehabilitation therapy.

Alice still couldn't say her other daughter's name without bursting into tears. Abby suggested to Dana that she hold off for some time until Alice was stronger physically and mentally before attempting to find out more about her twin.

Dana had tried to think about Darcy and what had happened. Then that morning she received a phone call from Abby. Abby asked Dana to come see Darcy.

Mac argued against it, but Dana dug her heels in. He finally gave in, but he insisted she not be left alone with her sister. Dana explained that the doctor had told her she wouldn't be seeing her sister face-to-face, but through a two-way mirror.

Dana felt a shiver of apprehension as they entered the building. Even though this hospital was a brighter and cheerier place than the one Darcy had previously been in, it still gave her a closed-in feeling. She tightly gripped Mac's hand. He gave her an answering squeeze.

Abby was waiting for them. She smiled warmly. "I realize this is difficult for you." She touched Dana's arm. "But I think you need to see something."

"Did something happen to Darcy?" Dana asked.

"More like Darcy's taking matters into her own hands." She opened a door. "This is a two-way mirror here, so she can't see you."

Dana blinked several times as her eyes adjusted to the dim light.

The room was painted a sunny yellow, with a table and two chairs set in one corner. One chair was occupied by a nurse's aide, who watched Darcy.

Dana gasped in shock. Dana wanted to cry when she saw the deep gouges marring one of Darcy's cheeks from her brow bone to her chin. The wounds were angry looking. The way Darcy always seemed to be.

Thanks to an intercom system, she could hear Darcy humming under her breath as she walked around the room. She held a hairbrush in one hand, slowly running it through her hair. The smile on her lips was like the expression in her eyes—vacant.

"What happened to her?" Dana asked, stunned by the change in her sister.

"Darcy was responding very well to a new medication we were trying. Unfortunately, she experienced a bad episode a few nights ago," the doctor said quietly. "She somehow heard about your marriage. She started screaming that Dana would no longer have her face because she was going to destroy it. Before anyone realized what she was doing, she'd clawed at her face."

"Couldn't surgery eventually correct the scars?" she whispered.

"They're much too deep. Actually, sad as it sounds, she's been much calmer since then." Abby hesitated. "I know you're still worried that your sister's condition is hereditary. I'd like to assure you it's not. I'm sure you've heard of the term 'bad seed.' Unfortunately, your sister seems to be one of those bad seeds. Darcy doesn't recognize any difference between bad and good. She has no conscience. I'd say you received enough conscience for both of you. I can promise you that she will always receive the best of care here. With the emotional problems she has, she will never be able to leave," she added quietly.

Dana took one last look at her sister.

"I guess you're right. She's calmer now because she believes she destroyed my face."

Mac understood Dana's silence as they returned home. Sensing she needed some time alone, he took Duffy for a long walk. When he returned, he found Dana outside on the patio curled up in one of the chairs.

The smile she gave him eased his mind. He wasted no time walking over and kissing her. She lifted her arms and looped them around his neck.

"We do have one thing to thank Darcy for," she said.

He was surprised by her statement. "The woman put you through hell and you're thankful? Want to run that by me again?"

She fingercombed his hair away from his forehead. "Because of her, I had to find someone to help me. Because of her, I found you. I am so grateful I have you."

Mac gathered her up in his arms and swung around, sitting in the chair and settling her in his lap. She automatically rested her head against his shoulder with her face buried against his neck.

"That goes double for me." His voice was hushed and filled with love. "With you I know I can do anything."

Dana lifted her head enough so she could look at him squarely. Her smile told him just how much trust in him she felt. He felt humbled by it.

"I always knew you could."

* * * * *

where love comes alive—online...

eHARLEQUIN.com

your romantic
books

- ♥ Shop online! Visit Shop eHarlequin and discover a wide selection of new releases and classic favorites at great discounted prices.

- ♥ Read our daily and weekly Internet exclusive serials, and participate in our interactive novel in the reading room.

- ♥ Ever dreamed of being a writer? Enter your chapter for a chance to become a featured author in our Writing Round Robin novel.

your romantic
life

- ♥ Check out our feature articles on dating, flirting and other important romance topics and get your daily love dose with tips on how to keep the romance alive every day.

• • • • • • •

your
community

- ♥ Have a Heart-to-Heart with other members about the latest books and meet your favorite authors.

- ♥ Discuss your romantic dilemma in the Tales from the Heart message board.

your romantic
escapes

- ♥ Learn what the stars have in store for you with our daily Passionscopes and weekly Erotiscopes.

- ♥ Get the latest scoop on your favorite royals in Royal Romance.

SINTA1

COMING NEXT MONTH

CMN1200